ACKNOWLEDGEMENTS

This book could not have been written without the help of a group of very good friends who shared with me many of the best days of our lives. To Gord, and Bill, and Ed, my thanks for a lifetime of memories of adventure and challenge, and for the tales with which we entertained one another. To Tom and Neil and Ernie, Bob and Howard and Jerry, my thanks too for the many more great experiences that are part of those years.

My heartfelt thanks too to daughter Marilyn, who guided me through the move from typewriter to computer, and whose patience on my long distance phone calls for help has kept my word processing more or less on track.

And I must acknowledge my good wife Mary's uncomplaining patience with the paper blizzard surrounding her during the weeks of trying to put this book together.

TABLE OF CONTENTS

PREFACE 1

BEAUTY OF THE HUNT 3

HUNTING ADVENTURES 11
    I'll Kiss the Ground 15
    Grizzlies 20
    The Yellow Bug 24
    The Frozen Boy 33
    Flower Wheels 36
    Memory Snapshots 37

MY STORIES
    The Early Days 40
    The Elevator 45
    The Dime 50
    The Teaching Years 52
    The Hundred Mile Skate 56
THE UNIFORM YEARS 61
    Humor in Uniform 67
    Navy Leave 71
    Life in the Dark 74
    The Talisman 79
    Convalescence 80
BRITISH COLUMBIA
    Mabel Lake 90
    Goose Tales 92
    Bear Tales 95
    Ravens 97
    We Challenge Thieves 99
    The Water Wall 109
    The Storm 111
    Mabel Lake in September 113

WALROD TALES 116
    The Ranch 117
    The Relief Camp 122
    Bears and Boats 124
    Grey Owl 126
    The Ice Train 128
    Strip Tease 133

KITZUL TALES 134
    Riding the Rods 138
    Placer Mining 142
    Logging 145
DEEP SEA FISHING 152
    The Egg War 160
    Terror At Sea 162
    The Russian Experience 168
    Ships, Charters and Films 172
    The Cable 175
    Ripple Rock 178
    Winning the Fishing Lottery 180

ED WHITLAM'S STORIES 183
    Underground Coal Mining 186
    Hardrock 191
    Wartime 199
    Work and Play 201

PREFACE

This book grew slowly over time, as a gathering of experiences and memories shared over more than fifty years with a wonderful group of friends.

Having been blessed throughout my life with the inclination, health and curiosity to live actively in the great outdoors, I have travelled many thousands of miles in the back country, forests and mountains of beautiful British Columbia, armed first with a rifle, in recent years with only a camera. I shared many of those miles with companions who were skilled in hunting, in woodcraft, in living, on whom one could depend in any emergency, who contributed more to my life than they can know.

There was Ed, who could drive impossible trails with such verve and skill he got us into and out of impassable areas; there was Bill, whose eyesight was so keen he was almost always the first to spot distant game, the first even when he was the driver on high mountain trails; there was Gord, always calm, always dependable, a driver who was never known to miss a pothole in the road, a great practical joker and teller of campfire tales; there was Ernie, who combined superb hunting skills with a love for HUGE campfires that lit and warmed the cold night woods for dozens of yards around; there was Tom, whose brief exposures to his beloved outdoors revealed an Indian's stealth and a sniper's skill; there was big Neil, who walked the woods at a pace that had his companion trotting, who had speed and stamina to challenge a running moose, who stripped off his boots and socks the moment he arrived back in camp, and spent his evenings barefoot around the campfire, even on snowy nights; there were others; there was my beloved wife, who on our retirement happily moved from the city to our remote lake-side home, and has seemed content to share that paradise with me for the past twenty summers, and never begrudged my hunting times.

During our hunting years our parties of three or four spent hundreds of hours together, confined a day at a time to a truck cab on long trips, sitting for countless evenings around campfires or closeted in the shelter of a tent or camper. During those times many

1

tales were told, tales that built gradually over the years and were easy and fun to bring back to life through these printed pages.

This will be a book of little stories. All of them are true. Their stage is set around our evening campfires, a stage on which we were privileged to share some of the most beautiful scenery on earth, a stage on which were played many adrenaline filled hunting adventures.

If you should find an error or two in the technical descriptions of my companions' adventures, the errors are mine. Sometimes there were long periods of time between the telling and the writing, and since I relied on memory for many of their accounts, I occasionally groped for technical detail, but never for fact.

Our hunting stories are not unique. Anyone who has spent many years hunting big game will have similar tales to tell. I hope those of you who have shared comparable experiences will enjoy returning in memory to night time campfires, mountain sunrises, breathtaking feats shared with lifelong friends.

And for those of you to whom this way of life seems strange, I hope to share with you a few of the memories we were privileged to gain in walking through some of our earth's most beautiful surroundings, and give you some appreciation of the magnetism and challenge of the hunt. Nothing else could have taken us to the places we have seen, the challenges overcome, and we would have missed so much!

I have limited our campfire tales for now to those told by Bill and Gord and Ed and me. They are a chronicle of our times.

THE BEAUTY OF THE HUNT

During my hunting and camera years I spent hundreds of hours and walked hundreds of miles of forest and mountain country in quiet, intense concentration on my surroundings. This is concentration far removed from backpacking or hiking, in that one moves slowly, studies every scene opening before him, registers every twig snap, bird call, squirrel chatter, elk bugle, wolf howl, slap of beaver tail, feels the tension and excitement of fresh grizzly sign, and of sharing these mountains and woods with moose, deer, elk, beaver, predatory wolf, wolverine, black and grizzly bear, bobcat, mountain lion, as well as scores of smaller animals and birds.

One sees dozens of beautiful lakes and ponds surrounded by glorious autumn colors, and witnesses the sun's first gleaming shaft of light lancing high mountain horizons in spectacular surroundings. Those years have left me with a legacy of scenes and experiences that flash through my memory almost every day. I'd like to share some of them with you on the following pages:

There was the morning Gord and I drove north from Germanson Landing in northern B.C., came around a curve and stopped in wonder at the sunlit beauty of an unnamed lake sheathed in mirror ice so clear and glassy it flawlessly reflected every hoarfrosted twig and branch of its shoreline woods, backed by real and reflected snowcapped mountain and deep blue sky.

Imagine if you will the most beautiful lake-mirrored mountain you've ever seen, exchange deep blue water for the steel blue mirror of gleaming ice, then dress every tree in twinkling white tinselled Christmas lights, add a touch or two of tinsel around the shore, duplicate the whole sparkling scene upside down in the lake surface, and you'll have some idea of what we saw.

We laughed later as we carefully studied with a magnifying glass the photos we took that morning, to see if there might have been a moose in our lens, as we certainly forgot to look for one at the time.

* * * * * * * *

I think of the tiny lake Ed and I found beyond the end of the trail featured later in my lost hunter story. Here again was the indescribable beauty of every twig and branch an inch thick in sparkling hoarfrost reflected in a beautiful little blue lake with deep mossy banks and a tiny, spruce treed island in its center - a challenge to an artist.

The real feature of this memory though is the perfect curve of a tall birch tree with its head bent to the ground, forming a white thirty foot arch that precisely framed our first view of the scene. We stopped in awe, realizing we were probably the only people who would ever see that spectacular picture in its frame! Ed's exclamation, "This is the gateway to paradise!" set the scene forever.

* * * * * * * *

There is a basin high in the Rocky Mountains that is probably one of the most beautiful places on earth. It has never appeared in National Geographic or glossy travel brochures, and may have been seen by only a handful of people in history.

Tom and I came upon it one September morning when we abandoned our 4x4 rig to continue climbing on foot to check for game high on the mountain. We were attracted at last to the hint of a basin, and as we came over the lip and entered the narrow gateway of vertical rock we stopped in wonder at the magnificence of the view.

The bowl dropped away below us, to level off in a green expanse of alpine meadow, interspersed with a scattering of short, compact mountain pine. A hanging glacier half a mile away dominated the skyline on the opposite side of the bowl, and from it a lacy waterfall fell into a mossy banked, bright watercourse that meandered through the meadow and pines and disappeared through a cut in the bowl at our feet.

This sort of Eden should have been full of game - not only the elk we were hunting, but with herds of deer in the meadow, a grizzly or two on the rocky slopes, a beaver dam on the stream, and possibly a herd of woolly mammoth feeding below the glacier! But there were none of these, and we were free to sit and drink in the beauty of this paradise without being tempted to despoil its serenity.

I have two memories of long abandoned mountain top forestry lookout cabins: The first is in the East Kootenay area of the Rocky Mountains. The tiny white cabin looking down across the miles of forest attracted Bill and Ed and me to challenge the abandoned, snow-swept road to the mountain top. The cabin door stood open in invitation to Nature's creatures there, and it was obvious that a family of porcupines had called it home (and larder) for years.

I don't know what porcupines find so attractive in plywood, but they have a voracious appetite, not only for the wood, but apparently for the glue as well in plywood doors, signs, walls, and cabinets.

Here, it was hard to believe how much they had consumed! Huge holes with neatly tapered and serrated edges left the insulation bared in most of the interior walls to window height. The plywood table top was almost gone, as were the counter top and doors and shelves of the cabinets.

We closed the door, because they had a hole in it big enough to permit easy access. The silly things would have had a much more comfortable home if they hadn't consumed so much of it!

* * * * * * * *

The other deserted ranger cabin looked down for many years from the bare rock top of a tall mountain in the Chilcotin Plateau. It was a favorite spot for Tom and Ernie and Neil and I to sit and glass the hundreds of square miles below, getting the lay of the land, map-marking trails and compass bearings to swamps and lakes, and just enjoying the magnificent view.

We were surprised one year to see the cabin missing, so fought our way up the abandoned road to check it out. When we reached the top we were treated to an art gallery on that bare, windswept rock that will remain one of my most curious memories.

The cabin had apparently been struck by lightning, and burned fiercely. Mountaintop gales had stripped away the ash and debris, leaving only a few bits of charred wood and handfuls of black nails. But - the aluminum roof had melted and splashed and dripped and run over the bare underlying rock to form fantastic patterns of frozen aluminum, shiny films duplicating every grain and crevasse in the rock, delicately fine tracery of metal thread firmly connecting strange three dimensional forms, accented here and there with odd blobs and black nails and bits of black charcoal protruding from the patterns.

We carefully pried, peeled and lifted many unique shapes off the rock, held them up for one another to admire, traded one or two, and brought them home to hang on our walls and attract the artistic appreciation of our visitors.

We don't often remove artifacts and other long abandoned treasures that we find, but the top of that mountain was so remote, so often buried deep in snow, we felt we were not likely depriving anyone of the thrill we felt in this find by taking away a few of the gems.

* * * * * * * *

The more bulky artifacts we found in the woods included two abandoned bulldozers and a wrecked airplane.

The first 'dozer was a really old fashioned machine that was obviously in working order until it threw a track on a steep side hill. As far as I could tell thirty or forty years later, there had been no attempt to replace the track, and I can imagine the dismay of that pioneer owner abandoning his machine so deep in the woods. However, it was now pinned to earth by a huge tree growing in the four foot space between the motor, blade, and the side arms. That made a very strange picture!

The other 'dozer, also miles from a road, was much bigger and more modern, but certainly would not move again until all the wiring was replaced. Every inch of every wire on the motor was stripped of its insulation by rodents, probably squirrels. Those yards of shining copper wire looked pretty, but would represent a disaster to the man who must have come back for his machine.

The airplane lay scattered on a mountainside near Germanson Landing. It had been a small plane, but its torn, twisted wreckage covered a large area. a shocking illustration of the fragility of man-made articles. We confirmed that the wreck had been reported and checked out years before.

A humorous (to me) battle between man and animal was over the high pressure line pumping water up to a stubborn fire in a coal mine. As I took advantage of the narrow slash cut through dense undergrowth to follow the half mile of heavy three inch red plastic hose, I noticed that it was bandaged every few yards with heavy tape, that between the bandages there were frequent tiny high pressure jets of water, and that several abandoned lengths of hose were lying on the trail.

Talking later to one of the workmen, I learned that porcupines also have an appetite for plastic hose. Every time one of them sank his teeth into that line, he got not only a high pressure drink of water, he created endless problems in keeping the line in working order.

* * * * * * * *

I have walked several miles of the continental divide forming the southern half of the boundary line between our two western provinces. It was interesting to stand on that high ridge and with one foot in each province, look west, down into British Columbia, and turn east to Alberta, a few inches away.

Tom and I had seen elk on that high ridge, and as we glassed the slopes below in both directions we laughed at the futility of looking for elk on the Alberta side of the border as we were licensed to hunt in only half of the area spread out below us.

The boundary markers were about two hundred yards apart. They had a concrete base, with each pylon about sixteen inches square at the base, tapering up for two feet to a six inch top. Each was sheathed in a grey metal, probably zinc, with the British Columbia crest on its west side and Alberta crest on the east.

Many of the pylons had been well covered during their fifty years here with the pencilled graffiti of a surprising number of passers by. The writing was as legible from 1923 as it was from 1980, as the simple lead-pencilled words seemed to be etched into the metal. They varied from simple names and dates to lengthy, sometimes philosophical paragraphs on the beauty of the view, the luck of the hunt, and the back-packing camp of a honeymoon couple. One story told of a shot fired from this pylon to bag a trophy elk on the slope below. That had us sitting there picturing that triumphant hunter right on this spot in 1947, wishing we could duplicate his feat thirty years later.

The earliest date we found was 1923. As we visualized the long, meandering line of an untold number of these metal and concrete pylons being built or placed on this high divide, decades before helicopters, we wondered at the labor involved in putting them there. It could only have been done with long strings of pack horses, and was one more example of the tremendous jobs that were done by pick and shovel, wheelbarrow and fresno in building thousands of miles of railroads and highways, digging basements, canals, and building dams, before the days of huge earth moving machinery. It's impossible by today's standards to appreciate how much those early people accomplished in settling our land!

* * * * * * * *

One often comes across traces of our pioneers in strange places, and those tiny, tumbledown little log cabins bring a lump to my throat when I think of the people who lived there so long ago. Some of them commanded beautiful but overgrown views, some were buried so deep in the woods they could only have been trappers' cabins. The wealth of artifacts in some indicated that the people who left them intended to come back, possibly struck by tragedy that caused them to abandon their home in a hurry.

I think of one such creekside cabin, miles and miles from anywhere. As I came in the door, a smooth sheet of birchbark hanging on the opposite wall caught my eye. On it was a little poem of welcome to that lady's home, written in such beautiful green script, I felt a bond with the person who wrote it so long ago. Her welcome still seemed so current that after I carefully explored treadle sewing machine, cupboards, dishes, cookstove, coal oil lamps, pioneer furniture, I tiptoed out, leaving it as I found it, wondering as I closed the door what she was like and how she lived away back then in such a remote place. As I think of it now, I hope her little home is still undisturbed, but I'd never be able to find it again to check.

8

Those little lost cabins of our early pioneers could never impress me as much though as finding the cabin of The Three Bears. Someone, and I have no idea who it was, found a well preserved but very old ten by twelve foot, mossy log cabin and spent hours and days of painstaking work in lovingly converting it to the fairytale cabin of Papa Bear, Mama Bear, and Baby Bear, then walked away from it without asking for any sign of credit. It was left as a treasure to be explored in wonder by any lucky wanderer who might stumble across it.

There was nothing fancy about it. In that natural, mossy, old, rather dark cabin you could believe that the three bears had left it only a few minutes ago. It lies in a mossy glade below our logging road and above the lake, about ten miles from our cabin. Only a tiny footpath beside a tinkling stream gives cause to explore the hidden glade below, but if you do, you are treated to a delightful experience.

Having discovered it, we took our two visiting grandchildren to see it last summer. Eight year old Goldilocks really completed the picture as she moved in wonder and awe from one discovery to another.

She sat in the big chair and the middle sized chair and the tiny chair, and liked Baby Bear's chair the best. There was no porridge in the three bowls on the table, but there were nice dry mattresses of moss on each of the three wooden beds. There were cooking utensils on the stove, a nice photo of Mama and Baby Bear on the wall , a plastic spider and real spiderweb on the window, and hanging from the ceiling a toy bat that flapped its wings back to its resting place when you pulled it down. It was all so real and yet so rustic, I think Susie expected the three bears to come home at any time.

Going outside again to the beautiful glade, we found their car parked at the side of the cabin. It resembled the Flintstone model, but was upgraded with wheels sawn from the round of a log, a willow frame and seats, and a mossy roof supported by willow corner posts. It looked sturdy enough, but we didn't want to add to the fairy tale by having Goldilocks risk a ride in it.

If I'd written the script I couldn't have timed it better as a big horned owl now drifted silently over our heads and settled in a tall tree, looking down on us. It

was an eerie, live extension to a wonderful day. I think
Susie could have been convinced that if she went down to
the beach she'd find a pea green boat with the pussy cat
waiting for her friend the owl to join her on their sea
voyage.

A typical fire ranger's mountain top cabin, now obsolete and abandoned.

HUNTING ADVENTURES

This chapter covers some of the more adventurous aspects our hunting years: During the approximately forty postwar years I shared on hunting trips with different friends, we hunted moose and elk in several widely spaced areas with different rigs and equipment. Moose hunting was generally north, from Prince George and Vanderhoof, Stuart Lake and Germanson Landing to Fort St. John and on up the Alaska Highway. Elk hunting was in the East Kootenay area of the Rockies, in the southeastern corner of the province. My last hunting years were for moose on the Chilcotin Plateau, west of Williams Lake. My comrades were all expert hunters, and in addition to our quota of big game, we brought back memories of many thrilling experiences.

Our early years utilized an old jeep towed behind a truck and camper. We had rebuilt the jeep, with a stiff plywood four man cab, capable of carrying a moose on the roof. It had racks for rifles, axe, shovel, chainsaw, and little room for comfort. It had windowed sides and a heavy glassed tailgate, hinged at the top. Access to the back was gained by raising the tailgate to a vertical balance, extending well above the roof.

On one early November trip north we decided to split the party at Quesnel. Two of us would take the jeep on the Blackwater road for the seventy five mile shortcut through good moose country to our hunting area south of Vanderhoof. The other two would take the camper on the long trip around through Prince George and Vanderhoof to meet us there that night. The Blackwater was too hazardous for the camper.

We drew straws, and Gord and I won the trip through the Blackwater, while Jerry and Howard were stuck with the long highway trip. Gord and I moved back into the camper to pack our gear and prepare the food we'd need, while we were still barrelling down the highway with the jeep in tow.

Gord was standing at the end of the table buttering bread and I was sitting at the side of it with my razor sharp hunting knife slicing ham for sandwiches when Howard suddenly slammed the brakes on our speeding truck.

Gord and I were both thrown. Gord fell forward over the table, and with each hand on a slippery slice of buttered bread, he came down heavily almost full length on it. In the meantime I used my arms on the table to remain in my seat, but my hand with that very sharp knife upright in it disappeared under Gord's sprawling body.

I'll never forget my feeling of dread as we disentangled ourselves, as I expected that knife to be buried to the hilt in his chest. However, knowing it was there, he had made a super effort to stay above it. There was not a scratch on his body, but we found a two inch slit cut in the chest area of his shirt, to show how close he came to disaster.

He kept and showed off that shirt for years, and every time he pointed out how he had avoided my knife, I pointed out how very sharp my knife was to do such a neat job on his shirt.

Following a successful hunt that week, we found when we reached the highway that it was too icy to risk towing the heavily loaded jeep. With four quarters of moose inside and another whole moose on the roof, there was barely room for a driver, as I found when I took my turn at jeep driving. My front seat companion (a front quarter of moose) kept shoving an icy cold elbow against my ear as I carefully guided the heavy load down the icy road.

Mid morning the next day we reached dry pavement, and stopped to hook the two vehicles together. We had trouble getting the socket of the jeep's tow bar over the ball on the truck, and decided to use the axe to drive it on. I raised the heavy jeep tailgate to its vertical position, got the axe, and was just handing it to Jerry when a big eighteen wheeler roared past from our opposite direction.

That's the last I remembered until I woke up in the ditch wondering why Jerry had hit me with the axe, and found the other three bending over me. When they found I would live, they laughingly explained that the blast of wind from the semi had smashed the tailgate down on my head and sent me flying. They also pointed out it was very fortunate I wasn't standing a few inches closer to the jeep or I'd have been hit with the window instead of the frame, and if my head had stayed on I'd have been wearing the tailgate frame for a collar.

A year or two later we had about fifty miles of high, rough logging road to drive out from Blue River to reach the highway. The road was so full of potholes we decided to drive the jeep out rather than wreck the truck transmission by towing it. Gord and I were elected.

Driving in heavy morning fog on a narrow section of the road hanging high above a drop that disappeared at about ditch level in the mist, we heard a heavy diesel logging truck speeding up behind us. We had no room to pull over, and knowing he could see only a few feet ahead of him on a road so narrow we couldn't get out of the way, we had only seconds to live!

A split second before the pounding roar overwhelmed us and sent us in a crumpled mass over the edge, the edge revealed a diesel train speeding past on a railroad track hidden in mist a few feet below!! That noise was so close and so overpowering, we both felt the impact and both knew we wouldn't live through it. We were born again as we carefully and thankfully continued our trip.

* * * * * * * *

On a trip north one year with a heavy truck and camper, three of us got into a pretty scary situation. The smooth, hard frozen dirt surface of the road gave us no trouble with traction as we climbed a long, steep hill one frosty morning to hunt an extensive plateau. We started back at mid afternoon of a sunny, warmed up day, and as we came over the crest of the hill the truck went instantly out of control. After fifty sliding feet it went into the high bank rather than over the side.

We bailed out, to find that we could scarcely keep our feet under us, on what could only be compared to a buttered surface. The sun had melted the frost out of the top quarter inch of slippery mud overlying a hard frozen road that gave no bond at all to the surface. Grease!!

Gord decided that if Bill and I walked beside his rig to try to keep it on the road, he would try to avoid a runaway sleigh ride. We chained up, but chains made no difference to his traction on buttered ice.

That was a very long, greasy, scary mile down that hill! Most of the time the truck completely ignored Gord's steering efforts. Bill and I walked or trotted beside the outside front fender, and every time it wandered toward the drop-off, wheels cramped and throwing mud, we put our muddy shoulders to it and managed to shove it back. Gord got a muddy high five from both of us when we reached the bottom!

Another year we were hunting moose in far back country near Hudson's Hope. The area was wooded, with long, straight seismic lines cut through the timber, straight as an arrow for miles. They were the only "roads", and were impassable to road vehicles. We were hunting the area on foot, with only Jerry's converted Volkswagon bug there as transportation.

About a foot of wet, heavy snow covered a ground surface of slush and mud and water that hadn't frozen before the heavy snow blanket kept it liquid in spite of temperatures now well below freezing. As we walked, the top frozen crust would support us for a few feet, then we would break through to slosh through slushy water that occasionally went over our boots. We all had wet feet.

The bug had a terrible time. As it plowed through the snow its wheels were in the mud and water below, and as it threw that muddy slush under its fenders and around its brake drums and steering rods it all froze quickly. Jerry knew he was in trouble when he had difficulty steering, and one of us pointed out that while three of his wheels were turning, his right front wheel was just skidding along like a sleigh runner.

He maneuvered it to an area where he had lots of wood for a fire, and spent the rest of the day with a fire as close as he dared to the frozen wheel while he chopped ice and frozen mud from around it.

We moved that night.

I'LL KISS THE GROUND

Anyone who has hunted big game in real wilderness country, who has got out of his truck and off the roads and hiked the timber, would probably be lying if he told you he never lost his way. And if his wilderness is trackless, where all he can see from the forest is the trees, where there are no grids roads to look forward to, he would certainly be lying if he told you that he didn't feel at least a touch of panic when he realized that he and his compass didn't agree.

Some hunters really panic when the going gets tough, and literally run themselves to exhaustion and death. Others manage to maintain or regain control, light a fire when night comes on, and eventually walk out or are found by searchers.

It happened to Howard, on one of our moose hunting trips in the wilderness south west of Vanderhoof. This story tells how it happens, and how it feels, as we experienced it, and as he told it:

"The terror that had chased me for hours in a stumbling, clawing scramble through the black, endless jungle of jackpine and windfalls had crept up on me slowly, as slowly and surely as the dark of the early winter night. I had felt twinges of it earlier, after I left the moose track and took a compass bearing to intercept the old trail that would lead me back to camp.

"I knew I had followed the moose too far, that I had paid little attention to direction and distance, but the tracks were SO fresh whenever they crossed the faint skiffs of snow remaining from this morning's brief flurry. The moose didn't seem to be hurrying, and every time I decided "enough" there was always that one more ridge or copse just ahead where he logically had bedded down, drawing me along for one more chance to jump him. It's hard to turn away from a moose that you are sure is just over the next ridge, but I finally left him, and reluctantly set out for camp.

"Cas and I had hunted the old trail for about five miles west of camp a couple of days earlier. It should be north of me now, and I wasn't too worried that I had less than an hour's light left, as when I hit the trail I could easily follow it to camp in the dark.

"I had to run lines with my compass, as every time I pulled it from my pocket to check I found I was circling left, heading 15 or 20 degrees west of north. It was when it became too dark to pick out a good target on my next bearing that I felt my stomach churn and fear chill my spine, as I should have hit the trail by now.

"A hundred fear-loaded worries hammered into my head as I hurried on: West is forever, trackless all the way to the Pacific a hundred and fifty miles away; I would die out there; the trail is north, I HAVE to find it; it's almost too dark already to see; it can't be more than a couple of hundred yards ahead, I'd better run; I should have hit it long ago; could I have crossed it already, without noticing it? No, impossible - or is it?

"I don't know how long I travelled in a mindless scramble through the black forest, bending and snapping branches, running through open timber, stumbling over roots, cursing my way through unseen thickets of jackpine, feeling my way around tangled windfalls. I dipped suddenly into little draws and climbed up steep banks, floundered through half frozen hummocky swamps, guessed my way around waterfilled potholes and sloughs. It was when scrabbling on the ground to find my cap, torn off by a branch, that I realized that I was doing what hunters who die in the bush do, and tried to talk some sense into myself.

"Hold it! Take your time. Think! Where am I and what are my options? I should build a fire and make camp, but this forest is so vast they'd never find me. I'll have to get out by myself.

"Fire three shots: - * - * - * - Listen! Nothing!! Oh God, don't let me die out here in this wilderness! Let me see, the logging road we drove in on runs more or less north and south, about ten miles east of camp, probably at least fifteen miles east of here. The trail runs approximately east and west. There's nothing else. Where in hell can the trail be? I've come north far enough to have hit it long ago. Can I have passed the end of it?

"God knows what direction I've travelled since I started to run. If I go east I could go right past camp, but I should hit the logging road eventually. I MUST have passed west of the end of the trail. If I go east and south I might hit the trail before the logging road, but if I DIDN'T pass the west end of trail, south takes me farther from it and I don't know where the logging road ends. God, I'm lost! No, keep your head. Try for another hour, travelling back east and south, but no more running! If you don't hit anything, build a fire, make camp and try for the logging road tomorrow."

Eight or ten miles away, Cas had walked into camp at dusk that evening, unloaded his rifle, and greeted Bob and Gord as Gord poured him a drink.

"Where's Howard?" he asked.

"Coming in from dressing a moose, I hope," Bob replied. "During that skiff of snow this morning we ran into a fresh track, and followed it southwest about a mile. Gord and I left it there and came back to hunt the country behind the big swamp, but Howard wanted to stay on the track a while longer, as he figured we were pretty close to it. He said that if he didn't get a shot by three o'clock he'd head straight north and hit the trail running west from here, and come in on it."

They prepared supper, sat around for another half hour, stepped out in the night and fired a shot toward the west, and listened intently as the echoes died and were swallowed up by the lonely sigh of the chill night breeze in the black forest.

"Brrr! It's dark and empty out here!" Bob exclaimed.

"It might be a long night. We might as well eat," Gord replied as they trooped dejectedly back into the camper.

They lingered over their meal, each worrying in his own way about their missing companion, thinking what it would be like for him fighting his way through thickets of jackpine and windfalls and swamps in the dark, wondering whether he'd make a camp, dreading the decision to go out to look for him.

As they were finishing supper, Cas asked, "What bearing did you say he was going to take?"

"Well," Bob replied, "He said if he didn't get a shot by three o'clock he'd head straight north and hit the trail about five miles west of here."

"Where's the map?"

Gord reached a topographical map down from a shelf

and spread it on the table.

"Where did you leave him?"

Bob studied the map for a moment. "About here," he replied, marking the map with a pencil.

"Damn, I'll bet he's missed the end of the trail. See where it swings north and ends up at this little lake? If he followed the moose anywhere down into here, then swung north he could miss the far end of the trail by a hundred yards, or half a mile, or two miles. It wouldn't matter how far he missed it, there's nothing out there but hundreds of square miles of wilderness. Look at this."

The others huddled over the map as Cas traced the faint dotted trail that was Howard's lifeline.

"I didn't notice that gradual swing north when we were hunting it a few days ago, and I'll bet he didn't either. We didn't talk about how far it went, and I doubt if he ever checked it on the map, or noticed that it doesn't go out there very far. I'll bet the next week's cooking that he's gone past the end of it."

"I hope he keeps his head, and makes a camp. I'd hate to have to sleep out there tonight, but if he doesn't settle down he could be anywhere by morning, and what a night that would be," Bob shuddered.

"I think he'll camp," Gord replied, "and he's good with a compass, so I don't think he'll get out there too far. But camp or not, I think we'd better do all we can to bring him in tonight."

"Yeah, we'd better get organized," Cas replied. "The trail is hell for mudholes and water, and we'd bog the truck down in the first half mile, so about all we can do is hike out as far as the trail goes, fire a shot every mile or so, and see if we can raise an answer. If we can't raise him we should be back by one or two o'clock. We'll have to think then about one of us driving in to Vanderhoof at daybreak to report him lost while the other two head back out to see if they can pick up his trail. I wish that skiff of snow had lasted, and hope it doesn't snow tonight."

Cas and Bob won (or lost) the toss. Gord prepared a thermos of coffee and grub while the other two selected a flashlight, rifle and shells, boots and jackets, and prepared for their long ordeal. They fired another shot as they moved away from the camper, stopped to listen, then faded away into the black night. Gord turned gloomily back to the camper to wash the dishes and try to get some sleep.

"As I stumbled to a stop, the terror that had drenched me for hours began to drain from my bones. God, can this be it? Crouching to get a better skyline on the straight little slit in the black forest, I could faintly see a line of stars hinting a narrow break in the wall of trees for fifty feet both right and left.

"With trembling fingers I lit and cupped a match, and in the bright glare glimpsed a few feet of frost sparkled grass with a pathway of bare, frozen ground. I raised the match to look for the parallel path of the ancient trail, but was plunged back into darkness as the match blew out.

"If this is it I'll kiss the ground," I muttered as I fumbled for another match. The flare of the second match revealed the twin path of a muddy, grassy trail, and just as it died I spotted a bootprint. On hands and knees I lit the third match, and felt tears come to my eyes as I studied the print and recognized the pattern in the frozen mud as my own Greb sole, made when I walked this trail, miles from camp, a few days ago.

"As I remained kneeling on the ground I could feel the despair drain from my body, to be replaced with a warm infusion of relief, happiness, contentment. I was safely delivered from the horror that had hammered in my head and heart for hours, of eventually losing my lonely fight for life in this endless wilderness, that my body would never be found, except by the bears and wolves and other predators who stripped all woodland carcasses to scattered bones.

"The faint, far-off "Puttt" of a rifle shot miles to the east brought me to my feet, and I smiled as I answered their shot and took my first stiff, tired strides to meet my companions."

* * * * * * * * *

GRIZZLIES

During our hunting trips my companions and I have many times had to contend with the presence of grizzlies, but luckily have always avoided direct confrontation. We have, however, sat around many campfires and heard enough hair raising grizzly tales from neighboring hunters to fill a book. When you have meat hanging in the woods, you have to expect a challenge at any time, and you had best be prepared for it.

There was the guide who had a pair of Americans hunting moose in the Cariboo country. When they returned to retrieve a moose they had hung in the woods a couple of days earlier, they found a grizzly had hauled it down and was feeding on it.

One of the hunters threw up his rifle and fired, and the bear tumbled backward out of sight into a little draw. The hunter yelled, "I got him!" and rushed forward, to be met by a charging grizzly who for some reason rushed right past him to attack the other two.

The guide got one shot away before the bear was on him, roaring and slashing and biting. His first bite was right through the stock of his rifle, the next one tore off an ear, and he had his teeth locked through his victim's shoulder when he finally died of eight more shots fired into him by the frantic hunters.

* * * * * * * * *

Hunting one day with Gord in the Germanson Landing area of Northern B.C., Gord shot a big bull moose that fell in an area of heavy second growth evergreens that restricted our view to a few feet. We knew there were several grizzlies in the area who had cleaned up on the remains of every kill we had seen that week.

Over half a mile from the road, Gord and I worked hard to pack two loads of meat to the truck that afternoon, and had to leave half the moose out there overnight. We were positive the next morning that our meat would have been claimed by a grizzly, and knew we had to be within thirty or forty feet of the site before we could see it. That's far too close to challenge a grizz to "his" meat, but we had to do it.

I'll always remember our stalk that morning, rifles loaded and cocked, safety off, working through the heavy growth of small evergreens, covering one another and expecting a whooshing rush of a grizzly at every step.

Well it was anticlimactic to eventually reach our moose, and find we had no more serious challenge for the meat than three or four whiskyjacks. The second half of the moose reached the road far faster and with far less labor and trouble than that of the day before.

* * * * * * * * *

Tom and I tracked a wounded elk one day for over two miles in heavy alder and underbrush in the Rockies. It was bleeding heavily for the first mile or more, and we had expected to find it at any moment. However it seemed to recover as it travelled, and we eventually lost it after a very stiff climb, no more trace of blood, and a mixup with many other elk tracks. We searched the area for hours until we were satisfied it had not lain down, and reluctantly left it.

On our hunt that evening we passed within a couple of hundred yards of the hillside where Tom had shot the elk, and were horrified to see a huge silver grizzly literally flow up the trail in the opposite direction to that taken by the fleeing elk, mill about for a few minutes when it came to the end (beginning) of the blood trail, then flow at twenty miles an hour back down the trail again.

He had come across the blood trail and taken it in the wrong direction at first. We spent some thoughtful hours on what we'd have been up against if that grizz had been tearing along that blood trail, nose to the ground, at the same time we were, sometimes crawling on hands and knees through thick undergrowth.

* * * * * * * *

I shot a big bull elk in a mountain draw, and three of us managed to get the meat packed out that afternoon. When I went back next morning for the antlers, the kill site had been rearranged and carefully covered. Fortunately the antlers were not considered a worthy trophy by the bear, but I sure earned them twice in getting them out of there.

Bill and Harold came in to camp one night, a bit shaken. They had come across a house-sized area of scraped ground in the woods where a bear had worked hard to scrape up enough material to build a big mound in the center. Since it seemed to be days old, they spent a few minutes in kicking the mound apart to uncover the pretty ripe remains of a moose kill.

When they came back through the same area a couple of hours later they were horrified to find that the mound had been carefully rebuilt by a grizzly who was no doubt pretty upset at their interference with HIS food. They travelled the scary next half mile with one walking forward and the other walking backward, rifles cocked.

* * * * * * * *

Here are a couple of bear tales experienced by neighboring hunters:

There was the fellow who drove alone the twenty five miles out from Prince George to Giscome at daylight, for a couple of hours moose hunting before he had to go back to work. He bagged a moose, field dressed it, winched it into a tree and hurried back to town. When he came back that evening he brought only his wife's little 25 caliber rifle, as he'd be packing the meat a couple of hundred yards to the road and didn't want to carry his big rifle.

Well, as he approached his kill a big grizzly stood up on his hind feet and roared a challenge. In a panic the hunter fired a single shot, and as the bear dropped in an apparent charge he dropped the rifle and fled. When he reached his truck there was no sign of the bear, but rather than go back in there, he drove to the nearest hunters' camp and recruited four hunters to go back with him.

They found the bear had dropped dead, killed by that hurried little 25 caliber bullet passing through his throat and severing his spine. One lucky shot from a 25 caliber rifle killed a bear instantly, ten close-up shots from hunting rifles were needed to stop another mauling a man.

* * * * * * * *

A couple of local Kootenay area hunters on a weekend elk hunt were travelling light, sleeping in the open back of their pickup. They had bagged an elk that day, hung it in the woods, brought the liver back to camp, and hung it safe from rodents in a sack on the side mirror of their truck.

Awakened by a swaying truck, they froze at the sight of a big grizzly tugging and pulling at the sack a few inches from their heads. Imagine their relief when it tore loose before the bear looked around for help, or a substitute meal.

THE YELLOW BUG

Bill and Ed and I hunted together for many years. Ed had a Volkswagon bug that was unique in many ways, and bore no resemblance to the standard bug:

It had been stripped to frame and engine, the frame was shortened 21 inches, the engine was changed to a more powerful VW engine taken from a van, and the transmission was changed to a rather rare VW "mountain" transmission. Roll bars were welded in place, the body was clad with heavy gauge steel panels fabricated from old fashioned refrigerators and freezers, cut and placed to take advantage of curved corners, painted a bright yellow. These body panels were so strong that in years of very rough use they scarcely showed a mark. A soft top and side curtains were rolled above and on each side of the windshield most of the time, put up only in severe weather.

That bright yellow, compact, high clearance, powerful little bug climbed mountains and forded streams and washouts and followed long-abandoned trails or bulldozer tracks and blazed new trails to take Bill and Ed and me to the top of the world and back. We loved it, and it still looks almost as good as new as it continues to service a second generation of mountain wanderers.

Its combination of light weight, power, speed and wide traction rear tires took us to virgin territory on the tops of mountains, through muskeg, mud and snow that was impassable to our expensively equipped competitors in their 4x4's and fancy rigs. However, since we frequently found ourselves in territory that no one else could reach, we relied on ingenuity, luck, and Ed's nerveless, expert driving to keep us out of trouble.

* * * * * * * *

We were hunting one year north of Fort St. John and west of the Alaska Highway. The country was a mixture of moose meadows and timber, and we hadn't seen a road or trail for miles. That was not a problem, as the little bug zipped us across meadows and through leads in the scattered timber as we scouted for moose.

The low lying meadows back there were becoming bigger as we went along, until we finally entered one that seemed a couple of miles wide. Speeding along in our crossing however we suddenly noticed that we were throwing a rooster tail of water behind us, and realized that we were into muskeg!

We knew if we stopped, or if the bug stalled or got stuck we'd lose it, as there was no way anyone could reach us with a vehicle. We'd be lucky if we could cross it ourselves on foot. Ed poured the coal to it and headed for a little jackpine "island", where he pulled up on relatively firm ground.

We could see water glistening in our trail. Testing the ground, we sank over our boots as we scrambled back from a probably bottomless mixture of peat and moss and water, and could visualize the bug slowly sinking out of sight in it. The far "shore" seemed a mile away. After considerable discussion of our non existent options we concluded that the only way out was to go for it at full speed, and hope for the best.

We spent some time on our island, clearing a runway. Ed backed the bug to the end of it, we loaded up, crossed our fingers, and took off. Well, we could have kissed that little machine, as with a rooster tail of water flying behind us, we raced across ground so soft it wouldn't support a man, and reached firm ground at last.

We took a second look at untracked meadows after that experience.

* * * * * * * *

We set up camp one year below the Flathead plateau, and fought our way up the precipitous trail to the top in the dark of our first morning there. A short distance after we reached the top we passed the dim shapes of bulldozers and construction machinery, with evidence of large diameter pipeline construction. Looking back on it now, we were foolish to go on, but we were anxious to get back twenty miles or so to good elk country, and there were no signs to indicate the trail would be closed.

Heading back for camp that evening we were within a couple of hundred yards of the drop-off when we were stopped by a big black trench intersecting our trail!

We checked our side of the ditch right to the drop-off and could find no way to get to the other side. We went back and followed the ditch, open all the way back to an impassable area. It was six feet deep and about six feet wide, with earth piled on our side. The pipeline crew had gone for the night.

Ed checked it over carefully, and figured he could jump the bug across if we cleared some dirt and built a ramp, but he was a bit concerned about upsetting on the steep side-slope of his runway. So we figured that if one of us rode the running board on the high side, rolled off into the new earth bank just before he hit the ramp, and he turned down the hill as he braked on the far side, we probably would make it. I volunteered for the running board.

We spent some time with our shovel moving dirt and preparing the ramp, checked the route for rocks, drove back fifty yards, crossed our fingers, and took off!

We must have been doing 30 when I rolled off the running board and ended up in the dirt pile. I got to my feet to see Ed's brake lights down the slope on the far side of the ditch, and knew that he and the little bug had done it again.

We watched the next day as those huge ditchers and bulldozers worked to cut their ditch straight down what appeared to be a sixty degree slope. Too steep for machines to work independently, a big bulldozer anchored above slowly let out the heavy winch cable holding the ditching machine working fifty feet below. It looked like very precarious work, but as one studies the hundreds of miles of mountain pipeline he realizes that this is quite a common experience.

* * * * * * * *

Up the same road on the same plateau a couple of years later, we discovered as we were returning that we had blown a brake cylinder and were rapidly losing our brakes. By the time we reached the drop-off we were using only our emergency brake to stop, had no facilities up there to repair the problem, and couldn't even consider going over the drop-off without brakes.

Our camp was just a speck two miles below. We would not only have to risk leaving the bug up there over night with its load of valuable equipment, we faced a very stiff climb back up in the morning with tools and repairs. We decided to drive it down.

Selecting a big dry snag from the scattered pine

trees on the plateau, we cut it down and trimmed it to a sixteen foot, fifteen inch diameter log. We chained the log to the rear axle, tried it for drag, and hauled it to the edge.

Ed found as he started over that the log would hold him, and he needed just a touch of power to move. Bill and I rode the running boards, ready to drop off if it started to run away, and we did drop off in switchbacks and very steep places to lighten the bug and give the log more drag.

We reached bottom with the log scraped and scruffed, and the links of my nice light chain stretched and bent, but we did get the little yellow bug down safely.

* * * * * * * *

The Rockies in south western B.C. are underlaid with vast coal beds, and over the years many virgin wilderness areas were scarred with the tracks of exploring bulldozers that cut and fought their way to the tops of mountains, stopped here and there to scrape away a few feet of overburden, and went on, snooping and sniffing for coal. When they found rich beds, some of our best wilderness elk country disappeared behind "NO HUNTING" barriers as mountains were ground down and sifted, train loaded or discarded in great black piles of waste that could change a beautiful mountain into a denuded, shapeless black hill.

Some of our hunting ranges survived, or have survived to date, but scarred here and there with old, overgrown, gullied bulldozer tracks. These were the highways that Ed and his little yellow bug sometimes used to transport us to high mountain ridges, where we could look down on miles of hunting country and know that we were alone up there.

We explored one such 'dozer trail one afternoon. It was steep, crooked, and gullied with a years-old watercourse that had left a two foot trench wandering from side to side down the steep, narrow, shale covered, somewhat overgrown track.

It was a very difficult climb. Ed maneuvered and straddled and crossed that watercourse countless times, shifting gears up and down and maintaining a high RPM as we climbed to a lofty ridge that appeared to be prime elk territory. After a brief exploratory hunt, we decided to camp at the bottom of the mountain and be back up there before daylight the next morning.

Well, we were well up the mountain, leaping and bouncing up that awful trail in the dark when there was a sudden, loud BANG under us! Bill and I thought we had caught a rock, but Ed stopped instantly. We found that we had locked our differential, and nothing for it but to get the bug down the mountain and loaded for the nearest repair shop.

The track was only a few feet wide, too narrow to turn on with locked rear wheels. We got out our come-along (hand winch), and enough rope to tie the front end of the bug to a tree above, winch it up, and swing the front end in the air over the edge and around so it was pointed down the trail.

Now we had a REAL problem. As we tried to push the bug, one of the huge rear tires tried to turn forward while the other tried to turn back, and in spite of all our efforts, we couldn't unlock it or release it. There was no way on earth for another vehicle to get up there to rescue the bug, so we had a choice of abandoning it or improvising some way to get it down ourselves.

Ed and Bill jacked it up and removed the backward turning wheel while I got the chainsaw out and cut a four foot length of 5" diameter alder that, growing out of the face of the vertical bank, was shaped like a hockey stick. We cut notches in it for rope bindings and a socket for the brake drum, and Bill, a commercial fisherman and rope expert, bound that alder skid under the drum and tied it to the frame so securely that it lasted for a rough, grinding three mile slide.

The bug required expert packing to store all our gear, but it was now a shambles as we dumped rifles, jackets, spare rope, come-along, shovel, axe, into it as we finished using them. When I went to put the chainsaw away, the only space I could see for it was the driver's floor area, but I didn't worry about that since Ed wouldn't be driving the bug down anyway.

We started our long push with Bill and I behind, pushing hard while Ed shoved from the side, steering with one hand on the wheel. It was real hard going for a while, especially since we had to cross the watercourse to the mountain side of it. There was a five hundred foot drop off the other side. We had to dig a trench for a hundred feet along the wall, as there wasn't room otherwise to avoid putting the right side with its skid into the mid-trail ditch.

As the down trail steepened, we found it much easier pushing. Soon Bill and I were trotting as Ed rode the running board, then we were running, then we were stretching in huge strides as Ed climbed in to apply the brakes. As Bill and I dropped behind and watched Ed squirm into the seat we heard him swear at the chainsaw blocking the brake pedal. With our hearts in our mouths, we saw the last of Ed in a leaping bug with three wheels and a skid and no brakes disappear around a curve at 40 MPH in a billowing cloud of dust.

We listened, heartsick, for the crash as the runaway bug went over that five hundred foot cliff, hoping that Ed could bail out but knowing he'd be smashed up anyway if he did. But all was silence until we heard a faint "Haloo" and a request to look for his cap on the way down.

Bill and I grinned and slapped high fives in relief, then trudged a half mile down the trail, marvelling at Ed's steering as we traced his skid marks. We found one place where the skid left the ground in a leap of over twenty feet!

Ed was busy repacking the bug when we returned his cap to him. One item he had not yet repacked was the wide rear wheel which had apparently fallen off the hood and was lying in the bush in front of the bug. (We had lain the wheel, loose, on the hood before we started down).

Well, Ed was still shaking his head in disbelief as he told us the story: As he was fighting to control the runaway bug, bouncing and swerving down the gullied track, the wheel with its very wide tire slid off the front of the hood, and he ran over it! He didn't know whether it turned upward as he passed over it or if it remained flat and compressed under the bug's metal body pan, but it threw him up in the air for a long, airborne leap and a two wheel landing that he barely managed to control. (That would account for that long leap that Bill and I noticed on the way down).

Then, unbelievably, as the bug finally slowed down on levelling road, the wheel rolled past him in the foot or two of space available as though someone were steering it, crashed into the bush on the next curve, and laid there!. By all odds it should have gone over the edge, and we probably would never have been able to find it or recover it from the timber so far below. We sat there for a few minutes marvelling at the triple miracle of Ed's survival, the bug's safety, and that wheel lying there in front of us! (And if you doubt any of this, I'll gladly supply Ed's and Bill's phone numbers).

We still had a long way to go. The skid was wearing, but still secure, so back to the three man, heavy pushing for a while, easing to easy going and even running now and then, a couple of winch jobs across creeks, and finally down to road that was decent enough that I walked the last half mile and brought up the camper and bug trailer.

We winched it onto the trailer, replaced that marvellous, worn-to-an-inch skid with the wheel, tied it down, and headed for Cranbrook. There we rented stall space in a garage, found a used VW differential, and spent a day getting the bug on the road again.

Bill and I taking a rest, part way down the mountain.
Note the skid replacing the right rear wheel.

That's me winching the bug onto its trailer. Note the skid, and its drag mark.

Bill (left) and Ed, contemplating a trip to Cranbrook. Bill is sitting on the tire that Ed ran over.

The bug, in typical bug country.

Ready to go over the drop-off without brakes.

Bill and Ed, cruising the Flathead Plateau.

Bill and I playing crib on a hot September noon siesta.

Ed, loaded with elk in meat sacks.

This is not an aerial view, it is mountain top country we wandered with the bug.

On the road north to the Alaska Highway.

A few days later, and 60 degrees colder.

Bill defrosting the windshield on a very cold morning.

Gord (left) and Bill, with the moose in Ed's trunk that almost didn't come out.

THE FROZEN BOY

The weather was deteriorating rapidly as Bill and Ed and I pulled in one November afternoon to the Giscome area east of Prince George, on a moose hunting trip. We had my truck and camper, towing the bug on its trailer. The road was deeply rutted, water filled and greasy, and was being loaded with snow as a cold front blew in by late afternoon. The temperature dropped fast as evening drew on, but as the snow built up it insulated the mud and the water filled ruts and ditches, so we had wind, deepening snow, mud, water, and near zero temperature to contend with.

We had to drop the trailer, unload and chain up the bug and drive it separately, and chain up the truck as the storm grew and the temperature continued to drop. Anxiously looking for a sheltered campsite as darkness approached, we came upon an old abandoned logging company maintenance garage, the size of a farm stable. The big doors stood open, with a camper already sheltered inside. On enquiry, we were welcomed in by the other hunting party, who backed their rig up to make room for us.

Following supper and a few hands of crib, we made up our beds and settled in for the night, with our camper furnace throwing a good heat. We had been asleep for two or three hours when we were awakened by shouting outside. As we sat up we heard something like, "Hey, wake up! I'm coming back. I need ...."

None of us could agree on exactly what was said. We could see no one outside, and finally decided it must have been someone from the other hunting party, probably drunk. After puzzling over it, we went back to bed.

We were awakened again an hour later by the same voice shouting, "Hey, get up. I need to come in!"

We opened the door to find a snow covered man carrying a snow covered boy. In a blast of cold air we took the boy from him and helped him into the camper. As we hurriedly donned pants and shoes we found that the boy was barely conscious, and the man was disoriented and beyond exhaustion.

We turned up the furnace, lit the stove and started getting the ten year old youngster's clothes off, only to find them to have been soaked and frozen on his body. He

33

was terribly ill clad for this weather, with light underwear, denim trousers, light jacket, a plastic type of cowboy boots that were wet and frozen and partially filled with icy snow surrounding partly frozen light socks.

It was a quarter hour after we got him stripped and massaged and wrapped in blankets before he brightened enough to accept a hot drink of cocoa laced with honey. His uncle (it turned out) was not in much better shape. As he took off his boots and jacket and hugged the furnace blast he told us their story over coffee and sandwiches:

He had picked up his ten year old nephew in Prince George that morning for an exciting first day of moose hunting for the boy. They had driven through light snow for about ten miles back on this road, hunted until noon, and decided to head for home when snow started falling heavily.

The road and weather conditions worsened rapidly. After being stuck, struggling out of a mudhole, jacking and chaining up, they had fought snow, mud and water for the whole afternoon and for hours after dark. They were both wet and exhausted when they finally abandoned their car in a deep mudhole about six miles back, and started their twenty five mile hike for home.

When we drove that road the next morning, it was interesting and heartbreaking to track their progress and read their ordeal in the snow.

The deep mud ruts were still only partially frozen, and water lay under the snow in many places. Their car was deeply mired in a big watery mudhole, with many tracks around it showing how hard they had tried to keep it moving.

They had started from the car walking independently, but the boy's tracks wandered and he fell frequently. Then the tracks came together for a mile or two, as though the man were assisting him to walk, but he still fell, and sometimes they both did. Then the boy laid down in the snow in several places, and the man's tracks showed that he had difficulty getting him on his feet and moving again.

They began to pay no attention to water, walking through icy pools and puddles instead of going around them. Finally only one staggering set of tracks showed that the boy was being carried - and those tracks revealed several falls and went through water holes too.

The final body mark in the snow was about a half mile from our camp, where the man had laid the boy down and left him, to come to the big shed he remembered or saw in the distance. I don't know what help he expected to find there but he was lucky to find it occupied.

He had shouted for us to get up, then instead of coming in to us for help he had hurried back to get the boy and carry him that last half mile. They were both very close to becoming statistics.

A 4x4 truck, chained up all around, turned up about midnight. It was the boy's father, looking for them. He had his heater going full blast and the cab very hot, and since our charges were feeling much better, warmed by our furnace and drinks and food and the prospect of a warm bed, we felt they wouldn't be too uncomfortable on the long ride home in their partially dried clothing.

We found a hunting rifle, barrel plugged with snow and the action frozen in ice, leaning against the wall beside our truck the next morning, a last reminder of the man's disorientation. He had carried his rifle for all those terrible miles, then forget he had it when he was home free.

We returned it to him on our way through Prince George later in the week.

* * * * * * * *

The old shelter building, with Ed and Bill and the two hunters who made room for us.

Fighting mud and slush on the Frozen Boy's trail. The bug bogged down pushing snow.

FLOWER WHEELS

I can't leave our hunting stories without telling of our "flower wheels". They are a rather rare phenomenon that may be familiar to some of you who have travelled snow country. They need just the right combination of weather and snow:

Bill and Ed and I were coming down from Fort St. John on a road that had an inch of fresh, soft snow. Our truck wheels picked up what snow there was, leaving a bare track on the highway, throwing the snow as slush under our fenders.

The slush built up and froze, until our tires were cutting their own path through the ice under the fenders. Every few miles we found that we couldn't turn the front wheels out of their slots to steer, so we stopped to chop them free.

Strangely, as we travelled that day the hubcaps attracted water spun up from the pavement or dribbling from the fenders and as it was thrown off by centrifugal force it froze in long, clear icicles. They spread out in a perfect ten inch sunburst that formed such pretty flowers on each wheel we looked forward to each ice chopping stop to see the how big they had grown.

The flower wheel. Note how the fender is iced up, and how the tire picked up snow off the road.

MEMORY SNAPSHOTS

We have shared a few of our hunting memories with
you on these pages, but have covered only a fraction of
them. If my beaten up old binoculars could only have
stored and reproduced some of the pictures they've seen,
they'd have included the following:

The beauty of a majestic bull elk as he surveyed the
world far below, his wide spread antlers and toffee
colored coat gleaming in the dawn's first high alpine
patch of light...

The pure white mountain goat standing on precipitous
rocks a couple of thousand feet above, attracting our
view by the crackling of a dislodged rock falling for
hundreds of feet...

The huge, glowing black grizzly tugging and jerking
as he hauled a full grown elk carcass into the woods...

The lens filling picture of a bald eagle soaring a
hundred feet above as I lay back to study him from my
mountain viewpoint, when on steady outspread wings he
reached one leg forward, dipped his head, and extended a
talon to scratch an itchy spot on his white chin...

The struggle of a royal bull elk to keep his harem
together as he moved them along a high ridge while being
harassed by two younger bulls seeking to steal a cow or
two. (One of them did)...

The four elk calves racing and leaping, chasing and
gamboling across a precipitous, rocky mountainside that
we had walked precariously, and knew was impossible for
them to even trot upon...

The tense, thirty minute, motionless staring match
between me and a young bull elk half hidden in brush
three hundred yards away, as I tried in vain to verify a
third tine to his antlers to make him legal...

The high flying V's of Canada geese passing over
snowcapped mountain tops on their long flight south...

The coyote trotting confidently across the new glare
ice of a little lake, who, when the ice cracked under him
with a resounding ring, scrabbled desperately to get
traction before racing, tail between his legs, back to
the shore he had left...

The flock of ducks who did a hilarious job of
skiing, skating, and clumsy flopping about as they slid
fifty feet across the same ice on a glide-in landing...

The majestic, full curl ram wandering in the virgin silence of the high rock face of Quintette Mountain fifteen years before that beautiful mountaintop melted away under the blasts of dynamite, thunder of big diesels and chatter of machinery chewing and gnawing its guts out, to spew them into miles of belting conveying them down to the processing silos of Tumbler Ridge. That glorious, powerful ram was replaced in my memory of Quintette Mountain years later by my grandson learning the beginnings of his all-star hockey career there, and if things must change, he is a worthy symbol of it...

And there are some closeups that never needed to get into my binoculars:

The humbling experience of chasing myself on my first ever hunting trip, when in snow and heavy hoar frost I failed to meet my companion as arranged, climbed a tall tree in a vain effort to spot him, walked another half hour, came upon fresh tracks and ran along them to catch up. They took me in a wide circle right back to the tree I had climbed!...

The wolverine who snarled and stood his ground over the discards of a moose kill until I was very near and had released my safety catch, then grumbled and muttered from under a brushpile a few feet away as I nervously set up my pre-planned blind...

The snow white ermine that joined me for a half mile walk along a trail, skipping and bouncing along cheerily over and under the roadside brushpiles...

The fat, rust colored grizzly sow swatting the rump of a laggard twin cub into the shelter of roadside woods as we approached...

The silent drift of a big horned owl settling into a tall tree in the glade of The Three Bears, and staring at us with its big round yellow eyes...

The scene at our jeep as I returned to a noon rendezvous to find a meal half prepared and suddenly abandoned, and a red cap hanging on a branch across a wide meadow to signal my companion's location and reason for his hasty departure...

The countless squirrels who could be depended upon to wait patiently until I was well settled into a good vantage point, then wake the woods around me with their yelling while pointing me out to everything around..

The countless squirrels who, in a silent forest, could drop pine cones at a tempo that had me searching for a strolling moose...

The belligerent big bull moose that walked right in on us as we finished dressing and hanging a moose in the dark of an October night...

The beautiful little wilderness lake that was so full of hungry two pound fighting trout we could have filled our truck with them...

The beaver that slapped the water like a pistol shot about twenty feet off shore as I was stalking a moose, and jumped me right out from under my cap...

The morning I sat on a high mountain ridge as the sun's first bright beams lit my world, and, studying the brightening panorama below, got real jumpy at the flits of movement in my peripheral vision fifty feet to my left until I identified them as Bill's five hundred foot shadow moving on a pine tree as he approached...

The pack of timber wolves that broke the silence of my lonely evening vigil with a sudden gale of sound that filled the woods around me and grew with every racing second as they passed me by.

Words can convey very little of the true depth of one's memories of the hunt to those who have not participated in them, but I hope these pages have given you some appreciation of the fact that no true hunter regrets the time he may have spent in "fruitless" days of wandering our beautiful forests and mountains, and that a freezer full of meat is the very least of his concerns.

If only we'd had Marty Stauffer's camera crew!

* * * * * * * *

So, for now we leave our hunting trips that formed the background for our years of friendship and the tales we told to one another, to take you to the tales themselves, as told by me, and Gord, and Bill, and Ed as we really got to know, respect and appreciate one another over the years:

We'll start with mine.

THE EARLY DAYS

My childhood was spent in Saskatchewan, where I grew up during the windblown, drought stricken, dust stormed depression years of the "Dirty Thirties". We were a close knit family of wonderfully supportive parents, four girls and two boys. We children had been born during their homestead years, fifteen miles west of Hanley and forty miles south of Saskatoon.

Dad had first come from Ontario to Saskatchewan on a harvest excursion train in 1904, and had stayed during Hanley's pioneer years as a center for the land rush that brought thousands of homesteaders to the Prairies from Eastern Canada, United States and Europe. This flat prairie land stretched from the rocky wilderness of the Canadian Shield to the foothills of the Rockies, north to the parklands and forests and south to the American border and beyond. It had been a bountiful home to Indians and buffalo for thousands of years, but during the two and a half centuries before our time there it had come under rule by charter of the Hudsons' Bay Company as part of their vast empire covering the north-western third of the continent.

During most of the white man's era (north of the American border) the Indians enjoyed relatively bountiful and peaceful times. Most of their contact, if any, with white men involved trading furs and pemmican to the trading posts scattered along the rivers from the prairie parklands to the far northern tundra. Fur trading posts were the only centers of commerce, and rivers were the only highways until the early 1880's. However, when the Canadian Pacific Railroad cut through the rocks of the Canadian Shield, swept over the prairies and on through the Rockies, it brought with it a flood of settlers who spread a vast patchwork blanket of black soil and golden grain over the ancient buffalo grass.

They built hundreds of villages and towns along the spiderwebs of rail lines that spread in all directions during the next twenty years. Hanley, built on the main line, was central to and an early staging point for these. Those who were destined for farming brought carloads of farm equipment, horses, oxen, cattle, with them. The cost of shipping from Minnesota to Hanley was $14 per freight car load. The settlers travelled free.

Early accounts tell of the carnival appearance of Hanley during the "settling seasons" of those years. Homesteader trains came in frequently, sometimes two and three a day, disgorging settlers and their carloads of effects. Some were to stay and settle in the Hanley district; most were to trek by horse or oxcart to locations up to a hundred miles away.

As a youth, Dad hauled freight and lumber from the railhead by horse and wagon, worked for his older brother in his new general store, and returned to Ontario in 1910 to marry my mother and bring her west.

Their homestead was in an area of light soil and stunted poplar trees. During those first years of turning over the sod of buffalo grass or prairie wool, grain grown on light soil germinated and matured faster than that grown on heavy soil, avoiding the risk of early frost, so light soil homesteads were at a premium. As those first years passed, though, and the sod of early plowing was broken down, a combination of dry years and strong winds blew away the thin layer of humus and brought the true sandy nature of the soil to the surface. Those homesteaders who had sought this type of land began to regret it.

My early memories of this land, after I was born in 1915, were of sand dunes in the fields, stinging sand abrading our bare legs as we walked to school, fence lines buried to the top wire in golden sand with little curliques of drift forming hot, dry patterns of waves on the land. On the roads, hundred yard stretches of sand wallows that could swallow a car to its axles were covered with layers of straw, so roads alternated between firm sand ruts and long stretches of straw surface. Paint was sandblasted off the buildings, and Mother recalled how her windows were "frosted" to dullness by blowing sand.

After a sandstorm a favorite activity for us children was to hurry out to the fields to search for arrowheads among newly exposed buffalo bones lying white on the sifting sand. We had gathered a large box of Indian artifacts by the time we left the homestead.

Well, we left the homestead in 1922. Dad rented a farm on the outskirts of Hanley for a couple of years, then we moved into town, where we six children spent the relatively prosperous years of the late 1920's and the depression and drought years of the early '30's, as we grew up and scattered to further education and careers.

Our little town was brand new when my father arrived there in 1904, and only twenty years old when we children moved there in 1922. However, I can't relate it in memory to new towns as we see them today, as it seemed forever grey, weatherbeaten, old, with its wooden sidewalks, scattered homes, false fronted stores facing dusty streets.

My earlier memories of a hustling, prosperous town surrounded by miles of golden grain, thundering trains, crowded streets, stores filled with Saturday night shoppers, faded away as I reached my teens. It now dominates my memory as a desolate scene of dust, wind and grasshoppers, of once-familiar farm homes standing empty to the lonely smell of vacant rooms, flapping wallpaper, broken windows and creaking doors of abandonment and neglect, tumbling mustard and Russian thistle rolling across barren fields in dust laden winds that buried fences, machinery and dreams.

The dust was everywhere, as black storm clouds of it drifted from as far away as Nebraska, Iowa, and the Dakotas, as well as from thousands of square miles of the Canadian Prairies. Permeating our very existence, it sifted through our windows and doors to film our sills and floors, dishes and clothing. Every sweeping yielded a dustpanful, every table-setting was preceded by a dusting of not only the table but of the dishes, which were then placed upside down on the table until they were served. We became accustomed to the moaning of the pervasive wind, to living with grit, to making do. We boys did our work and played our games, and found ways to pass the time.

On days that were too dusty for ball games, a favorite refuge was the large culvert under the railway tracks. It was about sixty feet long and four foot diameter, always cool on those hot dry days. With a deck of cards and a handful of matches, we learned to play poker for matches in the cool calm of the culvert as the moaning wind and dust and tumbleweeds passed us by. We discovered a way into the curling rink, and spent many summer afternoons there playing cards or just sitting and talking. The earth surface remained damp and cool for weeks after the ice melted, and mushrooms shared the pleasant earth in that cool, quiet shelter.

Looking back on it now, it is hard to believe we could be happy there, but we children grew up in a happy home, each of us busy in our own little world of school and work and play. We were not involved with the world beyond our brown horizon, so we accepted life as it was dealt to us, and made the most of it, spared the perspective of our parents who knew how much their life was changing as good times faded, year by year.

Businesses failed, salaries were cut in half, cars were put away or converted to horse drawn "Bennett Buggies", named after the Prime Minister of the time. Many people were forced to ask for relief in the form of food, clothing and fuel, and trainloads of food such as cheese, apples and dried codfish were donated and distributed from more prosperous communities in Eastern Canada.

We had a good hockey arena, built before the depression, and reputed at the time to be the best small town arena west of Winnipeg. We children had learned to skate and play hockey on an open air rink before the arena was built, but our parents never skated there. After all, they were elderly folks, almost forty years old!

They bought skates though for the opening of the arena, and we children were amazed with their grace as we watched them skating beautifully together to the Skaters' Waltz as the new sound system wafted music over the crowd.

Hockey was a winter madness on the prairies, which provided a large share of National Hockey League players for the six team league of Montreal Canadiens, Toronto Maple Leafs, Boston Bruins, Chicago Black Hawks, New York Rangers and Detroit Red Wings.

People sat glued to their radios every Saturday night listening to Foster Hewitt's play by play. Favorite teams and favorite stars had a huge following, and almost every boy dreamed of being one of them some day. The only boy in our town who had a reasonable prospect of going to the top in hockey had his career cut short by the war. He was killed over there.

I went through kids' hockey, the high school team, senior team representing the town in an eight team league, and made the Normal School team in Saskatoon playing in the university league (where three players did go on to NHL). I think I was reasonably close to moving up, as I was called in by the manager of the Saskatoon Junior Quakers of the elite Canadian Junior League and offered a tryout for the next year's team. (I was eighteen).

It was a choice between teaching or hanging around for a year on the slight prospect of making hockey a full time career, and I chose not to do that. I'll never know whether I'd have made it, but can at least look back on my writeup as a "hockey star" in the Normal School Year Book.

Our grandparents lived in a little home on the edge of town, and during my years from six to sixteen I did their chores every day. Chores included splitting and piling wood, filling the woodbox and coal scuttles, carrying water two blocks from the town pump, emptying ashes, weeding garden, shovelling snow, shopping for groceries six blocks away.

Grandpa was quite crippled with an arthritic hip, and walked with a cane. He had lost an eye to a flying nail many years earlier, and while his glass eye looked very natural, he was unable to close his eyelid over it. This meant that he slept with one eye open, and he was often sleeping in his rocking chair by the kitchen stove when I arrived to do the chores.

Very early in my days of knowing Grandpa, he impressed on me that even when he was asleep, he was keeping one eye on my activities. I suppose I was nine or ten before I could ignore that wide open eye staring at me and seeming to follow me everywhere as he slept, snoring, in his rocking chair.

I remember my tears, when, as a senior teenager I looked upon him in his coffin, saw him for the first time with both his eyes closed, and felt that he was truly, fully asleep at last.

* * * * * * * *

THE ELEVATOR

We boys living through the dusty, depression plagued apparent emptiness of a 1930's small prairie town would have scoffed at the suggestion that we were deprived. Dust and wind, Russian thistle and grasshoppers were the only life we knew.

We could keep busy all day in all seasons, with hockey, curling, baseball, soccer, and after-dark games like kick the can, hoist the sail, garden raids. If the wind and dust blew the ball game off the field, if our only baseball developed a big flap that would have to be taken home to stitch up again, well there were lots of empty buildings to play in. If the shoemaker still hadn't stitched up the old soccer ball, the blacksmith shop was good for an hour or two, watching flying sparks from glowing, hissing metal while we kept an eye open for bent scraps that we could save to freeze as handles into sand-and-water filled jam pail curling rocks for late fall curling on the slough. If extreme cold closed down the skating rink, we could be sure the road apples would be frozen hard for street hockey games.

And an empty, abandoned grain elevator was a natural challenge to the instincts of boys to find danger, excitement, and trouble. By the time we were in our early teens, four of the town's eight elevators were locked and abandoned to dust and depression and our ingenuity.

One afternoon Geoff Wrenshall, Charlie Smith and I found the lock on the crawlspace door of the Pioneer elevator was not secure. Furtively we opened it, worked our way down through the grain pit, up a ladder, and through a trap door to the main floor. Our hearts pounded as we looked around with the realization that we had all this abandoned man-sized world to ourselves. No one was watching over us to say "Don't touch that! Don't play there! Be careful!"

Looking up, we could see bin walls and conveyors, pipes and cables fading away into the gloom, to reappear far above in the dusty beams of light from unseen windows. A ladder spiked to the side of a bin rose endlessly until it disappeared near the roof. No one suggested climbing it. None of us had ever seen a ladder longer than sixteen feet, nor been up in a building higher than a barn loft or our second floor bedrooms.

Early in our exploration we discovered the manlift, which had carried operator Jock Kippen to the top in his rounds of greasing pulleys, checking bins and shifting conveyor pipes. We sensed at once the challenge of solving the operation of the lift, but looking up through the gloom to the window lit beams far above, we also sensed the potential terror in that long dark journey none of us knew anything about. We checked it very carefully before we tried our wings.

The manlift was a small open platform about the size of a warehouse pallet, with an A frame on each end which slid up guide rails. Steel cables fastened to each end of the platform went to the top, over pulleys, and down to counter-weights. A thick stationary rope through a hole in the center of the platform was fastened to the floor below, and to a beam 80 feet above. A foot pedal actuated a pair of spring loaded brake pads squeezing the guide rails. An 8 inch steel pin through the lift frame and into a guide rail locked the lift in place.

It was in an elevator like this where we boys played.
We had no green grass or trees in our town then.

After a final check, the three of us stepped on the platform and took white knuckle grips on the frame as Geoff pulled the pin and released the brake. Nothing happened! After a moment of indecision, Charlie reached up and pulled hard on the big rope. We rose about six feet, and sank slowly back to the floor.

"Mr. Kippen must have put counter-weights on the cables to match his own weight," Charlie exclaimed. "That way, he could go either up or down without much of a pull on this rope."

"Well, he's a pretty big man, but we three must outweigh him. Maybe if we all pull on the rope, we can go all the way to the top," I replied.

None of us could spare more than one hand for the rope, but we soon established a rhythm, and rose steadily with pulls and glides. I looked over the edge only once, and instantly had a two handed grip on the frame, inadvertently breaking the rhythm on the rope. There seemed to be nothing supporting us in that stomach-churning glimpse of our long, vertical trail of rails and swaying cables leading to the distant floor. I heard a murmured "Geeze, don't look down!" and realized Charlie, too, had looked over the edge.

We were all staring straight ahead as the light slowly brightened. Finally, in good light, we came level with a catwalk as our platform bumped to a stop. With weak knees and queasy stomachs, we transferred our grip, one trembling hand at a time, from rope and frame to catwalk rail, and stepped across the six inch wide, bottomless abyss.

Slowly, carefully, we hand-and-foot-walked our way along the lightly railed walks spanning the dark bins beneath us. When we reached the windows, however, the dread was all worth while, as we stared in awe at our first highrise view of our local world. We were fascinated at looking down at our familiar streets and houses, and the tiny people moving here and there among them. We could easily see elevators and a hint of houses in the several towns up to thirty miles away.

When we stepped on the lift to go down, things were different. Now we had a considerable weight advantage over the counterweights. As we released the brake, the platform sank beneath us, and gradually gained momentum until we were whizzing down at a breathtaking speed.

Geoff applied the brake in lots of time, and we reached bottom safely.

"Wow, did you ever imagine a ride like that!" shouted Charlie. "Let's go again!"

"Yeah," I said, "but why do all that work for a slow, one handed trip up? If just two of us go, we get a free ride."

"Then we'd have to pull ourselves down!"

"Not if one of us goes up the ladder."

The boys thought that over for a moment, then Charlie said, "Great, but it's your idea. Guess who climbs the ladder?"

"Okay, I'll go first. If it works, we'll take turns."

I watched Charlie and Geoff make a nice, smooth takeoff on their second flight. I stood by the swaying rope, listening to the rumble and swish and hiss of pulleys and cables, looking up to see the platform recede to postage stamp size. As they came to a stop, two brief flits of shadows moved far above as the boys stepped from the lift to the catwalk.

I took a deep breath and started up the ladder, saying to myself, "If you don't look up now, or down later, and if none of these rungs are loose or missing, this shouldn't be too bad." And it wasn't, except for the heart thumping step from the ladder to the catwalk. I was clinging to the rail pretty tightly when the boys returned from the windows.

Our second trip down was faster than the first, and as we gained confidence we enjoyed fast rides in both directions, two up, three down, two up, three down, with even the ladder man hurrying faster with each trip he made.

Word spread, and soon many boys were finding their way into empty elevators, and riding the lifts. This almost ended in tragedy one day, when Frank Hamre, Shorty Trask, and a couple of others went to our elevator for a few rides.

Frank jumped on the lift by himself, pulled the pin, and released the brake. He instantly shot upward at high speed, realized he was going far too fast, and applied the brake, only to find that the brake wouldn't stop a 90-pound boy on a lift set for about 220 pounds. In desperation he grabbed the pull-rope which was whizzing through the bottom of the lift. This burned most of the skin off the palms of both hands, but slowed him enough that he wasn't thrown off when he hit the top. The boys spent an awful hour getting him down again.

The story soon spread all over town, and this made our elevator operations much more difficult. One of the self-appointed guardians of the empty elevators was Alf Butler, the section-gang foreman, who lived right across the tracks from them.

We were there one evening when our lookout spotted Mr. Butler crossing the tracks, and we escaped just ahead of him. He chased us as we fled and scattered, and he was just behind Doc Chasmar as Doc dived under a fence and raced across the stubble field beyond.

Butler quit when Doc cleared the fence, but we were puzzled to watch Doc, with his dog at his heels, run and run and run until he stopped, exhausted, at the fence half a mile away.

He slowly returned, and we walked into the dusty field to meet him.

"Boy, that was some run! Why did you run so far?" we asked.

Doc blushed, wiped the perspiration from his face with a dusty sleeve, and reached down to pet his dog.

"Well, I knew old man Butler was reaching for my shirt when I dived under that fence. Then as I ran through the stubble I could hear him right behind me all the way across this field. How would you like to face him alone, away out here?"

"What are you talking about? Butler didn't even go through the fence!"

"No, but my darn dog did, and I was so sure it was Butler right at my heels, I didn't dare even look over my shoulder until I gave up and quit, at the second fence."

"You know, Doc, this old dog probably has a lot of miles in him yet. I'll bet, if you'd had stamina enough, the two of you would have run all the way to the border."

We all laughed as we ducked a double handful of dust scooped over our heads.

* * * * * * * *

THE DIME

Growing up in the prairies during the hungry thirties, we six children had never been farther from home than the annual forty mile trip to Saskatoon. We had never seen a real lake, a forest, ridden in a boat, slept in a tent, caught a fish.

I can now recognize Mother's courage the year she decided to give us a holiday at Waskesiu, far to the north in Prince Albert National Park. Our car was an old pickup truck, our road was a dusty two day trail of dirt and gravel, our only driver was my 17 year old brother, (and I doubt now whether he had a driver's license), our supplies consisted of a borrowed tent and whatever Mother packed out of the kitchen.

Riding in the open back of a truck for two days on those dusty roads was a never-forgotten adventure. The Prince Albert tourist camp with its varnished log cabins, white stone paths, and tall, fragrant pines, where we pitched our first tent on the pine needled ground, was the most beautiful sight we had ever seen. We went on the next day to Waskesiu and if last night was beautiful, this was heaven!

For more than a week we camped under the pines, walked the beaches, played and learned to swim in the lake, watched the fishermen come and go, marvelled at the surf in a storm.

I cranked the truck on the morning we crossed the Prince Albert bridge from camp to gas up on the way home, and must have forgotten to remove the crank, for we lost it. It took our last dollar to replace it at an auto wreckers - and that was the dollar that Mother had budgeted to feed us on the way home.

Someone among us had 25 cents, which bought enough food to keep us from dying of starvation on the road, but most of that went to sustain our brother, the driver. The rest of us feared that we couldn't last that long day without a meal.

A flat tire added to our problems. Flats were so common then that we didn't dare pass the next town without patching it as a spare, but without a cent of cash and none of today's facilities such as credit cards, bank cards or instant credit checks, Mother had to convince a garage man that her two dollar cheque drawn on

a distant bank wouldn't bounce. I'm sure he thought he
was performing an act of charity. She didn't have the
heart to pad the cheque and ask for change.

And after a big supper, with everyone talking at
once to tell Dad of our wonderful holiday, one of the
girls found a dime in her purse! We joked for days about
all the good things that dime would have bought if she'd
found it when we needed it.

* * * * * * * *

THE TEACHING YEARS

When I graduated from high school in 1933 the prospects of further education or of finding a job seemed to be zero. The graduates of the three preceding classes, almost without exception, were still in town, the girls living at home, the boys hanging around garages and pool hall, doing odd jobs for a pittance when they could find them.

My older brother had gone to Cold Lake Alberta to live with our uncle there. He spent the early winter cutting wood, and late winter on a trap line. My two older sisters were teaching school, but at a salary of $500 per year.

During the summer the government offered to accept a promissory note for the one hundred dollar Normal School tuition fee, to be repaid eventually from one's teaching salary! There was very little monetary incentive to choose teaching as a career, but there were no options either.

My uncle, as assistant fire chief in Saskatoon, was one of the few people we knew with a steady income, and he and my aunt devoted the ten depression years to helping students who could not afford to live away from home. I was one of thirty boys and girls who, in twos and threes, were invited for a year of free room and board in their lovely home in order to attend school in Saskatoon.

So, with a promissory note for tuition and almost no cash, I earned a first class teacher's certificate in 1933-34. As a matter of fact, for most of that long, cold winter a friend and I not only walked three miles to school and back, we delivered 1200 eight to twelve page advertising papers every Friday night. We each earned one dollar for working in blizzards and below zero temperatures from 5:30 P.M. to 1:30 A.M. and that dollar a week was our total spending money! At the same time I played hockey in the university league, and we both played baseball during the season.

The supply of school teachers far exceeded the demand, so my first weeks of writing applications drew no response. I had just about given up, when I was offered a job in a school with only six students, at a salary of $200 per annum and free board. I would move every month to a different boarding house, with the host being

52

credited $15 toward his taxes.

There were only six pupils in this school because the district had been almost abandoned in the hayrack exodus to the north country. Hundreds and hundreds of farmers whose crops had been blown away or eaten by grasshoppers year after year had loaded their families, furniture and implements on a couple of hayracks, tied a cow on behind, and left everything else, to travel two or three hundred miles north to the land of lakes and small homestead clearings in the forest, where dust storms were unknown and the world was green.

Well, I accepted the offer, but before the contract was signed, Mother and Dad went to Prince Albert on business, then another twenty miles north to visit the McIntyres, old homestead neighbors who had moved north via hayrack to a quarter section on the Little Red River in the Spruce Home district.

Dad phoned me that night to say that their school was looking for a teacher. I caught the train, met the school board, and was hired at $500 per annum to teach SIXTY THREE children in TEN GRADES in a one room, one teacher school!

All the schools in the north were bulging with children, as dust bowl refugees streamed north and settled every quarter section of land. There was no money or time to accommodate the extra children, so they just piled up, sat at double desks, and jammed the space in schools built for half their numbers. I never heard of any school with as many as mine, though fifty was a common number.

This was beautiful land to anyone who had lived in the drought and wind and dust of the prairies. The only time I had seen it before was described in my earlier story titled "The Dime", and as I fell in love with this land again I knew that if I wanted to stay here I had to beat the seemingly impossible challenge facing me.

Well, I guess I did, for I stayed on the job for six good years, loving the district, the people, and looking back on it now, even the job! I met, romanced, and in 1938, married my lovely wife there, and Mary and I have celebrated over fifty years together.

This was a very different land. I had grown up to unlimited horizons, where only the earth's curvature or the latest dust storm limited my view. Here, the farms and the fields were small, and my view was seldom as long as a mile, with trees still covering half the land. But the crops were good, the air was clear, and there were lakes and rivers and woods as a regular part of my environment. My boarding house was a log cabin, and I walked a mile to school on a path through a sweet smelling, bird singing forest.

My first impressions on checking out the school were the obvious poverty of equipment, and the terrible overcrowding. The library was a small, half filled bookcase of old, dog-eared books. The desks were all two-seaters, jammed in with narrow aisles, the front desks only a few feet from the blackboard and the back ones scarcely leaving room to pass behind.

I suppose that first school morning represented my graduation from youth to adult, though having just passed my 19th birthday I wasn't old enough to vote or drink a legal beer. And as I stood at the window watching the roads and trails and paths filling up with long lines of lunchpail swinging children, I didn't feel old enough to face the challenge that their certain arrival represented either.

A few mothers arrived with beginners, and adding to the confusion of sorting children into some semblance of order was the problem of separating mothers from six year olds who were even more terrified of that turbulent mob than I was. When we got organized and settled down, I found there were sixty-four of us, with sixteen beginners!

I wouldn't have believed it at the time, but in that same crowded room six years later I was to graduate those sixteen children of my beginner class into grade seven and hand them on to the next teacher as a nice, smart class of well disciplined children that any teacher would be proud of! During that time about thirty-five children "graduated" from the top grades, and thirty more started.

Teaching and learning seemed impossible under those conditions, and it would have been, under a spoon-fed curriculum. It required organization on my part to keep lessons moving in all classes without much individual instruction, and initiative on the children's part to work and study together, and help one another.

These were not the conditions we trained for at

Teachers' College. Very little of the fancy lesson plans and structured lessons carried over from the formality of teacher training to the quiet, heads down, work together horde of barefoot farm children packed together.

It took a while, and it was not easy, but eventually the great majority of the students worked well together all the time, and all of them did most of the time. I had no serious discipline problems, as through a combination of working with the children rather than at them, and participation in school and community in an active sports program, they worked with me and with each other.

I was rewarded by sharing my time with children who liked school, earned good grades, enjoyed learning, and the satisfaction of seeing many of them step with no trouble from that crowded room into senior high schools and on to university and professional careers. This was exemplified this year when, more than fifty years later I met one of those children at a golden wedding in Vancouver. Now a lady in her 60's, she came up to me and said, "Finally I can give you a hug," put her arms around me and gave me a big one, then told my daughter how much my years there had influenced that whole generation of children. That felt pretty good!

* * * * * * * *

There was a great group of young people in the community, with no alternative in those days but to make our own fun. We all cross-country skied, we built ski runs and a toboggan run on "old baldy' hill eight miles away and skied to it on weekends, we skated for miles on the Little Red River, we went to dances in the community hall and at the several lake resorts within a few miles, and we played baseball on our community ball team that was rated as one of the best in the north country. We even built our own outdoor hockey rink.

* * * * * * * *

Mary and I were married at Spruce Home after my fourth year there, on my salary of $550 per year. The depression still had a strangle-hold on the world's economy, and World War II was still a year or two away.

THE HUNDRED MILE SKATE

The Little Red River never gets big enough, or deep enough, or turbulent enough in its two or three hundred mile length to create much of an impression on anyone who sees it. In fact I suspect that many people pass by it or cross over it without ever seeing it at all. However it has remained vividly in my memory for over fifty years as the locale of one of those youthful adventures one never forgets.

The river rises almost imperceptibly in swampy ground some sixty miles northwest of Prince Albert, and seems to have so little notion of where it wants to go that it changes its mind and direction hundreds of times as it meanders slowly south. It grows to a twenty foot width and four foot depth before being engulfed eventually by the North Saskatchewan River a mile or two below Prince Albert.

During its early journey it passes through hills and forests, then creeps along in willow lined loops wandering aimlessly through the farm fields of Northside, Spruce Home and White Star, to slide back into pine clad hills for a few miles before emerging on the Saskatchewan's north bank.

Those of us living near the Little Red never apologized for its size or lethargy, as in those depression plagued 1930's days of our youth it provided us many pleasures. It supplied swimming holes in summer, miles of willow cover for exciting partridge, rabbit, and prairie chicken hunting, even places where we could lie on our bellies on a bridge or log and snare fish if we were lucky.

But the river got its biggest play in winter, when it provided us miles of beautiful skating. I still glow when I think of those skating parties scattered over four or five miles of river, with frequent gatherings around our blazing central fire. It was exhilarating on Saturday and Sunday afternoons, beautiful on crisp moonlit nights.

On our first fall skating party one Wednesday night in November 1936 we found the ice on the Little Red to be slick and smooth and endless, under calm frosty weather with no snow. As we effortlessly skated miles of river that night, John Boden, Jamie Nicol and I decided to skate to Prince Albert the following Saturday. We had a fairly accurate estimate of one hundred miles of river looping the eighteen miles between our farm homes and the city, but one hundred miles didn't worry us, as we were twenty one, in perfect physical condition. We estimated we could easily average twelve to fifteen miles an hour in eight hours of skating.

We walked to the river at eight o'clock Saturday morning, laced up our skates and shouldered our backpacks containing shoes and lunch. Heavy willow growth lined our first couple of miles of skating, and we exulted in the ringing cut of our skates on the clear dark ice as we cut around the curves and long twisting loops of the river. We were all looking forward to a glorious day when John, a few feet in the lead around a high banked curve, suddenly broke from a glide to a couple of stumbling steps before sprawling on his belly. Jamie and I had time to avoid a fall, but had to run several steps to keep our balance. The surface of the ice was filmed with sand, in an area that had been beautiful Wednesday night!

Of course! That big wind on Thursday must have blown sand from the high bank, and it didn't take much of it to change ice to sandpaper. Somewhat crestfallen, we picked our way along a hundred feet of sandy ice, reached clear ice again, and were soon ringing along at a good rate, but only for a short distance. Now out of the heavy willows, we found that almost every exposed bank had dusted sand onto the ice. We skated easily and swiftly for a hundred yards - or a quarter mile - then suddenly had to run like heck to keep from tripping on sand. In most places we couldn't see the sand, but we learned to anticipate it, and varied our progress from easy skating on beautiful ice to gritty skating, to a running walk on ice that didn't permit any glide at all. Sometimes we had long stretches of easy going, but when we passed under the Prince Albert-Waskesiu bridge late in the morning we were far behind schedule, and by the time we got down toward White Star we knew we were in trouble.

With skates so dulled with sand we couldn't get a normal push, our inner thigh muscles and tendons soon were aching from edgeless skating. We were back in wilderness now, miles from roads or habitation. Since our edges were completely gone, and we were concerned about making it out before dark, we took to walking shortcuts. Wherever we could see by the tree lined banks that a long loop of the river circled back and passed close, we just walked up the bank on our skates and across to the next stretch of river. By the time we got into the pine clad hills north of Prince Albert, dusk was approaching. We were at least two hours behind our estimate, which would have been accurate under good ice conditions.

Then we ran into a long series of beaver dams, each with hazardous ice above the dam and open water below. Now relatively clear of sand, we were trying to make up time, as it would be almost impossible to walk out through the hills and pines in the dark. Skating fast, one by one we went through thin ice, no two of us at once, and all on different dams. We each tripped as the ice gave way, scrambled out from shoulder deep water, and not only soaked all our clothing, but backpacks and shoes as well.

Though we were miles from shelter in freezing weather, a fully clothed plunge through ice was not all that traumatic. I have felt greater shock in a bare skinned plunge into a chilly swimming hole. Wool underwear, though wet, still insulates, and heavy outer clothing, even with an eventual coating of ice, is still protective.

Below each dam the branches of trees and willows came to the river edge, or over it, forcing us to skate as best we could along the narrow fringe of ice beside open water, frequently breaking through and wading a step or two, scrambling over bad ice before reaching doubtful support again on a hundred yard pool above the next dam. Every dam dictated a difficult fifty yard detour on skates through the almost dark forest to avoid the very thin ice and brush of the dam itself.

It was full black dark by the time we reached the Saskatchewan River. As we emerged from the high banked, tree lined Little Red, the slick black ice on the broad expanse of the Saskatchewan reflected the lights of the city on the opposite shore as flawlessly as from glassy water. Every light formed a sparkling jewelled path of welcome to the city.

We had been told during the week that city people were skating the Saskatchewan everywhere without restriction, so we felt that our journey was almost ended. We had only to skate the quarter mile across that beautiful ice, angling the mile or so upstream to the area below the firehall, take off our skates, climb the riverbank, and walk uptown.

Dead tired, aching, exhilarated, ice coated, glowing with relief and fulfillment, we were angling upstream and about half way across when suddenly the ice cracked under us with a ringing snap! As we slid to a stop, we gaped with amazement and bone chilling fear at the light reflections twenty feet in front of us roiled by a wide expanse of fast moving water! Had we skated another six feet we'd have broken through and been swept under the ice.

Slowly and carefully we backed off and headed back for the north shore, only to find more open water between us and the shore. We turned downstream, and moving separately, slowly and cautiously, we skated almost all the way back to the Little Red before reaching safety. In a temperature somewhere between 10 and 15 degrees (F) we walked ashore, took off our skates, fished wet shoes out of ice coated packs, walked up to the road, and started our cold, dark, two mile hike for the bridge, and town.

A car stopped, and when the driver asked if we wanted a lift, we told him that we couldn't get in his car as we all had soaking wet clothing. His response was, "Hell, all the more reason. Get in!" He took us to a big downtown hotel managed by a man John knew, who sent us down to the boiler room.

That big boiler room in the basement of the steam heated hotel had hundreds of feet of steam pipes looping back and forth, too hot to touch. We stripped naked, hung jackets, packs, pants, shirts, shoes, socks, mitts and longjohns over those hot pipes and sat back in that hundred degree boiler room for the pleasantest heat-soaking hour you can imagine. It was one of those memories that sticks with you pleasantly through a lifetime.

When our clothes were dry we dressed, had a meal, and caught a ride with a Saturday night shopper as far as the Spruce Home corner. We walked (shuffled) the three long, long miles home from there, our thigh and leg muscles unable to step out, counting every aching step.

Our adventure would have been such a snap if the wind hadn't blown that sand, and we had been able to freely skate the hundred winding miles of river.

    We were very lucky. We never tried it again, but two of us still reminisce about it. Jamie was killed in the war.

* * * * * * *

This is me on the Little Red River.

THE UNIFORM YEARS

The following chapters share with you a few of my memories of the war years, without getting into the blood and guts of combat. We are still assaulted daily with Hollywood's version of World War Two, Vietnam, the Indian Wars, the Civil War, the Gulf, and a dozen others, so if you are interested in that phase of war I'd refer you to your TV Guide.

Those of you who were there will relate to many of our experiences, and may enjoy stirring up memories of days we can never really dismiss from our lives.

Who can forget, for instance, the day we said "Goodbye" to family and friends and headed for war? Or the realization, whenever or however it came, that our own war days were over, that we had survived it, and that although we were leaving so many of our best friends over there forever, we were going to come home to those loved ones we had left behind so long ago? - Or - those hundreds of good and bad experiences in between that still drop in on us from time to time, unannounced.

These pages tell a few of mine:

By the summer of 1942 the war had escalated into a worldwide conflagration, fiercely fought on every front, but going against us everywhere. The Japanese were advancing ruthlessly south eastward through the Pacific Islands, forging rapidly through Burma toward India, and threatening Australia. The Germans and Italians controlled all of Europe, almost all of North Africa and the Mediterranean, and the Germans were pushing relentlessly across western Russia, having conquered and destroyed thousands of square miles of Russian territory.

The Japanese navy was in command of the Pacific. In the Atlantic, German U Boats were sinking dozens of ships every month. Catastrophic convoy losses were common, with the U Boat fleet growing by the week as new U Boats were coming into service faster than they could be sunk. German battleships were lurking in French and Norwegian ports, tying up precious allied naval strength guarding against a breakout assault into the Atlantic. The North Atlantic supply route to embattled Britain was in serious jeopardy, and any convoy could anticipate U Boats and fear battleships.

In late August 1942, when I reported back from Infantry Officers Training School to the Prince Albert Volunteers Infantry Regiment, training at that time in Vernon B.C., the Second Canadian Division had just been decimated in the abortive raid on Dieppe. On my first Saturday afternoon back with the regiment, knowing that I could share very little time with my little family in the foreseeable future, I walked down the hill into Vernon and spent hours looking for a place to rent for Mary and the baby. The town was sold out, and I returned to camp with the unhappy prospect of having a real problem getting them out there from Prince Albert to live.

Luckily I didn't make a deal that day, as on Sunday morning the colonel called a special regimental parade and informed us that he had orders to send a fully manned rifle company overseas at once to replace some of the casualties suffered at Dieppe by the South Saskatchewan Regiment (SSR). The 120 NCO's and men would be hand picked from our active service ranks, but he told us officers that he was calling for volunteers. He said he would be out of his office until 1500 Hrs. and that if we wished to volunteer we should put a note to that effect on his desk.

We went our separate ways that beautiful end of August Sunday afternoon, and each of us in the privacy of our own emotions we wrote our notes and placed them on the colonel's desk. He told us in a meeting that evening that every officer in the regiment had volunteered, and that Major Tucker, Captain McLellan and Lieutenants Treleaven, Stewart and Hadley had been selected.

Once overseas, Tucker and McLellan were transferred to the First Canadian Division and went to Italy with the Edmonton Regiment. Tucker was wounded and McLellan was killed at Ortona. The other three of us stayed with the SSRs. I was hit by shrapnel in Normandy, Bumps Hadley was killed there when his jeep ran over an anti-tank mine, Murray Stewart was killed by a sniper in Holland. Our regiment suffered over two hundred percent casualties before it was over. Fortunately, none of us could see our future, but we knew our prospects. It was an established fact that infantry platoon commanders suffered the highest casualty rates in the war.

We took a few days to get our company selected, organized, and equipped for overseas service, then moved with them to Regina, where we were joined by several other infantry companies destined to reinforce the SSRs and other regiments decimated at Dieppe. Given four days embarkation leave, I took the first train to Saskatoon, where Mary met me with our one year old Marilyn.

I spent most of my leave trying to sell our car. Mary didn't drive at that time, and with heavy gas rationing and the prospect that the Japanese conquest of all the rubber producing land would cut off the supply of civilian tires, there was no point in storing it. However, for the same reasons, there was no market for it, and I finally sold it for $200 and hurried to buy the rest of my overseas equipment.

Mary, Marilyn and I, just before I went overseas.

It was fortunate that I was kept so busy during those last days, as the emotional trauma of the closing hours was almost beyond endurance anyway. I'll never forget taking my last long look at Marilyn sleeping in her crib, my leave-taking of Mary, and closing the door on them to get into the car for the drive to the station, the troop train, and war.

I suppose our troop train could have been the five hundredth to steam its way across Canada to Halifax, and people living along the main line must have thought of them as never ending. However to every individual on those trains, heading for an ocean crossing to war, it was a very personal experience. Fresh from leave-taking of loved ones, they felt every click of the wheels carrying them farther from home, watched the endless scenery flowing past the windows, and wondered if and when and how they would look on it again. But at the same time they felt the purpose, excitement and exhilaration of the future.

Eventually our train puffed slowly through the confusion of busy Halifax rail yards and crept to a halt on a long dock, walled on one side by a huge warehouse, and on the other by the towering steel wall of an ocean liner. We quickly formed up our trainload of troops on the dock, listened to embarkation orders, marched up the gangplank and dispersed to assigned quarters.

Our ship was the Awatea, Australian, formerly on the New Zealand run. It was a beautiful ship, with its rich panelling and gleaming appointments only partially hidden by plywood and other protective materials. Anti aircraft and antisubmarine gun emplacements had been added, and like big steel ravens' nests they spoiled the symmetrical lines of the ship. However its destiny was no longer as a beautiful liner, but as a troop carrier, partially self defended. (It was to be sunk a few months later in the North Africa landings.)

We were awed the following morning as, loading completed, we pulled out to an anchorage in the harbor. We were surrounded by dozens of ships sitting darkly at anchor - rusty freighters, sleek grey cruisers and destroyers, and some twenty five liners like ours in their camouflage war paint, obviously loaded with tens of thousands of troops - army. air force, and a few women's service units including CWAC, RCAF(WD), and WRENs, uniformed in army. air force, and navy colors respectively.

There was a great deal of harbor hustle and bustle as tugs, supply boats, and personnel craft hurried here and there among the ships, and from ship to shore. Ships talked to one another in the always seemingly urgent language of aldis lamps flashing their messages from shore to ship and ship to ship across the harbor.

The flashing lamps gradually took effect as ships began to raise their anchors and move ponderously toward the harbor mouth and the open sea, destroyers hustling about among them like nervous dogs herding sheep, barking in their peculiar, high pitched calls among the slow moving, silent liners.

All our decks were crowded as we watched the rocks and islands of the harbor mouth slide by, and the buildings of the city blend into a haze, fade away and finally disappear. Looking around us as we rolled into the grey open sea we realized that we were a very large convoy, as ship after ship surged into position in three long lines. The lines were hundreds of yards apart and extended ahead and astern as far as we could see.

As the day wore on and the convoy settled down, a walk around the deck enabled us to count some twenty six liners within our sight. Looking carefully we could see the superstructures of a couple of destroyers away off on our flanks, but having counted them as we formed up, we knew there were six of them out there somewhere, and a cruiser leading the convoy. Little enough protection against the wolf packs of U Boats then at peak strength lying in wait for us, and the rumor that was to haunt every convoy - that the Scharnhorst or the Gneisenau or the Graf Spee - or whatever big battleship was the current concern - was roaming the ocean ahead of us. Our rumor was the Scharnhorst.

Ours was a fast convoy, made up entirely of troop ships. Troop convoys must have been a nightmare of worry to naval personnel, as if a pack of U Boats got among them they could sink half the ships in a convoy and scatter the rest to be picked off one by one. And if an enemy battleship got free it could easily knock out our light escort ships, and like a hungry wolf in a herd of lambs, pick off the ships at will.

We took six days to make the crossing, travelling probably twice the distance from Halifax to Glasgow in getting there. The whole convoy constantly zigged and zagged its way across the ocean, never maintaining a steady bearing for more than ten or fifteen minutes at a time. We became accustomed to the list of the ship, first to port, then a few minutes later to starboard as we leaned over, creaking and groaning, in fast turns. Surrounding ships had to make their turns in unison to avoid collision, with the six day marathon dance choreographed by our convoy master somewhere up ahead.

The ships were totally blacked out at night. We were even forbidden to smoke on deck. It was an eerie feeling to stand out there in the pitch blackness of an overcast rolling sea, hear the swish and hiss and slop of breaking waves rolling along the side and the hum of wind blowing through the rigging, and other than the occasional quiet murmur of voices, not another sight or sound of our own ship or the dozens of ships and tens of thousands of men around us.

Standing at the rail, our own ship's passage was marked on the surface by the phosphorescence of roiling water, and if we looked closely toward our near neighbor we might see the disembodied white of a bow wave, and a few hundred feet behind, a smaller moving blob of white. These ships kept strict radio silence and had no radar yet, so each ship towed a log on several hundred feet of cable. This created enough wake that the lookout on the following ship could make it out, and keep his distance.

We enjoyed one big storm at sea. At least those of us not subject to seasickness enjoyed it. It caught a few of us in the huge, tile floored washroom at morning ablutions. Several of us were standing in our hobnailed boots at the row of basins along one wall when a combination rolling wave and turn of the ship listed it so quickly and so far that we all slid in a row, helplessly, across the slippery tile floor. Just before we crashed into the far wall the ship listed steeply in the other direction, and we slid in a row back to our basins again. This time we hung on, laughing.

We had to pass down long corridors and flights of stairs to our dining room. We laughed at the people ahead, as in the enclosed, horizonless corridor the walls seemed to remain upright, but all the people walked along with a thirty degree list to starboard, slowly moved upright, then slowly leaned thirty degrees to port. On the long companionways we had to work to go down the first few steps as the ship rose, then raced down the next ones as they dropped from under us. My whistle, hanging on its lanyard on a hook in our cabin spent the day as a slow pendulum keeping time to the contented squawking of an old hen hidden somewhere in the wall.

Finally one morning the misty distant shores of Northern Ireland appeared on our starboard. A few hours later the grey misty rocks of Scotland rose slowly out of the sea, changing as we approached to the most brilliant green we had ever seen.

As we passed up the Clyde and into Glasgow harbor we crowded the rails for our first views of stone houses and tiny green fields, so neatly bordered by rock walls or hedgerows. We laughed to see a tiny green train racing along and to hear its high pitched whistle, so different from our big, deep throated Canadian ones.

This too was a very busy harbor. We crowded to stare at a monstrous ocean liner with a huge hole, larger than a house, torn in its bow, right down to the water line. We didn't learn until weeks later that this was the Queen Mary, which while crossing with a load of troops had accidentally rammed and sunk an escort cruiser. Such were the perils of the sea that she had steamed right on, not daring to stop to search for survivors and risk the lives of the many thousands that she carried. She was eventually repaired and returned to service carrying thousands of troops, generally Americans, on each of her fast, lone Atlantic crossings. The big, fast ocean liners, Queen Mary, Queen Elizabeth, Normandie, Ile de France, were safer travelling alone.

So there we were, Convoy No. 228, safely in Glasgow Harbor, thanks to good luck and the protection of the Canadian navy, which did most of the North Atlantic convoy escort duty. We debarked directly into our troop train, and developed the beginnings of our admiration for those little green trains that raced at high speed the length and breadth of the island and carried us during the future years to so many places.

* * * * * * * *

HUMOR IN UNIFORM

We sometimes found something to laugh about during those years. Here are a couple that weren't laughers at the time, but are funny in retrospect:

When I was shipped to England in 1942 I had just graduated from officer training school, and joined the South Saskatchewan Regiment with only a week in the field as a regimental officer. I still had many things to learn about military rules and regulations, and one of my first lessons was an embarrassing one.

Each and every day a regiment is in camp the adjutant posts on Daily Orders the designated duty personnel including a lieutenant Orderly Officer. The

Orderly Officer is responsible for various inspections during his twenty four hour tour of duty: the cookhouse, various messes, barracks, the posting and changing of the guard, and for the orderly room and all camp functions between Last Post and Reveille. He is, in other words, the officer responsible for the whole camp during the night.

The very first time I was stuck as Orderly Officer came a couple of weeks after I joined the SSRs, posted near the channel coast. Since there were many responsibilities, plus ceremonial duties in the several changes of the guard during the twenty four hours, I was nervous, but fairly confident.

Well, the day and night went fine until about 02:30 on our very rainy morning, when a dispatch rider from Brigade HQ was ushered by a guard into the orderly room. He handed me a brown, heavily sealed envelope addressed to the colonel, and marked *"TOP SECRET!"*

I knew it was important, but for that nervous decision-making moment I decided that since it wasn't marked *"URGENT!"* I wouldn't wake the colonel, but would guard it carefully and deliver it to him at 07:00.

When the colonel slit open that envelope, all hell broke loose! The message, to test the SSR's ability to get their troops out and mobile in a hurry in the middle of the night, ordered us out as a full battalion on a ten mile, fully armed, full pack forced march, to pass a certain reference point two miles down a muddy wooded trail at 04:00 hours.

The Brigadier General and his staff stood out on that muddy trail in those woods, in that rain, at 04:00, and at 05:00, and I hope that by 06:00 they went back to HQ for breakfast. We started thinking about it at 07:00.

Whatever happened in the higher echelons of command, I was let off the hook with a well earned lesson: that anything marked *"TOP SECRET" is URGENT*! However, the battalion wasn't let off the hook, as instead of being the first 700 men over that muddy trail, they were the third, three mornings later, and by that time it had been churned to knee deep mud. And instead of the incredible luck of missing that march (as Orderly Officer), I was in the middle of it, and had to listen with secret guilt to all the cursing of the heavily laden, rain soaked, mud spattered men. They didn't know they were three days late, and I don't think many of the officers knew until two years later.

Shortly before D Day we held a regimental dinner, with our Divisional Commander, General Burns, as guest of honor. General Burns was our Brigade Commander in 1942, the Brigadier who, thanks to me, was amazed to see nothing happen as he stood out in that long black rainy night.

During his after dinner speech the general told a very humorous anecdote relating to the SSRs, and I knew from the first sentence what the story was going to be. I'm sure that as he told it, my shining red face identified me as the culprit.

* * * * * * * *

I still chuckle when I think of one of our Infantry - Tank training exercises:

We were doing a combined attack in the rolling hill country of England's South Downs, practicing live ammunition tank cannon fire supporting infantry, and infantry attacking anti-tank gun emplacements as they moved up together. The real key to the drill was good communication and coordination between platoon commanders and tank commanders.

As in all exercises of this kind, we had umpires moving up with us, officers independent of our units who kept throwing new problems at us, then umpiring our reaction, assessing and removing "casualties", and reporting on results.

As we were moving up toward a ridge with an old sheep herder's shack on it, the umpire with my platoon shouted that we were under machine gun fire from the ridge. I called on the tanks for smoke, and the tank just behind me fired a smoke canister from his cannon. (A smoke canister is about the size of a large grapefruit can, primed and fused to fire from the tank's cannon and to give off a large volume of smoke for some minutes on landing. Two or three of them, strategically placed, can screen off the enemy and enable your own troops to attack under its cover, bursting upon their positions without coming under accurate counterfire during your approach.)

Well the first canister hit the ridge just below its crest, and trailing an erratic line of blue smoke, it bounced and tumbled and rolled a further two hundred yards beyond the crest, where it was useless to us. When the second canister did the same thing, the tank commander evidently got the brilliant idea of bouncing the next one against the old sheep shack for a backstop, swivelled his turret, and fired.

The canister hit the ground about ten feet in front of the old shack and disappeared through the wall on first bounce. There was an old corral about fifty feet to the right, and immediately after the shack shot he swivelled further and drove a fourth one at the corral.

He was apparently so intent on swinging his turret and aiming for his fourth shot that he never observed the results of his third, as the canister no sooner went through the wall than about ten men in various stages of undress poured out with the smoke, saw our ominous tank-infantry advance below them and fled for the shelter of the corral just as he let them have it again!

They turned out to be an English anti-aircraft battery, with their guns just behind the ridge. They were night crew, asleep in the shack (their billet) when that can came through the wall, passed between the bottom and top bunks of two sleeping men, hit the opposite wall, and burst into a million cubic feet of smoke. They really thought we were after them when we fired the next one at them. And it turned out that our first two canisters bounced pretty close to their guns, and smoked them out too.

It wouldn't have been so funny if we hadn't taken the second poke at them. We were lucky the poor fellows surrendered instead of shooting back, and doubly lucky no one was killed.

There was hell to pay of course for the mix-up. Somebody blundered in assigning our exercise to ground not cleared of personnel, but that fight took place away over my head, so I wasn't involved.

None of us burst into laughter in the midst of that frightened, furious crew, but it made a good mess story later.

* * * * * * * *

70

NAVY LEAVE

We were treated rather generously with our leaves, being granted a six day pass including free rail travel to any destination in Great Britain every three months. Depending on season and personal interests, London was a favorite, with Edinburgh, and Torquay on the Devon coast close seconds. Most soldiers varied their travel, and during their years there they came to know Britain better than ninety five percent of the natives.

Some, however, developed intimate interests in London, and never varied their leave from a quick trip to the clubs and pubs of the battered old city. This type of leave didn't interest me, and I travelled the length and breadth of the island, including all of the above, Cornwall, Blackpool, The Isle of Man, Folkstone and Dover. My most memorable leave though was at sea.

Navy leave was granted by request to officers who sought sea adventures rather than than hotel adventures. We were attached to the Royal Navy for all purposes except actual duty, and had all the privileges of the ship that the navy officers had.

My navy leave application was granted in the fall of 1943, and I was assigned to a converted trawler doing convoy escort duty through the English Channel and the Irish Sea. My trip was from Plymouth around Land's End, to Cardiff. Plymouth had been saturation bombed, and most of the city and port facilities were in a roofless, burned out shambles.

During my stopover in Plymouth I was scheduled to spend a day on North Atlantic anti-submarine patrol in a huge Sunderland flying boat, but the whole area was in the midst of a massive storm, so my flying trip was cancelled. I did, however, get a small craft trip out to the Sunderland anchored in the harbor, and a very impressive guided tour through the huge craft. I would have loved a day at sea in it!

Our trawler was pretty small, as navy ships go, with a complement of four officers and about twenty other ranks. It was armed with a four inch gun forward, several 20mm cannon, and a deck load of depth charges. In addition to U Boats, its chief enemy was "E" Boats, those very fast torpedo craft that could sweep in from nowhere, sink two or three ships, and be gone again at high speed. The Captain told me that they averaged E Boat attacks on about one convoy in six, but our weather was so stormy there was only a slight chance of seeing them on this trip. U boats of course were a constant menace.

And was it stormy! As we rounded Land's End and headed north into the Irish Sea the wind-swept rollers were so high that our ship rolled and corkscrewed and pitched its way up massive hills of water until we could see all of the dozen ships in our convoy spread out before us, then down into hissing, seething valleys so deep we could see nothing but a foaming horizon close in around us. We had only a few feet of freeboard on the main deck, and tight lines were run the length of the deck so sailors had something to grab when green rollers swept down the deck and crashed against the wheelhouse.

I enjoyed most of the first day of the storm, with the freedom to explore the ship, stand on the bridge and watch their new electronic devices in action: Asdic showing the profile of the sea bottom (and a submarine if you passed over it), and the magic new radar just installed, whose green screen showed the blips of all the ships in our convoy, and the profile of the shoreline when we were close enough to it. I appreciated the privilege of this freedom to explore, as on our Atlantic crossing we had no way of satisfying our curiosity regarding the sailors' world.

My undoing was my first trip to the head on the deck. When the walls of that tiny cubicle closed in around me, then performed such wild gyrations in all directions that I had to hang on, I could hardly get out of there fast enough. For the rest of the three day trip, I was OK if I stayed out on the gale-swept deck, but I had trouble staying inside.

A particular problem was mealtime. The officers' wardroom was away back in the fantail of the ship — that little overhanging bulge that curves up from the propeller and rudder, then curves another fifteen feet back and up to the deck. To reach it we had to descend a steel ladder onto a grilled walkway that was open to and above the engine room, and walk the open grill back thirty feet over the engines to the wardroom door.

Well, as I inhaled my last deep breath of fresh air on the deck and came through the door I was immediately assailed by the hot, hot oil stink of the pounding engines. Then in the heat of the engine room I descended that pitching ladder, hung on as I negotiated the hot noisy roller coaster of the grilled walkway, and finally burst through the wardroom door into cool fresh air again.   I had long ago lost my appetite, but knowing I had to eat, I sat down at the table railed off into individual place settings by four inch rails fastened to the table. It was like eating out of a shallow box. The mess waiter set a bowl of soup in front of me just as everything dropped from under us for forty feet at falling speed, paused a moment, then rushed upward again in a dizzying climb that left my stomach behind.   (I wished it would.)

The wardroom was so far out on the stern of the ship it was like being on a hundred foot teeter totter. On the second drop, as I hung on to my bolted down chair I decided I'd better get out of there, but still had to negotiate the swaying grill, hot oil stink, pitching ladder and top door before I hit the deck and that blessed roaring gale.

I never lost anything over the rail, but didn't eat much either. What surprised and puzzled me was that all three of the ship's junior officers were at least as seasick as I was, and confessed they always were seasick in big storms. Nevertheless they had to carry on with their duties, and as I stood at the rail inhaling most of that wind, I felt sorry for them working inside.

We finally shepherded our convoy into Cardiff harbor, eased our way to a dock, and tied up beside a destroyer.   I'd like to have done a destroyer trip, but they were off limits for navy leave since an army officer on one got a trip all the way back to Canada when his ship was suddenly detatched from channel convoy duty and assigned to one crossing to Halifax.   Not much chance of that kind of luck for our little trawler!

So that leave ended happily with Good Bye and Good Luck to the officers and crew, an overnight train ride through the mountains and wooded hills of Wales, a change of trains in London, and back to camp near Worthing on the channel coast.

* * * * * * * *

LIFE IN THE DARK

The world at war was a world of night time darkness for six long years, a fitful darkness that could be total one moment, then flaring with sheet lightning flashes and blinding flares the next. Black skies were intermittently lit by strings of pearly lights floating lazily skywards to burst into twinkling sparks among the pencils of dazzling blue searchlight beams sweeping and probing the smoking heavens. In quiet times the darkness of our world was so all encompassing it was palpable as it wrapped us softly in its velvet folds, a world much darker than you experience on those rare occasions now when you are able to escape urban life to wilderness and starlight.

The lights were switched off in Britain with the first bombing raids. The illuminated map of cities, towns, railroads, highways, and even farms faded from sight, and enemy pilots had to depend on navigation and reflected waterways to find their targets and drop their bombs into darkness.

Large raids set off huge fires, as burning London and other cities became flaming beacons that for months could not hide themselves. In spite of that, the blackout was strictly enforced, as even one tiny beam of light from every tenth building could form a pattern, easily identified. Every window had an opaque, tight fitting blind. Every outer doorway had an entrance drape, so when the door was opened, the drape still blocked light escaping to the street, and you didn't push the drape aside until the door was closed. An escaping beam of light brought a warden's knock in minutes. Blackout patrol was one of the duties of the Veterans' Guard, and of the guard in military camps. Everyone cooperated if for no other reason than that a light might attract a bomb.

As the months and years of the war wore on, blackout became an accepted fact of life, a routine part of the night, an unbreakable habit. Outdoor lights became another dream to look forward to "some day". The song, "When The Lights Go On Again All Over The World" was very popular.

The lights went on again for me on our troop train's first night out of Halifax, returning wounded in late

1944. As we pulled into a small town in New Brunswick we were startled to see its street lights, neon signs, and unshaded windows lighting up the whole town like a beacon. As we crowded our train windows we realized how much we had taken darkness for granted, and how brightly the lights of a nameless little town signified to us our move to a different continent and a different world.

How did a nation function in darkness? Well, it started by making things as visible as possible without lighting them. White paint picked up the faintest starlight in contrast to dark surroundings, so doorknobs, stair edges, curbs, street impediments, were painted white. Telephone poles were white for the first six feet, and center lines and traffic lanes on streets and highways were maintained in pure white.

Autos, trucks, and military vehicles had their left headlight covered with an opaque lens. A similar lens on the right light had only a tiny quarter inch hooded slit about four inches long in it, providing a very small light beamed down on the center line, which traffic was able to follow at a reasonable speed. The single tail light was a dim red.

Civilian traffic was very light except for taxis. Taxi and military drivers became expert at driving in light conditions in which most people couldn't function.

Huge, fast night time military convoys were made possible by a clever little light. Each vehicle had its differential housing (the bulge in the center of the rear axle) painted white. A little pencil light mounted above the housing shone down on it, lighting it up quite clearly, but visible only directly behind the truck. In a convoy, the lead vehicle had its tiny slit headlight on, the rear vehicle had its tail light on, and all those in between were completely blacked out except for their housing light. The lead vehicle could maintain about a 30 MPH speed as it followed the white line, and each of the others could easily follow the white lighted housing floating along before it. From back in a convoy it made a very pretty sight as the long string of full moons floated along in the dark, winding around curves and up and down hills like a string of pearls being pulled on a black velvet cloth.

That string of pearls brings an unforgettable experience to mind: We were on a big training exercise in England, involving at least our brigade of infantry plus many auxiliary troops. We were away back in hilly, forested country that night, and we footsloggers were riding for a change, being carried by Army Service Corps vehicles.

Our regiment got a sudden, urgent order to be somewhere else, about thirty miles away. A hurried call to O Group, (a meeting of officers to receive plans and instructions and map coordinates), revealed that we were to move to an isolated position on the "Hogs Back", unload and move out from there.

My platoon, in three fifteen hundredweight trucks, was comfortably placed about a third of the way back in our hundred vehicle convoy. Riding in the cab with the driver, I was feeling quite relaxed as we followed the moon or moons floating ahead when suddenly a military policeman with a flashing red light stepped out on the roadway and stopped my truck and the whole convoy following!

As, horrified, I watched the last moon ahead fade out of sight I saw that a big army truck travelling the opposite way on our steeply climbing, winding road had rolled over in the ditch, and a Service Corps wrecker was ready at that precise moment to haul it back up on the road. While we waited the long minutes for them to get it up and cleared, I frantically studied my map and charted our route, realizing that my truck would now be leading the balance of the long convoy, and that we should try to make up time to catch them (if we should be so lucky).

I'll never forget that ride, staring bug-eyed out the windshield, trying to follow the white line flowing beside us at forty miles an hour, (we had turned on our little hooded headlight), trying to relate that line to the map, anticipating route changes and guiding the driver through them.

About mid way we hit a town (totally blacked out) just after the cinema closed. The streets were loaded with jay-walking crowds pouring out of the show, and I can see them yet as dim shapes leaping for the sidewalks as we roared through, horn blaring, little slit eye leading a long line of black, roaring trucks.

My nightmare of leading that long convoy into confusion ended when we came on the head end of our convoy just as they were starting to unload. The rest of the night was easy in comparison.

Darkness set the stage for startling pyrotechnic displays, made more startling by the contrast. As enemy night bombers droned overhead, antiaircraft guns hosed fire up in long streams of bright tracer with sparkling explosions in the distant sky. Searchlight beams formed waving batons of blue light directing the orchestra of antiaircraft fire. When a searchlight caught a plane up there the plane shone like a bright winged star, twisting and turning, attracting other beams which formed a gyrating apex of three or four straight blue lines smoking at the top in puffs of fire.

In the spring of 1944 we were camped under canvas between Dover and Folkstone. The weather was warm, so we slept with the large flap of our bell tents wide open.

Wakened by gunfire one night, I opened one eye to see long lines of tracer streaming from a moving red light in the sky straight down toward our tent. As I leaped outside and got the other eye open I realized that the tracer stream was not coming down, but going up from antiaircraft guns at the back edge of our camp. The red light they were shooting at turned out to be the pulsing exhaust of one of the first V1 flying bombs, headed toward London.

We were to see hundreds more of them in the next few weeks, as we were right on their flight path between the Pas de Calais launching area and London. It seemed that every few minutes we heard another staccato engine pulsing another in the endless stream of pilotless bombs on their way towards the destruction of the beleaguered city.

They were priority targets for antiaircraft fire, fighter planes, and the maze of barrage balloon cables through which they had to pass, as London defense forces tried to down as many as possible before they reached the metropolis. It was interesting to stand out at night to watch the fireworks and cheer the huge flaring explosions as one bomb after another crashed within our sight. One night we counted thirty five of them, but hundreds more got through.

In battle, tracer in small arms fire seemed to move slowly toward you, then flash by with a snap. Your own fire drifted toward your target, then arced up in the sky as it ricochetted. The flash of artillery guns danced like lightning storms along the horizon, and you hoped to be spared the thunder. And when darkness closed in again, undisturbed for a time, those quiet, chill little night breezes brushed your cheek with the ever present stench of death.

* * * * * * * *

THE TALISMAN

Servicemen who put their survival on the line every day in a theater of war depend frequently on a bit of outside help in one form or another. A lucky charm takes on great significance and becomes very personal, very important to the one who wears it or carries it through the hell of battle. His attachment to it becomes obsessive when it proves to him that it is working.

I wonder how many strange little objects, greatly loved, come home from wars and spend countless years adorning a place of honor, protected from wife and children, from house cleaning, carefully accounted for on moves.

My talisman was a little red coated toy soldier. I can look across the room at him now, after fifty years still standing rigidly at attention among the books on a shelf in our library.

Moving through heavy woods one evening during a training exercise in England, my eye caught a tiny red speck of movement fifty feet to my right. Since we were in a remote area, far from buildings, roads or trails, my curiosity led me to investigate.

Amazement mixed with compassion and fury when I found, deep in that forest, a tiny Grenadier Guard swinging from a branch on a string formed into a gallows  rope expertly tied around his neck. What warped mind, or secret enemy, had gone so far into that forest to perform his secret ritual of hanging a soldier in effigy?

In spite of his ordeal the Guard's expression never changed as I cut him down and removed the rope from his neck. I felt an immediate bond as I carefully put him in the breast pocket of my tunic, and I made room for him there wherever I went during the remainder of my war. I think I felt that since I had overcome infinite odds in rescuing him from hanging in those woods forever, he would probably wish to repay me through the hell I had before me.

And repay me he did, in full measure. He had busy

times, and one day his magic was taxed to the utmost as he guided me through a dozen miracles. Then, when he sensed that the future was hopeless, that the only way out was via stretcher, he still worked a miracle in his arrangement for that.

We had been living in rain and mud and blood, so that when I reached the field dressing station my filthy wet uniform was stripped from me and I was shipped back to base hospital wrapped only in a blanket. My helmet and a little cloth bag of my pocket contents were tied to my stretcher.

It was with great concern that I asked a nurse next day to empty the bag on my hospital bed. There, among waterstained pictures of wife and baby, paybook and inoculation records, my little companion slid out of the bag and lay at attention. As I lay there thinking of the scores of my buddies who would not waken to see this beautiful day, I acknowledged that any debt he owed to me was paid in full.

Our bond, after all these years, is still very close.

* * * * * * * *

CONVALESCENCE

What does it feel like to be hit by shrapnel? Well, the one that went through my upper right arm felt like being hit by a baseball bat, swung hard enough against my arm to knock me off my feet. The shell which landed twenty feet from me wounded two of us, but killed one of my men a hundred feet away.

The few of us left in our position that morning had survived tremendous odds and many miracles in being there at all. Being the only officer left, I had taken command of the company the night before, but with only twenty six men left out of one hundred and twenty five, I had fewer men in the company than I'd had in my platoon before the battle started. There only six in my platoon, and one died and one left by ambulance with me that morning, so I left only four of them. One of those four went through the war unscathed.

These were men I had worked with, trained with, lived with for years. I knew every one of them well, and counted dozens of them as good friends. They were superbly trained and ready, and I had looked forward to having them beside me as we fought our way through Europe. They have remained in my memory through the ensuing years, as a group and as individuals. I've never forgiven our "brass" for the complete lack of support that allowed them to be sacrificed in a bloody field of wheat.

There were no helicopters in those days, ferrying casualties to M*A*S*H* type hospitals, although our field hospital was comparable. Our jeep ambulance moved us back several miles to a very busy canvas field dressing station, where the severely wounded were hurriedly given emergency treatment to keep them alive for the thirty mile ambulance ride to the field hospital. The fellow in the stretcher beside me didn't make that journey, as he died a very rattly death while being administered to by only a padre.

Those of us who could be moved were sent on after a couple of days to a staging station near the coast, for our move by ship to England. We found ourselves in a small rural school, empty of desks, but with the children's work still on the blackboard since the explosive June day that had closed their school. I spent a couple of nostalgic hours studying their work from my stretcher on the floor, reminiscing about my days of teaching, so far away, so long ago, in such a different world.

Our move from the school to the ship was by DUKW (Duck), those twenty five foot boats with four wheel drive wheels under them, that were able to run about the beaches, out to sea and inland for short distances.

We were moved onto a LST, a big tank landing craft that could run ashore, open its huge bow gates and drop its ramp to unload tanks, trucks, and a multitude of waterproofed vehicles into four or five feet of water. Thousands of army vehicles came ashore on those Normandy beaches, and very few of them "drowned" as they ran through those few feet of water to the beach. LST's brought loads of armor across the channel to Normandy, they took loads of casualties back.

That huge, cold, oily steel deck must have been a couple of hundred feet long and forty feet wide, with every inch of it covered with stretchers, row after row after row. There were even a couple of rows folded down from the walls.

I could have been mobile by this time, but we weren't issued clothing, so were confined to our stretchers. As we lay there in the dark, with small lights moving here and there in the narrow aisles, we listened to an air raid on our harbor, with the pounding of antiaircraft guns and the crump of bombs, and could imagine the streams of sparks hosed into the sky and the fountains of lightning-lit explosions on the other side of our thin steel walls. One of our officers still on the beach in a Duck told me later in hospital how they lay there watching the stream of tracer from an approaching enemy fighter dance up the beach and shut off just as it should have wiped them out.

I had my first of several operations on my arm in the No. 8 Canadian hospital at Horley, in Southern England. It became badly infected after a few days, and during a couple of weeks of serious illness I very nearly lost it.

Our nerves had been through a great deal even after our arrival here, with operations, infections, needles and shots every three hours day and night, seeing friends die and hearing from new arrivals of the deaths of others in Normandy. It didn't make it any easier that this hospital was right on the flight path of a heavy stream of V1 flying bombs delivering their deadly loads to London every few minutes.

We had scores of barrage balloons in our area, and I recall many times lying awake at night and listening to the clattery engine of the fiftieth or hundredth bomb approaching. We would visualize the unending miracle of its passage through the balloon cables, hear the sputtering, uncertain motor pass low overhead, wonder how far it would go before it blew, and know we could survive at least until the next one.

When my staph infection cleared up I was fully mobile, and spent a lot of time visiting friends in other wards while waiting for my next operation. There were many stories of the miracle of survival, where it was a matter of pure luck, an inch of space or a second of time that determined who came back home to a long and rewarding life, and who stayed in Normandy forever, lying under a white cross in a neat green field.

I was granted a weekend pass after I got firmly on

my feet, and took a train to the seaside town of Brighton. As the beautiful countryside flashed by the train windows I felt so alive, so "born again" on this, my return to the land of the living, that one would have to have looked at death at close range to appreciate it. I could hardly keep my exultation to myself as I treasured every scene that was mine again, and was surprised and disappointed that those around me were paying no attention to our beautiful world.

Our hospital bulletin board listed a number of people, with descriptions of their accommodation, who volunteered to take officers on convalescent leave as their guests. A "castle" in Devon owned by a Lady Waring looked particularly attractive, as I remembered Devon as a beautiful county. My application for convalescent leave and for a visit to Lady Waring's estate were both granted. On arrival I found the place all I had hoped for, and spent a relaxed, very enjoyable week there.

Lady Waring was a widow in her 60's who was contributing everything she had to the war effort. Her estate was fairly large as English acreage goes, with a twenty room ivy covered stone house surrounded by walled gardens, small grain fields and a few grazing cattle. It sat a few miles outside the village of Salcombe, close to the Devon coast and the sea.

I would judge that the former staff of servants numbered ten to twelve, but wartime had reduced them to four: a chauffeur, a gardener, a youth who assisted the gardener, and one housemaid. However, all these people (and Lady Waring) worked very very hard, very long hours.

Lady Waring had endowed a small hospital in the village during the first war and had now gone back to full time hos- pital work for the war years. She left home dressed in a blue Red Cross uniform at 7:00 A.M. every day, and didn't return until near 6:00 P.M. The gardener had the several cows milked by 6:00 A.M, and he and the chauffeur bottled it. The chauffeur took two or three dozen bottles of milk and sacks of garden produce with him in the old Rolls Royce when he took Lady Waring to work. He delivered the milk and vegetables in the village before he came back, to work hard all day at agricultural tasks, then back to the village in late afternoon to pick up Lady Waring.

I roamed the grounds, walked the short distance to

the cliffs overlooking the channel, looked toward Normandy out there in the blue haze, spent quiet hours reading in the beautiful library or just sitting alone and absorbing the peace and quiet.

Toward the end of the week Lady Waring announced that she was having an old friend in for dinner, an American author who for many years had owned a summer home overlooking the sea a few miles away, and was now working as a war correspondent. I was impressed and delighted to learn that she was speaking of Paul Gallico, as I had always enjoyed his magazine stories and had only recently bought his delightful little book, "The Snow Goose".

Gallico had recently returned from Normandy, and was spending a few days at his Devon home. He was of course a most entertaining raconteur, and I spent a memorable evening with just the three of us around the dinner table and enjoying our pre war Austrian liqueurs by the library fire. He told an anecdote of an old French peasant that was so easily and beautifully told that I'd give a great deal to have it on tape. It no doubt became a magazine story.

On my stopover in London on the way back to the hospital I heard the first rumors of a new German terror weapon. There was no word about it in the papers, and none of the officers I talked to in the club had seen or experienced one, but people had talked to people who knew an area that had just been devastated by a mysterious new bomb that no one saw or heard before it struck. It was reported to be huge, was not dropped from planes, and travelled beyond the speed of sound. It was not until weeks later that the British admitted that huge V2 rockets were raining down on London from the stratosphere on their flights from Germany. If Hitler had developed his V1 buzz bombs and V2 rockets a year before the continent was invaded, he would have devastated England.

On my return to hospital I was transferred to Basingstoke for further surgery to splice my severed radial nerve. This hospital had three wings: neuro surgery, plastic surgery. and psychotherapy. All branches were experiencing a dramatic surge in patient load with the heavy fighting in Europe.

My ward contained about a dozen officers, all with significant nerve damage. About six of the twelve were paraplegic, and as I visited and talked to them individually that day I found a vast difference in their acceptance of their terrible fate. Some seemed to accept it to the point that they could be rational about their limited future. A couple were still fighting fate, and one poor fellow was unable to accept it at all.

He was hard to listen to in the daytime, but at night he became such a problem he got no sleep, and the rest of us got very little. By five o'clock in the morning I would be counting the minutes until I could get up and dressed and escape the ward, feeling sorry for the others who not only had to endure their own suffering, but had to go on sharing so much of that poor fellow's too.

And when I got out of the ward I was still not out of the woods. Most of the fellows I met in the corridors or reading rooms were from the burn wards, enduring endless months of plastic surgery. After a sleepless night it was difficult to be casual and nonchalant in greeting and chatting with people in the raw state of having no ears, almost no nose, hard, staring eyes in a tightly stretched, expressionless face.

To escape for a breath of air and a walk in the walled grounds was no better, for here your companions had at least temporarily lost their minds to the war. These were men who had been asked to endure more than they could endure, and since I'd had no training in dealing with the kind of world they lived in, I could only seek still another refuge. Since I could not leave the grounds, there really wasn't one, and I could only hope my stay here would be brief.

I had my exploratory operation on my third day. There was bad news and good news.

First, the bad news: The shrapnel passing through my arm had cut a groove across the bone of my upper arm and not only severed the radial nerve which runs down a channel in the bone, it had whipped out about an eight inch length of it. Since this was far too big a gap to stretch and splice, there was no way to restore the use of my radial nerve and the muscles and tendons it controlled in the back of my arm.

Now the good news: Since they could not restore my arm to full use, I would be sent home to Canada for discharge from the army and for further treatment. About four minutes later I phoned my "Coming Home" cable for dispatch to Mary.

Following my discharge in Regina, my move to Shaughnessy Hospital in Vancouver dictated our permanent move from the prairie to the coast. On my final discharge from hospital the following June, we started a new life in British Columbia.

* * * * * * * *

STARFISH TO THE RESCUE

My life has been in jeopardy many times. I can recall at least a dozen instances when there was no better than a 50-50 chance that luck would once again give me another draw.

"Luck" took many forms, but one of the strangest had to be starfish, those purple, five-armed marine animals who might move the six inch length of themselves in a day. My fondly remembered starfish lived many years ago on the rocks of the narrow arm of the sea separating Princess Louisa and Jervis Inlets, in a deep fjord of British Columbia's coastal mountains.

Malibu Lodge was built there, operated by Young Life, a youth organization. Our application to be part of the parents annual volunteer "Tool and Tackle Week" had been accepted, and Mary and I joined about forty other couples for a wonderful week of work and play at the beautiful lodge there.

The women spent their mornings in household maintenance, blanket and linen laundry and repair, baking and cooking for the crew. Most of the men were skilled tradesmen: carpenters, electricians, plumbers, painters, diesel and outboard mechanics, who worked hard to repair and repaint buildings and boats of all sizes, overhaul outboard and diesel engines, update the wiring and electrical generating system, Unskilled men built trails and worked as tradesmen's helpers. Great fishing, hiking, mountain climbing were available for the afternoons.

My assignment was to help Bud Olson build an 80x12 foot floating dock. We two weren't long in stretching the "tool" half of our days by several hours, reducing the "tackle" part to evenings, as we realized we would have difficulty finishing the dock before the following Saturday noon deadline.

A massive flow of water sluices four times a day through the narrow channel in front of the lodge, as the several vertical feet of tide ebb and flow between the two huge bodies of water that it joins. The lumber for our dock project was piled in an abandoned mill yard at the head of Jervis Inlet, and we had to negotiate about half a mile of that torrent with our twelve foot boat and ten horse motor for every plank of it.

Timing our daily lumber haul to the tide, we would

make our first trip to the mill at low slack, and spend an hour selecting four bundles of long 2x12" planks. We would pile the first bundle on the beach near the water's edge, and the other three at progressively higher locations up the beach. By the time the fourth was piled and lashed, the first would be ready to float, as the tidal current into Princess Louisa built up.

We would tie a 75 foot ski rope to the floating bundle of planks, and with Bud operating the outboard and me sitting on the center seat, feet braced, gripping the handle of the ski rope, we would ease the load into the current, race down the channel with it, then struggle with a laboring motor and taut rope as we swung toward the dock.

The bundle would pass us and try to drag us downstream, and we became quite expert at judging our drift so we could work our load into the dock, tie it to a piling, and with wide open motor fight our way back against the tidal current to pick up our next bundle just as it began to float. Four bundles would keep us busy sawing, boring, assembling and building for the balance of our work day.

On the last rainy morning of our week most of the crews had completed their assignments but Bud and I still had a few feet of decking to lay, and no planks left to work with. Bud was busy framing, so he asked me to pick up a volunteer helper and grab a dozen planks from the mill. The tide was wrong, but we couldn't wait for it. We weren't too concerned anyway, as we would have far less than a normal load.

As Fred and I, dressed in heavy rain gear and rubber boots, tied our little bundle at the water's edge and hurried to the boat, we looked at that heavy current racing past, and paused a moment to put on and secure our life jackets over our rain gear.

As motor operator on this trip, I worked our way along the vertical east wall of the channel where slower flow and back eddies allowed us some progress, but I could see that Fred had all he could do to hold the load as it fought the current. About half way through the channel, with the tow bucking and swinging in the torrent, our progress along the wall slowed to a crawl. Then, in spite of a wide open motor, we came to a full stop. We were reluctant to give up our precious load, but as the stern dipped and a surge of water poured over the transom I yelled at Fred to let it go. The handle of the ski rope snapped like a projectile into the motor, caught on something, and instantly flipped us upside down into the boiling maelstrom.

Our heavy boots and rubber rain gear dragged us down and fought the buoyancy of our lifejackets as we were tumbled and rolled and deeply submerged in the roiling boils and whirlpools. Desperate for air, swept along several feet under the surface, I was finally slammed upside down against the rock wall, and as I felt the jolt of solid substance I grasped instinctively at its smooth, slippery surface. Surprisingly I found firm, rough, scratchy handgrips that stopped me and held against the current as I scrambled to the surface.

Fred was clinging to the wall fifty feet upstream. We climbed and clung above the surface with hand and foot holds on an intertidal mass of sandpaper-backed purple starfish, so firmly suctioned to the smooth perpendicular rock that they supported us there while a speedboat raced across from the lodge, nosed its bow along the wall, and picked us safely off.

Those starfish saved our lives, as without their support we'd have been swept tumbling along beneath the surface until we drowned. Their backs still feel like sharp gravel imbedded in firm rubber every time I pet one.

* * * * * * * *

MABEL LAKE

Mary and I have spent the past twenty two years migrating with the birds, wintering first in Mexico, the past eighteen years in Arizona, summering in British Columbia. The following stories are based on our summer home, so I'll start by setting the stage:

We left Vancouver in 1972 to build our retirement cabin on the shore of beautiful Mabel Lake, in a relatively isolated valley of the Monashee Mountains, half way between "the gateway to the Monashees" and Three Valley Gap. With my apologies to all the "Mabels" of the world, I have to say that the name of our lake was unfortunate, and hope that eventually you will share with us a picture of a truly beautiful, dark blue, deep mountain lake surrounded by heavily timbered shores and snow capped peaks. It deserves a magnificent name.

Ninety percent of the shoreline of the twenty six mile lake is too precipitous for building sites, but half a dozen creek and river deltas and beaches provide space for a few cabins and a small resort community.

A dotted black line on the map wandering south from the trans Canada highway at Three Valley Gap represents a seventy mile logging road traversing true mountain wilderness for its first fifty miles. During that time it cuts above the Wap River valley, passes scenic, isolated little Wap Lake, cuts along the mountains for 26 miles above the east shore of Mabel Lake, and finally emerges as a paved road passing the farm fields along the Shuswap River leading to the logging and sawmilling town of Lumby, known as the "Gateway to the Monashees".

Ours is one of the three valleys of Three Valley Gap. Our cabin is on the point forming the east side of half mile Tsuius Narrows, one of about a dozen cabins on the wide delta of Tsuius (Meeting of the Waters) Creek, on the isolated east shore of the lake. We are connected to civilization on that side of the lake by a two mile trail climbing to the logging road heading thirty five miles south to Lumby, or thirty five miles north to Three Valley Gap. All of our road north to Three Valley Gap is rough, gravelled logging road, frequently passable only to trucks. The first fifteen miles of the road south are also rough, narrow, winding, coarse gravel, hung hundreds of feet above the shoreline, threatening a thundering logging truck around any curve.

That is our heavy supply route. The alternative is a two mile boat trip across to the resort and a fifty mile drive to the nearest city. We keep our pickup truck at the cabin, and our car at the resort. There is logging in the surrounding mountains, but no town or industry anywhere near the lake. The water and the air are crystal clear.

On the vertical grey granite and green forest shoreline across Tsuius Narrows from our cabin, a smooth fifty foot patch of almost pure white rock rises from the water. It is about half a mile away, clearly visible in daylight, a faint white patch in starlight. On those beautiful evenings when a full moon rises over the east mountains and bathes it in light, it takes on an almost spiritual glow, reflecting a sparkling path to us across the water.

Over uncounted centuries, untold numbers of Indians have stood where we stand on our sand beach, backed by towering trees, and gazed with reverence on that glowing rock. They honored it with paintings in bright red ochre, that in time grew to a twenty foot petroglyph of fish and bear and deer, spears and arrows and hunters, campfires and tepees, canoes and gatherings of stick people. Some of the art is crude, some is beautiful, all is easily interpreted.

Authenticity of the petroglyph has been verified by the Museum of Anthropology in Ottawa, and it has been included in a book on Indian petroglyphs in British Columbia. We feel privileged to have this memorial to our Indian culture so close to our home, and treasure it with deep respect.

Unfortunately, vandals in recent years have chipped away about two thirds of the Indian paintings from the rock, almost destroying their value and beauty!

* * * * * * * *

Mabel Lake, looking south from our beach.

Mabel Lake looking north. There's about half a mile of shoreline between pictures.

Osprey on the wing. Looking for fish.

Osprey on the nest.

Part of the Indian petroglyph. Tragically much of it has recently been destroyed by vandals who chipped out the face of the rock! This remains.

91a

GOOSE TALES

During our years at Mabel Lake, Mary and I have watched the migration of thousands of waterfowl, and the arrival of thousands more who spend their summers with us. We have learned the consistency of their habits, and can predict almost to the day when, and by what routes they will arrive. We also see the variations, and especially in the huge flocks of Canada geese we witness many curious actions in their flight patterns which puzzle us, but must make sense to them. Not yet quite understanding their language, we imagine what they are saying to one another, and amuse ourselves with our interpretations of what goes on.

One day a big flock came over the hill across the lake, with another flock following a quarter mile behind. As we watched and listened to their gabbling, one lone goose dropped out of the leading flock, flew at almost stalling speed until the second flock caught up, then joined their formation with a great deal of further talk.

Mary was quite sure she heard the leader of the front formation say, "John, drop back and tell that bunch that's been following us all day that we're going to swing down to the north end of Mabel Lake and rest and feed there until Sunday. If they take a northwest bearing they'll see the Shuswap after they cross the mountain, and should reach it before dark."

I didn't hear it quite that way. I thought he said, "John, you've been bitching all day: 'Too high, too low, too fast, when do we eat!' If you don't like the way I run this flight, get out and join the flock behind us!" So he did.

Another time a flock came over the hill with one lone goose two or three hundred yards ahead. As soon as they cleared the hill he set his wings and swung down for a glide to his right. Immediately the whole flock behind him protested with a tremendous noise, at the same time maintaining their flight pattern and direction toward the north end.

The loner was off by himself, and had to scramble and work to catch up. We think the conversation went something like this:

"I've had it! We've flown all the way from Lake Chelan, and this is as far as I go this afternoon!"

"Hey, stupid, can't you see how deep that water is? We're going to eat as soon as we quit, and you certainly can't eat there!"

"But I'm tired!"

"Well, eat fish. Goodbye."

An approaching flock caught my attention one day because a big white goose stood out plainly among the Canadas. They landed in the bay nearby, so with binoculars we studied them for some time, speculating on this happy foreigner, apparently fully accepted as a member of the flock.

It seemed too large to be a snow goose. Had it escaped from a domestic flock? How far, and for how long had it flown with them? Had it formed a permanent bond, or had it been unable to leave the south with its own kind, and joined these as a temporary convenience on the long trip north? We will never know, but there it was.

One day last spring was one of the busiest goose days. We counted ten flocks, of whom seven swept in low from the bay and literally flew through our front yard. They each had their own V formations, but followed one another in almost continuous passage, only a couple of hundred yards separating each flock. It seemed as though the Head Goose said that morning:

"Okay, today we practice close formation flying. Form up, and maintain your patterns. Three flocks to the mile. Don't crowd, and don't lag so you interfere with the following flight. And when we reach Mabel Lake, let's swing down and say 'Hello' to our friends in the cabin on the point. They should be back by this time."

Nature provides many different ways for her creatures to rear their young. The predatory type most frequently has babies born helpless, to remain in the lair or nest for weeks, fed many times a day by their parents, finally gaining fur or feathers and strength enough to venture out on first wobbly legs or wings to face the world, still under the protection of their parents. Man, wolves, bears, eagles, hawks and owls are samples of this class.

Game and prey creatures on the other hand cannot afford those helpless weeks, so their young are born running. Moose, deer, elk, antelope, ducks, geese, grouse, and hundreds more move their young out of the nest during their first few hours of life, and they are fast and elusive from their first day.

Grouse can fly when they are still like little winged golf balls being chip shot into the woods, and water birds can swim as soon as they hit the water. Some water birds, like wood ducks, mergansers, and Canada geese like to nest safely in trees, and the urging and eventual leap of those little fluff balls from the safety of a tree nest to bounce on hard ground and waddle happily to water is something to see!

Some, like mergansers, love to hitch a ride on mother's back. It's amusing to see her rafting ten or twelve bright eyed baby passengers about the lake, with the three or four leftovers paddling along and scrambling aboard whenever they get a chance to shove a sibling off the other side. However, from the first day, those that can't find room, or fall off, can swim along with her.

We have wood ducks and mergansers nesting in trees in our area. Nothing in nature looks more awkward than a big fat old merganser hen trying to land against the perpendicular trunk of a tree and hold on long enough to fight her way through the hole leading to her nest. But they manage. They usually choose to enlarge a woodpecker or flicker nest, and the ducklings seldom have more than a twenty or thirty foot fall when they leave their nest forever.

I can't imagine that geese normally build their nests much higher, but one year we had a silly goose who tried to build hers in the broken snag of a cottonwood tree, eighty feet above ground. The top wasn't very big, and our attention was first drawn to her attempts to land on it and stay put, while her mate flew around scolding and ordering her to use her goose brains. How were her goslings (if she could make her eggs stay there long enough to hatch), going to survive an eighty foot fall to hard earth?

However, she was stubborn, and finally mastered the aerodynamics of a landing on that few square inches of treetop. She spent an hour or two on two successive days sitting happily on that snag, no doubt leaving an egg each time.

Whether she ran out of egg room, or her mate finally prevailed, they disappeared after that, hopefully to nest in a more reasonable location.

* * * * * * * *

BEAR TALES

Mary and I were out fishing in front of our cabin last spring when a bear came down the beach, intending to swim across the lake at the narrows. He got in only as far as his front feet however when he backed up, shook that icy cold water off his socks, and walked back to the forest. But he DID want to cross the lake, so he tried it again, only to repeat the performance. We laughed as we watched him, like a thin skinned person trying to get up enough courage to jump into that frigid water. Finally, after several trips to the water's edge and back, he took a deep breath and made the plunge. He not only swam across, but changed direction near the far shore, and swam farther than necessary.

We spent a night in town a couple of years ago, and came home to put together an amusing bear story. Tracks and toothmarks showed where a bear had come into the yard, found nothing of interest in his upset garbage can, then followed his nose to a half-gallon plastic jug of concentrated fish fertilizer. He bit into this, penetrating the plastic with his four canine teeth, turned and started to carry it home. When the full strength of that concentrate leaked into his taste buds he dropped the jug and rushed back to take four big bites out of a bagged bale of peat moss. That dry moss must have felt pretty good as he chomped it around to clean his teeth. That was enough for him, for he never returned to our yard that summer.

Then there was a morning we were awakened at 5:00 AM by a loud thump. We got up to find a big black bear on the deck, with his nose pressed to the glass of the front patio door, only a few feet from us.

I turned to the gun closet and picked up my rifle and a clip containing two shells. By the time I was ready, the bear had walked around the corner of the cabin, still on the deck. I went out the patio door and followed him around the corner, expecting to see him going down the back steps, but I almost ran into him, standing on his hind feet and turning from looking in the kitchen window to face me. He looked seven feet tall!

I didn't want to shoot him, and certainly not on the deck at six foot range, so I shouted, "GET OUT OF HERE!!" He got down on all fours and ambled heavily down the back steps. As soon as he was clear of the steps I fired a shot into the ground, right beside him, thinking that would put him out of sight in two or three seconds.

Well, it did put a bit of hustle into him for about thirty feet, where he grabbed the first big tree, climbed it about six inches, and stayed there, hugging the tree and looking back at us. I fired another shot into the tree, about six inches from his face, and he never moved! (This was with a 30.06 rifle, with the boom echoing back and forth off the mountains.)

Well that was my second shot, so back into the house for more shells, thinking seriously now that that bear had to go! When I got back outside, (still in pyjamas and barefooted), the bear had come unstuck from the tree and was ambling through the woods toward the beach.

Rifle supported on the deck rail, I kept him in my scope, in and out of the brush, thinking, "Should I, or shouldn't I?" When he came out on the beach clearing he walked along a big log lying there, stopped in the middle of it, and looked back over his shoulder at me, giving me a perfect target.

I thought to myself, "If he steps off the log this way, he's dead; if he turns away I'll let him go." He turned away, and very dignified, ambled down the beach and disappeared.

Incidentally, the thump on the deck that woke us up was caused by the bear knocking over a garden dwarf. The dwarf has a basket of fish between his feet, is holding a big fish in his hands, and is looking up out of the corners of his eyes with a pleased expression on his face. Well there was no earthly reason for the bear to knock him over, as he was in a corner, well out of the bear's way.

We puzzled over it, until we figured out that the bear was after his fish! As we set the dwarf on his feet he was gripping that fish tighter than ever, and looking as if he was telling us all about it. I suppose we'll never look at that dwarf again without hearing him tell the story of his fight for his fish with that monstrous, colossal bear.

* * * * * * * *

RAVENS

We have had a small flock of ravens in our area for some years, a flock that never seems to grow or diminish from half a dozen birds. We have come to know them very well, and we think they know us, and recognize us as friends, or at least as neutral non-combatants. They range the square mile of our woods, with the occasional foray across the lake to the shoreline woods there.

Ravens have an extensive vocabulary through which they communicate a wide variety of moods and messages to one another. We have learned to recognize many of their phrases and calls, and to distinguish the different times and circumstances under which they are used to talk back and forth across our forest.

They even have a couple of distinctive calls for us: One they use from the tall trees in our yard at five o'clock on sleepy summer mornings to awaken us and keep us awake until Mary threatens to dust their tails with buckshot. The other is reserved for those rainy days, especially in May and June, when melt of the mountain snowpack threatens our creeks and lake with flood levels, and we count the falling rain. It isn't exactly cheering, but it is amusing to hear our friendly raven sitting in his favorite tree and counting in his raucous voice: "One bucket! One bucket! One bucket!" and to hear his companion a few hundred yards away counting them over there too.

I was treated one day to the most spectacular display of aerobatics I have ever seen. I was returning home by boat from the store and mailbox across the lake, and on rounding the point I glanced up at the cliff to check for action around the huge osprey nest silhouetted against the skyline there.

ACTION!! I shut the motor off and sat spellbound watching an osprey and a raven exceed anything I had ever imagined in speed, maneuvering, and smart flying in a long aerial dog-fight.

The raven had undoubtedly been caught in nest thievery, and was fleeing for its life. It was only trying to escape, but the osprey was cutting off every effort, and confining the arena to about a three hundred yard diameter around its nest area. In vertical distance however, they covered hundreds of feet.

97

I was accustomed to the slow, lazy, wing flapping flight of ravens, and the soaring, wind riding glide of osprey, but neither was recognizable here in this frantic, high speed chase. Both birds used a very fast, powerful wingbeat, as inches apart they seemed to fly as one unit in tight turns and full power dives, to disappear at forty or fifty miles per hour into the trees, only to emerge fifty feet away in a dizzying climb that took them hundreds of feet into the sky in seconds.

Each time they disappeared at such speed into the heavy forest I marvelled to see them emerge again unscathed. I couldn't believe how cleverly the raven dodged and turned and dived and climbed, and how cleverly the osprey anticipated his moves as she cut corners to stay only inches behind, forcing the raven to ever more clever evasion.

I was standing on the boat seat when the inevitable end came. For the fifteenth or twentieth time they had come from hundreds of feet up in a screaming dive down into the trees. I cast my gaze fifty feet forward, this time to see only the osprey soar upward on outstretched wings, and in a slow lazy gliding turn look down into the forest where her enemy undoubtedly lay shattered.

We saw a second battle only a couple of days later, this time between two ravens. They flew over the cabin making an awful din as they fought and yelled at one another, and headed across the lake at about a quarter the speed of the previous flight. This time one actually struck the other in mid air! As an explosion of black feathers floated slowly down to the water, the chase continued on to the forest across the lake.

What was so different was that at such a relatively slow speed, the fleeing raven was caught, and hit. Maybe he was fighting back, whereas the one chased by the osprey was only trying desperately to escape.

It was amusing to see a third raven hovering in the background. When the collision took place, she either cheered or swore a couple of times, turned and came back to our side of the lake, and sat in a tree muttering to herself.

* * * * * * * *

WE CHALLENGE THIEVES

Those hundreds of us whose lakeside cabins have been assaulted by thieves and vandals spend a lot of time in vengeful fantasy on what we would do "if only we could walk in on them, and catch them in the act!" Well Mary and I caught them in the act, and found that in the real world of cops and robbers, fantasy is hard to live up to:

My thoughts were troubled as Mary and I closed windows and vents against the dust of the mountain logging road.

"I'm sure worried about what we'll find when we get down to the cabin. I'll be glad when we get there." I muttered.

"You've been worrying ever since we left it."

"Of course I have. It's been sitting there isolated for six long lonely winter months, wide open to vandals, thieves, big trees in winter storms, snowslides sweeping chimneys off the roof. We're overdue for trouble."

Twenty miles later I eased our loaded pickup off the logging road onto the winding trail leading down to the dozen isolated, unoccupied cabins on the shore of the lake.

"Tired?" asked Mary, as she rolled her window down.

"Yeah, that's a long four hundred miles from Vancouver, and the logging road at the end of it doesn't help. Hey, those are pretty fresh looking tire tracks!"

"Probably a neighbor, in last weekend and out yesterday."

"I hope so!"

The cabin looked glad to see us as we drove in through a heavy carpet of golden leaves. As I was opening the back of the truck canopy, Mary called from the deck, "Come and look at this. The back door has been broken open!"

We hurried into and through the cabin, puzzled but pleased to find nothing missing, broken, or disturbed. No fires had been lit, no beds slept in.

I rechecked the open door.

"Whoever it was sure smashed this door open. Look at the splintered frame around the bolt. And hey! Here's a bootprint where they kicked it open!"

"Good heavens, look at the size of that footprint, and the height of it on the door. He must have been a giant!"

"And look at those cottonwood sticky buds stuck in his bootprint. They look damn fresh."

We quickly checked our outbuildings, and found the padlock smashed off our storage shed door. Here again, trail bike, outboard motors, canoe paddles, water skis, chainsaw, tools, seemed intact. A check on the neighbors found Doug Monteith's storage shed next door forced open, but again everything inside seemed undisturbed.

"Why would someone force all those doors, then not take anything?" Mary wondered.

"I'll bet we disturbed them, and scared them off. They might have assumed all these cabins belonged to weekenders, and wouldn't expect to be disturbed today. They probably heard us coming, hid, and took off. They'd be smart enough to park their truck somewhere else until they had a load ready to go out in a hurry."

Everything seemed peaceful for our busy first couple of weeks as we got settled in. Our one resident neighbor, Mrs. Alice Large, arrived and settled into her cabin half a mile up the winding beach road. The other dozen cabins in our isolated group belonged to weekenders.

On an early Monday morning Mary and I drove the fifty back trail miles to town, and came home late in the afternoon with a truckload of supplies. It had been a stormy day, with wind gusts and morning showers, and as we turned off the logging road to run the last two miles down to our cabin the wind was bending the treetops and kicking up whitecaps in the lake below.

"Look at those fresh tire tracks turning down our road from the north!" I exclaimed. "They're over top of our morning tracks, and made since the rain. Who would be in here from that direction?"

"No one who belongs here, unless it's a logging or forestry pickup. I hope it's not those doorbreakers again, because Alice is down there all by herself!"

When we reached her cabin Alice assured us that she hadn't seen anyone all day. Her yard is screened from the road, and since her car was parked under heavy pines, no sign of life would show to anyone passing by.

We unloaded her material and went on home about

6:30. As I idled up to the storage shed on the back of our lot I said to Mary, "I'm going to unload gas and cement, so you'll have to walk the rest of the way home."

To the sound of wind in the trees and surf breaking on the beach, she began gathering parcels from the truck as I went to unlock the shed. My heart skipped a beat as I stared at the lock, then hurried out to the truck.

"That big new lock is smashed, and it was OK this morning. They've been here today!"

"The house! I wonder what they've done to the house!"

As we hurried together through the yard we were startled to hear a heavy scraping sound coming from Monteith's shed, and looked over to see his door forced open exactly as it had been before. I had the feeling of having a bear cornered as the hair rose on the back of my neck. "We've got them, but look out!"

We continued to the cabin, found the door intact, unlocked it quietly, and rushed to the gun closet. I grabbed my 30.06 hunting rifle and a loaded clip of four shells.

"You'd better have a weapon too. Here, take the shotgun," I whispered. I broke open a box of 0 gauge buckshot shells, and loaded one up the spout of the 12 gauge.

"I won't take time to load any more. Do you know how to release the safety catch?"

"Not sure."

"Well, here, if you want to fire, you shove this little lever over so the red shows. It's on SAFE now. If the red is showing, it's set to go. Be careful!"

"Same to you!"

I slapped the clip on my rifle as we sneaked outside and around the corner of the cabin. I intended to stop short of Doug's shed and order them out with their hands up, but they were already backing out, dragging a load.

I pumped the action of my rifle to load a shell into the chamber. Startled, the nearest man looked over his shoulder and in the same instant made a tremendous running leap for safety. I have never seen as fast a takeoff as those two men made, one around each corner of the shed.

The one on my side was still in sight as I fired a shot over his head and shouted, "Hold it right there!" He didn't stop, but hurdled Doug's big woodpile in three leaping strides and disappeared in the timber faster than a scared moose.

As I lit out on the dead run for the road I heard Mary blast off with the shotgun, and when I had time to think a few minutes later I was nagged with worry as to why and what she shot with that load of buckshot that would kill a bear.

I got a glimpse of my man, jacket flying open, crashing through the woods behind the neighboring cabins. Where have they hidden their vehicle? With eight or ten driveways along that strip, I was convinced they were racing for it, and would come roaring and spinning out of someone's yard. I was going to be there to stop them, with a bullet through their engine or a tire if necessary.

Well I ran all the way to the last cabin, and saw no sign of them. But maybe they have a boat or their vehicle is hidden on the beach side of a cabin - so I ran through to the beach. No boat, no vehicle, but fresh tracks at walking speed where they had checked the cabins earlier.

I was still on the beach when I heard our truck racing up the road, and ran out too late to intercept it. Was Mary driving it, or had they stolen it? I had taken the keys out to unlock the shed. Could they hotwire the truck that fast, or had they taken Mary's keys from her? She had only one shell, and had fired that. Why? All these thoughts while I was debating shooting a back tire off the receding truck!

I had to let it go, and as it zipped around a curve I thought,"If it WAS Mary, she'd stop at Mrs. Large's", so I ran up there, to find her talking to Alice.

"Whew, am I glad to see you!" I panted. "What did you see?"

"Nothing, after you left, but I was worried about you thrashing around in the bush, so I came looking for you."

"Thanks, I wasn't too worried, with my trusty little rifle. What did you shoot at?"

"Nothing, really. I was just so darned mad, I thought I'd give them a little better sendoff, and fired over the second man's head just as he disappeared"

"Great. They sure got a running start. What about the cabin?"

"I went in and got four more shells, and locked up."

"Good! Those truck tracks turned off on the road to the old bridge. Let's run up there and see if they're camped. You drive, I'll road hunt."

"What do you want me to do?" asked Alice.

"You'd better stay inside, and lock your door," Mary advised. "We'll check with you later."

I got in the passenger side of the truck, moving Mary's shotgun and shells out of the way.

"Step on it!" I said. "If they're camped up there I want to get there before they do."

At the old bridge we found only fresh tire tracks, where they had pulled in earlier in the day and turned around. We turned back and drove slowly homeward, searching the woods carefully with our eyes.

"Well, they're in the timber somewhere, and can't get their vehicle out unless they pass us. I wish we had some help!" Mary exclaimed.

"If I had my chainsaw in the truck I'd drop a big tree across the two mile trail. The trouble is, it's too damn stormy to cross the lake and phone the police."

"I don't think we want them blocked in here with night coming on. If we don't catch them before dark I hope they're long gone. And what will we do with them if we do catch them?"

"I don't know. They're a pretty tough looking pair, and certainly aren't juveniles. It would be pretty tricky to transport them unless we tied them up. The ideal solution would be to take the paddles and lifejackets out of the canoe, force them into it at gunpoint, tow them into the middle of the lake and cast them adrift, then phone the police and ride herd on them until the police arrived."

"Well it's too stormy for that, and too close to dark."

"Let's go all the way back to the end of the road, and find that vehicle."

An old brown Dodge pickup was approaching from the creek as we reached the corner near our cabin. Mary swung our truck across the trail to block it as I stepped out with my rifle. The other truck stopped, and as I approached, the driver rolled his window down. He was alone, a big man with black curly hair and a heavy, short beard, about thirty.

"Who are you, and what are you doing here?" I demanded.

He raised his eyes from my rifle and shut his motor off.

"I've been fishing the creek," he replied in a matter of fact tone. "Not much luck though. I caught a couple of little trout, and threw them back."

"How long have you been in here?"

"Since about noon. I'd like to have been able to get over to the other side of the creek, where the current looks better. I drove to the bridge a mile or so up, but it's gone! What in hell happened to it?"

"Washed out in a flash flood. Is anyone with you?"

"No, I'm by myself. Drove in through Three Valley Gap this morning. I was going to fish the Wap River at the north end of the lake, but I couldn't get to it for high water. How do you fish the creek?"

"I don't, in May and June. Water's too high. Did you hear the shooting?"

"Yeah, half an hour ago. What's going on?"

"We've had a break-in and put a couple of fellows on the run. Have you seen anyone?"

"No. - Well, shortly after the shooting a boat took off from the brown cabin near the creek."

"What kind of a boat?"

"Oh, about a fifteen footer, fiberglass, with about a fifty horse Chrysler motor."

Mary had joined me during this conversation, and she now casually walked back to our truck, took out a pencil and paper, studied his license number, and wrote it down. He was eying her as I checked his truck. There was a fishing rod in the cab, a heavy jack and an old pair of boots in the back, nothing else.

I signalled Mary to move our truck, and the stranger started his motor.

"Sorry about your break-in problems," he called as he drove off.

"Did you believe all that?" asked Mary.

"I don't know. Funny for an experienced fisherman to be working the creek when the water's so high. He had all his geography right though, and his truck was clean. If he is one of them, he's a cool one."

"Well I sure didn't believe him, so I wrote down his license number."

"I noticed, and so did he. Well, anyway, what could we do but let him go? Let's check the rest of the road."

We drove the remaining quarter mile to the end of the trail at the creekbank and found nothing, so turned back home to check on what they had been doing.

Piled up in front of Doug's shed we found my hip waders and gas lantern, Doug's fishing tackle box, two rods and reels, two spare reels, and a five gallon can of gas. They were dragging his outboard out when we surprised them.

"Why would they do that?" I wondered.

"What?"

"Well, they passed up dozens of things in our shed of far higher value than this stuff. Why would they leave a $400 chainsaw to steal a $30 lantern. Why hip waders instead of expensive skis, or our outboard, or tools, or trail bike?"

"Don't forget they were only started. You can be sure our cabin was next, and we'd have lost your guns for a start, and heaven knows what else."

Just then Alice wheeled her car into our yard and skidded to a stop.

"That truck," she said, "When he passed my place about a quarter mile he stopped, waited a minute, drove another hundred yards, stopped again, then drove off fast."

"So - that S.O.B. fisherman was one of them after all! Let's go! Alice, come with us!"

We roared and bounced out the rough road and up the two mile hill to the logging road, but caught only tracks. Their tracks were easy to see, and while they had come in from the north, they went out to the south, toward Lumby.

"There's no use chasing them!" Mary exclaimed.

"No, they'll be miles away, and no way of intercepting them," I acknowledged

"At least, they're gone, and I'm thankful for that," said Alice.

"I suppose the two we chased saw our truck go by and saw me run up to your place," I mused as I turned around on the narrow road. "The coast would be clear for them to sneak across the road and a few hundred yards through the woods to their truck. You can be sure the driver got to it in a hurry too, when he heard the shooting."

"I'll bet that shooting scared him silly. He must have been pretty worried until his cronies showed up," laughed Mary.

"Yeah, he probably aged a little," I agreed. "Anyway, when they got together they would figure they couldn't get the truck out without it being apprehended, and those two had better not be in it."

"So the driver would send them through the woods, and he would plan to bluff his way past you, and pick them up a mile up the road," guessed Alice.

"Right, and it worked."

"Oh well, we're really better off not capturing them anyway, as long as they don't come back."

"I don't think they will. We sure scared the first two, and the fisherman would see we were still hunting hard for them, and meant business. No, I don't think they'll be back. If the lake settles down I'll run across first thing in the morning, and phone the police."

It wasn't more than an hour after I phoned the report and license number to the Lumby RCMP the next morning until a police car drove into our yard. Constable Ken Allen introduced himself.

"I almost jumped out of my chair when I heard that license number," he said. "Our Specialty Squad has had that old brown truck and that gang under surveillance for months. They are the Korler gang, two brothers and a cousin. They specialize in drug store break-ins, going after only the specially locked narcotic drug cabinets."

"Wow, they sound rough!" I exclaimed.

"They are indeed rough, very rough. One of them, a big fellow we call 'The Bear', has the reputation of coming out fighting if he's cornered, and we figure it would take at least two of us to take him in a fight. We haven't really tangled with the other two, but they all have records. I brought out some photos. See if you can identify any of them."

The three glossy prints each showed front and side view of men in typical prison pose. The first one didn't register at all, the second sent a charge of electricity through me, the third was a very doubtful 'maybe'.

"Well?' asked Allen.

"This one, without any question, is the driver-fisherman. This one I wouldn't identify in court, but he could be the one who went over the woodpile. This one doesn't do anything for me at all, but of course I never really got a look at his face, and only a flashing glimpse at this guy."

"Okay. I'd like your wife to check them too."

Mary came out, met Allen, and was handed the pictures. She, too, quickly confirmed the truck driver, but couldn't identify either of the others.

"Good enough," said Allen. "The truck driver is the one we call 'The Bear'."

"That pleasant, bearded fellow we talked to for so long yesterday would take two mounties in a fight? Thank God for my rifle!"

"You folks were very fortunate that you were armed before you met them. I hate to think what might have happened if you had walked in on them in your shed, or your cabin."

"Do you think they'd have really attacked us?"

"I don't think there's any doubt about it. They know how deep their criminal activities have been, and that if they were arrested they'd likely end up in the pen. In this isolated area, if you were the only people standing between them and freedom, I think it quite possible they'd make sure you were never able to turn them in, or testify against them."

I felt sick as I thought of what yesterday might have been.

"What will they do now?" Mary asked. "Last night was bad enough. I think we heard every drop of rain hit the roof, and every groan and creak of trees in the wind. I hate to think of tonight."

"I'm sure you have nothing to worry about. They know you have their license number, and that we will have it too by now. You showed that you would use your weapons, and they have nothing to gain and everything to lose by returning."

"Where do you think they are now?"

"I suspect they're camped out somewhere in a backwoods hideaway. That would explain the choice of stuff they were stealing. They dropped out of sight from Revelstoke ten days ago. This is the first of over thirty robberies that has involved anything but drugs, so I think they were stocking up their camp. We're sure they didn't come into Lumby last night, so they must be back in the timber off a logging road somewhere."

"If you knew they were in Revelstoke, why didn't you pick them up?"

"Because we haven't enough evidence to stand up in court. We've checked them into many towns, but they hit small towns that don't have 24 hour police patrols. They're clever and fast, hit the drugstore and are gone in minutes. So far we haven't been able to tie them in through a witness, a fingerprint, a photo or a shred of solid evidence. Once, we anticipated a raid, and had automatic cameras set up. When the alarm went off a couple of nights later the local mountie was there in minutes, but too late. When we developed the photos, everyone in them was wearing a balaclava and gloves, so we had pictures of three hooded men, and nothing for an arrest. That's why I was so excited when I got your call. You're the first people to witness them in a crime, and while it won't tie them up as long as the drug robberies would, if we can get the evidence here we'll pick them up, then see if we can make the other charges stick too. But first I have to get some fingerprints."

We watched him carefully dust and study everything in the booty pile, the handle of my axe used to chop our lock, the outboard motor, and discard them one by one.

"Nothing! Can you imagine them wearing gloves on a job like this? But that's why they've been getting away with all these jobs. Did you notice that they were wearing gloves?"

"No, but I wouldn't have noticed if they were wearing boxing gloves! Did you see gloves, Mary?"

"All I saw was running men. Where does that leave us?"

"Nowhere, I guess. We can't identify the men you saw committing a crime, and the one you can identify can't be charged with anything more serious than fishing, or driving a truck with no tail light. I'm just as pleased though, as we'd hate to take them to court on such a minor charge as breaking and entering when they have so much hanging over their heads. We'll get them!"

"How about a cup of coffee?"

"Thanks, I'd love one."

The Lumby drugstore was robbed the next night. Late in the summer, we read that the Korler gang made a mistake on a break-in, and that somewhere down the line the Mounties finally "got their man".

THE WATER WALL

After living together for over fifty years, Mary and I can have pretty good communication without much talking. We were watching TV recently when an advertisement showed a huge arch of water shooting over a car and falling harmlessly on the other side. We instantly looked at one another, Mary said, "Water wall!" and I nodded. It's a fifteen year old memory:

Those few seconds of horror seared that beautiful summer day forever into our memory. It is as though the re-run of the afternoon's action film has not been edited to the few important minutes of the performance, but still carries several hours of clear but inconsequential footage.

Why do I remember the cutting of that particular load of firewood: the hot sun on the mountainside; the blue lake away down below, filling the valley and disappearing north and south around forested shoulders; the selection and felling of half a dozen tall birch trees; the hot, hard but pleasant work of limbing and bucking and loading and cleanup? Perhaps it is because they were part of the first day of the rest of our lives, that only a miracle gave back to Mary and me.

Mary was waiting as I eased the heavily loaded pickup into our lakeside cabin yard and backed up to the woodpile.

"Hi dear," she called, "let's see if we can catch a fish for supper. I'll help you unload the wood this evening."

"Okay, but give me time for a swim first. It was hot up there."

Half an hour later we were on our beautiful lake, Mary facing me from the bow of the canoe, trolling a line while I paddled slowly. It was a frequently enjoyed, quiet, peaceful time.

As we rounded the point the quiet was pleasantly broken by the roar of Tsuius Creek, and our solitude by the appearance of a couple sitting on the beach near the creekmouth, their boat nosed into the sand nearby.

As we waved to them I became conscious of the distant sound of an inboard motor. The approaching roar grew rapidly in volume, and as I saw concern grow in Mary's face I looked over my shoulder to see twin sheets of water rolling from the bow of a big speedboat.

"Damn fool!" I exclaimed as I swung the canoe to meet the rolling wave. The beautiful boat swept around us, headed for the creekmouth, and shut down near the couple on the beach. I was fuming as I watched the driver talking to them.

"I suppose he likes to show off that big boat," Mary remarked, "but I'd rather not have to admire it from such close range."

"Hell, he was doing at least forty miles an hour, and with all this big lake to play in, there's no excuse for him to swish by within thirty feet of a canoe. I have a notion to go in and tell him what I think of his damn fancy boat and stupid manners."

"Now don't go getting all upset. We will probably never see....." Mary was interrupted by the scream of her reel, and as she set her hook and snubbed it up a bit a big rainbow cleared the water a hundred feet behind us.

"It looks like a dandy. Don't lose it!"

I was busy keeping the canoe in position with Mary's running line when we heard the burble of the inboard starting up. I looked over to see it swing out from shore, then almost leap from the water as the powerful engine roared into life.

"My gosh, he's headed straight toward us!" Mary cried.

"And look at that damn fool driver! He's standing up and looking back at the people he left on the beach. He's paying no attention... Hey!.... HEY!! .... HEYYYY!!!.... I shouted, then it was too late to shout.

"Don't jump! Get your feet back!"

In our last few seconds, as the tall sharp bow sliced at 40 miles per hour straight toward the canoe, several thoughts jammed my mind: One of us at least is going to be killed - the lifejackets are in the bottom - can I swim well enough to save her if her legs are mangled ?...

Legs drawn back, I looked up from the last thirty feet at that cruel bow rushing over us, then glimpsed the horror in the driver's face as he plunged a frantic full turn of his wheel. In the blink of an eye we were staring through a foot thick, fifteen foot high window of crystal water at every glistening detail of the bottom of the boat lying over in a broadside skid and rushing past at arm's length. It towered above us as it swished past Mary at high speed just as we were deluged by the collapsing water wall. Fortunately most of the tons of water in that huge wall arched over us and collapsed in a thundering cascade into the lake twenty feet beyond us.

The canoe, half filled, rocked crazily but remained upright. As I cleared the water from my eyes I saw the driver look back over his shoulder, and without a gesture toward his throttle, roar down the lake and flee into the distance.

The sudden rattle of Mary's fishing rod submerged in the bottom of the canoe shook us both out of the trancelike contemplation of loss of a loved one, or a lifetime in wheelchairs and hospitals. As she picked it up to fight her fish I began bailing out the canoe. We didn't speak until after she had landed a nice rainbow that brought us back to reality, and the realization as we paddled slowly homeward that we had escaped scot free, and our lives could go on as usual!

* * * * * * * *

THE STORM

It's a wild day at the lake, with no end in sight. Since early morning, roaring gale and lashing rain have swirled around from south to north and back again, testing our endurance and playing boisterously with our puny man-made resources. Several times the world was blacked out so we couldn't see in the cabin without a light.

This morning's gale announced its approach from the south with low, torn clouds sweeping over the hills, their bottom edges flapping like ragged sheets on a line. The lake developed a momentary ominous black hue, retreating toward us at high speed ahead of the hurried turbulence of a welter of churning whitecaps. Half a mile away the wavetops began to tear off and rise in frightening sheets of white water blown fifty feet high and lashing past at seventy five miles an hour in a sudden roaring explosion of wind and noise.

Abruptly our canoe and aluminum boat were picked up and flung rolling down the beach. As I rushed out to rescue them I was drenched in that horizontal blast of water as quickly as though I had plunged into the surf. The boat, upside down, skidded to a stop short of the water, but the canoe, fortunately also upside down, was well into it. As I dragged it ashore I searched frantically for paddles and oars, found three of them scattered on the beach, and one canoe paddle already fifty feet off shore and making good time.

Robbie File, struggling with his own boat down the beach, stripped off his shirt, checked his pockets, and with a strong stroke swam out and retrieved it. I dared not venture out to my dock, as huge green waves rolled over it and swept deck sections away, bobbing down the lake and disappearing in the spume, to be searched for on distant beaches another day. Our big boat, rearing and plunging, tugged and jerked at its anchor as though anxious to dance away and join them in their new found freedom. Hundred foot trees, with their backs to the wind, struggled to keep their skirts from being blown over their heads, or being undressed altogether.

Over the next several hours the wind dropped suddenly, reversed, brought sunshine for brief periods, returned and stormed from all directions, always with spectacular thunderous clouds boiling overhead or along the horizon somewhere. Twice, the whitecaps were still churning in one direction when a new blast hit the lake from the other, piling them up in confusion until they could reorganize and reverse their rolling sweep.

For over an hour this afternoon the huge black storm hung suspended behind the hills across the restless lake, booming its thunder almost continuously as it lanced bright firebolts into the black forest, as though pinning us down with a heavy artillery barrage while it sneaked its main force around to the south in another flanking attack. As its ragged sheets-in-the-wind marched up the lake again, presaging another violent blow, I hurried out to help Robbie batten down his trailer. We timed it well, as I rushed into the shelter of our own cabin just as the roaring wind and torrential downpour blasted us again.

And now, I really should have a light on to see what I'm writing, at four o'clock on this exciting, noisy, wildly beautiful summer afternoon.

* * * * * * * *

112

MABEL LAKE IN SEPTEMBER

The drowsy sunlit beauty of this mountain lake in the Indian Summer days of September seems beyond description. As though conscious of the picturesque scenery along its shores, the lake surface settles into a deep blue mirror, reflecting flawlessly every tree and fleecy cloud and skylined mountain, until broken momentarily here and there, and away over there, by the concentric rings of rising fish rippling the glassy surface.

Occasional wisps of mist up on the hillsides sit behind and silhouette draws and slopes, and set off dark green trees spectacularly against a white background. Our boat sits patiently and quietly at its mooring, so quietly that it doesn't stir its anchor chain off the bottom, and we could safely tie it for days on end by a piece of string.

On a boat trip down the lake we seem to hang motionless in airy space between the mountains and forests and fleecy clouds floating before us and those upside down around and beneath us, and we have to look back at our spreading wake to find substance. The occasional autumn leaf floating on the invisible surface looms up for hundreds of feet as a visible obstacle suspended airily in our path, and I have to fight the urge to steer the boat around it to avoid collision. A bank of fog becomes a low cloud in our sky, and we burst through it to the breathtaking beauty of a lone, still fishing boat mirrored several degrees above the distant horizon.

There's a smell of woodsmoke in the air from slash burning in distant logging clearings. In the quiet we hear the faint far off TOOT TOOT of the whistle punk's signals to the donkey engineer, cable hauling unseen logs up the slope to the landing. There is no one else around and we are torn between the wish to share this beauty with others, and our appreciation of the quiet isolation.

Mary and I enjoy travelling the high logging roads, pausing at an abandoned log landing to look across our hills to the endless columns of hill and mountain beyond, picking out the white exclamation mark of a waterfall tumbling for hundreds of feet off a forested ledge, looking down at our white curve of beach with the white speck of a raft or boat moored offshore, tracing the slash of the creek twisting its way through the forest which hides our cabin.

On a misty morning, with fog rolling through the trees and down the lake, we can climb through the clouds as we ascend the mountain, and in bright sunshine look down as from a plane on the sparkling white sea where lake and hills and vales lie hidden. Only the tops of high slopes and ridges project up as unfamiliar green islands, isolated from their base. We seem to be in another beautiful world, unable to relate these strange shapes to the land we know so well.

As the quiet days go by, the hills across the lake develop dots and splashes of red and gold and crimson among the evergreens, and the tall trees around the cabin become a golden canopy. Single leaves swoop and drift and dive and flutter on their hundred foot journey to rest. For the first few days they form isolated spots of gold in the yard, on the roof, the deck, the hood of the truck, the beach, the path through the woods. In the still air we sometimes have to wait a few moments to catch the next one starting its long, fluttering journey, and we wonder why that particular leaf chose that particular, causeless moment to let go. An occasional breath of breeze here and there creates momentary showers of leaves, and between the showers the now almost continuous flutter begins to form a carpet below. The yard becomes an ankle deep, crisp golden carpet, beautiful in the bright sunlight streaming its lights and shadows through the woods.

One black and memorable early fall evening though, we were reading by the fireplace when we heard the lake start to stir, with the musical ripple on the beach changing to the slop of waves, then the roar of surf. We heard the beginnings of the rain on the roof increase to a drumming downpour against roof, walls, windows, and as the sound grew I drew the drapes to look out into the stormy night.

In the window beam of light I was startled to see a flaming golden fire swirling into and across the glass. It took a shocked moment to realize that the drumming roar of rain had no water in it, but was composed instead of almost all those tons of overhead leaves coming down at once, churning in a gale-swept blizzard into everything in their path. It was eerie and almost frightening

114

to listen to and look upon in that dim shaft of light.

As the month draws to a close, the early Vs of geese come honking their way over the horizon and down the lake, frequently passing so close we hear the swish of their wings. We too are preparing to leave, to share in their migration south, and the cold rains and mountain snows of early October speed us on our way.

In the new and different booklet of beautiful memories that we take from the lake each autumn, sustaining us through the winter, Indian Summer is always a favorite chapter.

* * * * * * * *

Mary on the beach on a September morning. The golden trees across the lake are mostly larch, among pine, fir and cedar.

I leave you here, to turn the telling of tales over to Gord. The following few chapters, while told in the first person, are his stories, not mine.

* * * * * * * *

I was born in 1915 in a homestead shack in the sandhills south west of Dundurn, Saskatchewan. Dad paid the midwife by giving her a brood sow, so our family lost a pig and gained a son.

Dad was a homesteader, rancher, park warden. We moved during my first year of life from the homestead to a six section ranch fifty miles northwest of Prince Albert. I had a five year old brother Orville, and five years later, a baby sister Ruth.

My ranch years were exciting, happy ones, but I left at age 16 with Orville to prove up on our own homesteads in the Big River district, on the National Park boundary. After three years of breaking land and batching, I sold my homestead for $450.

In the meantime Dad had sold the ranch and moved to a cabin in Prince Albert National Park as a park warden. He patrolled for game poachers and fires in summer by saddle horse and truck, and in winter with a team of nine dogs. I spent a month or two at a time with him there, and gained experience fighting fires and patrolling forest country.

The Hungry Thirties had arrived by this time. Prince Albert National Park, with Lake Waskesiu as its crown jewel, was in the early stages of development as a beautiful resort when depression and politics placed a relief camp on the shore of that beautiful lake. (Prime Minister MacKenzie King represented the Prince Albert constituency in parliament.)

One hundred and fifty men spent their time building the Waskesiu golf course by hand and horse teams. My job there as a second cook introduced me to five summers in this beautiful area. I spent the winters with Dad in the park, and in doing odd jobs.

During the winter of 1941-42 I worked for Big River fisheries hauling fish by cat train from northern lakes into Big River. Ninety percent of our travel was on the ice of the rivers and lakes chain heading north west. We could travel only during the ice months, but ran day and night, around the clock, at four and a half miles per hour.

This then is the locale and time frame around which the next few tales will be told. Keep in mind that it is the story of a farm and ranch boy raised in the 'twenties and depression decades, in the lake and forest country of North Central Saskatchewan.

It would help your understanding of these stories if you could place them on a map.

* * * * * * * *

THE RANCH

The year I was ten, Dad bought a driving horse and sulky (a two wheeled cart similar to those used in trotting races) from a farm a few miles west of Canwood and thirty miles from home. He took Orville and me with him that cold late fall day, and when the deal was finished Dad started me off for home with the new horse and a pat on the head. He and Orville passed me in the truck a few minutes later as I began to contemplate that long thirty miles of cold road, sitting inches behind the horse's tail. I really knew how close he was when he raised his tail and dumped a load of steaming manure at my feet.

I was cold and miserable and feeling sorry for myself even before it started to rain, but when that icy rain began to fall on that long, lonely, desolate road I knew all the world was against me. I didn't dare get off and walk, and the colder and wetter and more miserable I got, the madder I got at everyone. If I'd been a crybaby I'd have been crying, as with chattering teeth I scrunched, shivering, behind the horse's rump.

As I approached Odegaard's little general store and post office about ten miles from home, I was surprised to see Dad's truck parked outside. When I went in, Dad sent Orville out to take over the rest of the driving, then handed me a parcel and told me to go into the living quarters to change.

Only those who have been privileged in their childhood to experience the indescribable feeling of pulling on a brand new suit of WARM, SOFT, FLEECE-LINED underwear in our cold climate can have any idea how I felt.

The change from misery to ecstasy was heightened when Mrs. Odegaard served me a hot drink and a big plate of steaming stew. I can still remember the feeling as I wriggled my bum and my back into the truck seat in that

fleecy underwear and watched Orville's hunched over form
as we passed him in the rain.

* * * * * * * *

Grandpa Main visited us one winter. On a forty
below zero morning he passed me in a hurry on his way to
the barn, exclaiming, "It's na a very heavy load, but
I've got a poor holt on it!"

* * * * * * * *

We had a round corral, about 60 foot diameter, built
of logs, with a snubbing post in the center. It had been
a rainy week, and a low spot in the corral had a long
puddle, mixed with ample quantities of soggy manure.
        Neighbor Shorty Robinson was a short, cocky, self
opinionated horseman who boasted he could handle any
horse. He arrived one day to pick up an unbroken gelding
he had bought from Dad. He was wearing his usual heavy
mackinaw pants, several sizes too large at the waist,
held up by suspenders.
        There were several horses in the corral, so Shorty
had a little trouble getting a rope on his. When he did,
the horse and Shorty were a long way from the snubbing
post, and before Shorty got to the post he lost his
footing to the running horse and landed on his belly.
The horse dragged him at full speed through the low spot,
and his heavy, loose topped pants scooped up a full load
of water and soggy manure. As he finally snubbed the
horse the stuff was oozing from inside his pantlegs over
his boots. We heard nothing more for years about his
skill with horses.
        Mother had made some dandelion wine, and bottled it
too soon, as it was so wild you could open it only by
piercing the cap with a nail, then aiming the jet into a
container. When she offered Shorty a bottle one day she
warned him about it, but he insisted he could handle it,
and popped off the cap. When he tried to control the jet
with his thumb it blew in his face, then blew his hat off
his head. At this stage he stuck the neck of the bottle
in his mouth, and almost blew himself up. Choking and
gagging, he surveyed the remaining inch of brew, and
sputtered a suggestion to Mother that he'd have another,
but that she could open it.

118

* * * * * * * *

We had about thirty head of horses. Mine was Old Blue, a retired race horse who still had a good turn of speed. I was bringing in the horses one day, and had them almost into the corral when two of them broke away and headed back on the trail. I was overtaking them to cut them off when one of them fell right in front of me! Old Blue went down at full speed, and I flew out of the saddle and down the trail on my belly. As a twelve year old, I was barefoot, wearing only bib overalls and a shirt, with nothing under. As I skidded down the trail for thirty feet my overall buttons came off and peeled off all my covering. I was scraped from chin to toes, and everything in between.

* * * * * * * *

During my school years I owned a team of five sleigh dogs that I drove every winter - to school, to cover my trapline, to visit distant neighbors. I fed a four pound chunk of frozen meat to each dog every night. They got no other winter food.

One Saturday morning I drove my dog team to the Gullikson's, tied them there, and went to town with the boys. Mrs. Gullikson, a kindly Scandinavian lady, had just separated the morning milking, and had two or three pails of warm skimmed milk to feed to her calves and pigs. She decided to be generous to my hungry looking dogs, and fed them about half a pail of that warm milk.

When I got back and hitched up my dogs they didn't seem too happy with the world, and I soon found the reason. It must have taken me three hours to drive them the three miles home, as we never went more than fifty feet at a time without one dog or another having to stop and leave a loose deposit in the snow. I was kept very busy, not only keeping the four dogs not involved with the stop from hauling the squatting one along in the harness, but lifting and swinging the heavy toboggan over or around each mess in the snow.

* * * * * * * *

When Orville and I left home to prove up on our own homesteads he was 21 and I was only 16. We were in the Big River district, just outside Prince Albert National Park, with the Sturgeon River forming the boundary between us and the park. We were about thirty miles from the park cabin where Dad and Mother lived after he sold the ranch and took a job as park warden.

A homestead in the wilderness during the Hungry Thirties could have pretty empty cupboards at times. Late one cold winter afternoon Orville and I were busy on the swede saw, sawing up a load of wood when two moose came out of the timber half a mile away.

The timber was in the park, within our Dad's warden territory, so no matter how short we were of meat, we had never hunted the easy moose, elk, and deer in the park. The Sturgeon River forming the park boundary flowed in a high banked stream through willows a quarter mile from our shack.

No one worried about hunting licenses in those depression days, but there was a definite hunting season, now long expired. The local game warden walked the narrow line between law enforcement and reasonable use of much needed meat, and as long as game meat was not being wasted or being fed to sleigh dogs, and was not flaunted in front of him, he didn't look too hard for trouble. Wild meat was hard frozen, stored under hay stacks for the winter, and hurriedly canned during spring thaws.

When those moose came out of the timber and headed for the river, Orville grabbed his long barrelled 30:30 and disappeared, leaving me sawing wood. Twenty minutes later I heard three fast shots, and Orville came back for the horses, saying he had both moose down. He had run down the river until he came to their tracks crossing the ice, peeked over the bank, and spotted them a hundred yards away.

Well it was a cold winter night, now dark, with a pair of moose lying in three feet of snow within sight of the public road. We had to get them dressed by lantern light and out of there that night, and didn't dare light a fire to keep us from freezing while we were doing it. We eventually got the job done, but it was a very long, cold night before we had the meat secured and got back to our cold cabin to build a hot fire.

* * * * * * * *

On the second winter of our homestead days Orville and I took out a permit to log and saw 50,000 feet of lumber. We hired two Norwegian homesteaders to do the falling and bucking. Orville and I skidded, loaded and hauled to Hank Matz's mill on Moonlight Lake.

Nyberg and Nystrand were exceptional woodsmen. Nystrand had built Orville's log cabin, and hewed the inside of each log so true that you could stand a 2x4 against any part of the wall and touch every log with it. We paid them off with birch lumber, which they cut with ours, and cured in their cabin attic. When it was ready they tore out their old floor, laid a rough plank birch floor, then hand planed it, cross planed it, sanded and treated it until that log cabin floor shone like glass.

When sawed, Orville and I hauled our lumber 12 miles to the homestead. We piled up 50,000 feet of it, and sold it at $15.00 a thousand delivered to a lumber yard in Canwood, 30 miles from home. I had a team at the homestead and Orville had a team in Canwood. I would load about 2,000 feet on a 5' bunk sleigh at night, and head for Canwood in the morning. Orville would meet me half way with yesterday's empty sleigh, take over my load and deliver it to Canwood, while I took the empty back for tomorrow's load.

* * * * * * * *

THE RELIEF CAMP

Waskesiu is an eighteen by seven mile lake in the pine forested hills of Prince Albert National Park, seventy five miles north of the city of Prince Albert. It is part of a larger lake chain, and the present day site of a beautiful resort boasting luxury condos, marinas, modern hotels, riding stables, golf course, and all the other amenities of a modern resort. In 1930 it was newly opened, at the end of a long, long dusty gravel road, with gravel trails winding through the pines to tent campgrounds and shack tent "cabins". (A shack tent has a wooden floor and four foot wooden walls, topped by canvas walls and roof).

The new resort was immediately struck by the onset of the drought and depression of the 'thirties, so that instead of building over the next few years to its modern beauty, it became the site of a large government relief camp.

Canadian relief camps were work camps, providing food and shelter and a pittance wage to homeless, hungry men who had spent a year or two or three drifting about the country, riding the rods, finding a meal wherever and however they could. The Waskesiu camp was established under quasi military conditions, with about one hundred and fifty single men and twenty to thirty teams of work horses.

The make-work project here was the construction of an 18 hole golf course in this forested wilderness by shovel and axe and horse team. Men were paid $5.00 a month (20 cents a day) plus board and room, board being all they could eat of top grade food, and room being a bed in a bunkhouse. Men with teams earned $10.00 a month. They worked a six day, forty eight hour week. Tobacco was free. Government policy seemed to be to feed the men better than they had ever experienced, but to pay almost nothing. The food bill was enormous in those depression days.

The kitchen-dining room was a long log building seating one hundred and fifty men. The kitchen crew consisted of a head cook at $30 a month, and a second cook and four helpers at $10 a month. (We bought our own tobacco). I started as a cook's helper, and moved after a month to 2nd cook.

Dining room discipline was strict. Talking at the tables was forbidden, except to ask for food to be passed. The men were in and out of the dining room in twenty minutes. In those homeless, hungry years for many, and home tables of meager variety for the rest, this camp provided steaks, roast beef and pork, bacon, ham, jams and jellies, pies, choices of breakfast cereals, milk, coffee, tea, in as many helpings as they had time and stomach for. Large bowls of apples, bananas, oranges, sat on a table at the exit door, and the men helped themselves to as much of this fruit as they wanted as they left the room.

Pancakes were mixed in a twenty gallon tub, and baked thirty two at a time on roaring wood stoves. I poured eight pancakes up one side of a grill, eight back, eight up, eight back, then immediately started turning them in the same order. As soon as they were all turned it was time to take them off in order and repeat the whole process, seemingly endlessly. Pancake breakfasts included bacon, eggs, sausage, hashbrowns, bread, jam, in huge quantities. We baked thirty two pies every day.

Many of the men who came to camp had spent a year or more riding the rods from Vancouver to Halifax and back, begging for food, always hungry. When they came into this endless, unlimited supply of wonderful food they couldn't resist eating everything they could cram into their bodies. Almost invariably new men showed up on sick parade after two or three days, were fed a dose of castor oil, and settled down to eating within their capacity for the rest of their stay.

Our old martinet of a cook took his usual stance at the kitchen-dining room door with his usual meat cleaver in his hand one morning when a new man sitting on a single end-of-the-table bench stood up and reached down the table for a plate of eggs. By the time he had it, the cook had pulled back his bench, and as he crashed to the floor with eggs all over him, the cook stood above him and roared, " No man in this camp stands up for food! If you want something, ASK FOR IT!!" This kind of discipline was readily accepted under the circumstances.

During those early days at Waskesiu the camp was plagued with bears. Their favorite target was garbage barrels, though they frequently invaded tents and shack tents. On my way to work one day I came upon a fifty gallon garbage barrel with a half grown bear feeding at it. He had both hind feet and one front foot on the rim, with his other front foot and his head away down in the barrel, out of sight. I threw a rock, and when it clanged against the barrel, the bear's front foot slipped off the rim and he fell in on his head, with only his back feet waving over the edge. He kicked and squalled and squirmed in that garbage for minutes before he got turned right side up and took off.

One of my jobs was lighting the big stoves very early every morning. I came in one morning to find a full grown bear sitting on one of the long tables. He had cleaned up on several helpings of butter, jam, honey and sugar on the pre-set table, and looked up from another sugar bowl when I opened the door. When I yelled at him he took off through the window he had broken to get in.

One night, while I was sleeping with my head against the tent wall, a soft bump on my head woke me up. I bulged the wall as I put my hand up to my head, and was immediately bitten through the canvas. One finger was cut, and a single hole the size of a bear's canine tooth was left in the canvas wall. I didn't go out to see how big he was.

* * * * * * * *

MORE BEARS AND BOATS

After three hot summer months in a kitchen cooking for one hundred and fifty men on two huge wood burning stoves, no air conditioning and little air, I quit and went back to Big River to help brother Orville cut and stack one hundred and fifty tons of hay on his homestead. In the meantime I had met Len Hunter of Hunter's Boats at Waskesiu, and been promised a job as boatman-fishing guide on the Waskesiu, Crean, Kingsmere, Adjawan Lakes chain for the next summer. So, after a winter with Dad patrolling the national park by dog team from his warden's cabin there, I returned to Waskesiu and five wonderful outdoor summers, three with Hunter and two running my own boats. I spent my winters with Dad, and on odd jobs.

We had a few storm scares out on the big lakes during those years, but my nearest call to disaster came the day I swung the big boat alongside a swimming moose, and all thirty passengers rushed to the same side of the boat to see it. The boat rolled its rail to the water, and as I visualized it turning turtle, everyone scrambled to the high side, and repeated the thrill. We settled down when they followed my orders to "SIT DOWN!"

The Park Board had a log picnic cook kitchen on Kingsmere Lake. Harold Beck had a fishing party there on an overnight trip, and since it looked like rain, they all settled to sleep on the floor of the kitchen. There were many bears in the area, and Harold laid his sleeping bag across the open doorway to keep them out. During the night, when someone rolled him gently onto his back with a hand on his shoulder, he assumed he was being wakened to go fishing. As he said "Okay" and opened his eyes, he was looking at twelve inch range into the brown eyes of a bear. He went straight to the bottom of his sleeping bag, and the bear left him there.

Mark Mellon was a park ranger on Crean Lake. His cabin was up on a hill overlooking the lake, with a path winding up from the lake to the cabin.

Mark and his big husky dog made one of their regular canoe trips out to Waskesiu one day for supplies. When they came back the dog ran up the trail to the cabin ahead of Mark, who had loaded himself down with a heavy back pack and a bag under each arm. As he came around the corner of the cabin a big bear and the dog came rushing around from the opposite direction.

Man and bear met right at the corner, and the bear had time only to duck his head and run between Mark's legs. However he was too big for that, and Mark was picked up and rode the galloping bear backward down the trail, scattering groceries in all directions.

* * * * * * * *

125

GREY OWL

We had an internationally famous attraction in our area during those years. Grey Owl was a well educated Indian of noble bearing who had gained an international reputation as an environmentalist, writer, and story teller. His isolated cabin on Adjawan, a small wilderness lake, was home to many species of wild animals with whom he had established a magical human relationship, made famous through his widely published stories and books.

Most famous of his animal companions were his two pet beaver, Jellyroll and Rawhide, who shared his cabin and used it as other beaver would use a beaver house, having their own canal running from a hole in the floor to the lake, and free access to come and go as they wished.

As Grey Owl's reputation grew, so did his stream of visitors, and he welcomed them to share in his love of nature. We ran daily "big boat" excursions to Adjawan, a twelve hour round trip with thirty passengers. This involved an eighteen mile trip up Waskesiu with the big boat, a mile and a half walking portage to Kingsmere Lake, an eight mile trip with five small outboard motorboats, then a two mile hike on a path through the woods. Here, Grey Owl, Rawhide, Jellyroll, and other wild animal friends took over the entertainment while I took an afternoon siesta before the long trip back.

Grey Owl was a wonderful speaker, with a soft voice as he spun his tales of nature and Indian lore, and a manner that made him a much loved and respected part of our times. On a lecture tour to England the previous year he met two elderly (sixtyish) English ladies who decided to make a once-in-a-lifetime trip to Adjawan to see his wilderness world at first hand.

Cliff Christianson and I were assigned to move them and all their luggage including seven cameras on their overnight trip from Waskesiu to Adjawan. Grey Owl knew the date of their arrival, and had told me earlier not to walk them around Adjawan on the normal trail, but to come through the woods across the lake from his cabin.

I suppose we all contributed to their fairy tale trip, as Cliff and I used a big freighter canoe to transport them through the lakes and portages. There was a rail trolley portage between Waskesiu and Kingsmere

Gord at Grey Owl's cabin. Note the beaver lodge just outside.

Cliff and Gord with the two English ladies, enroute to Grey Owl's cabin.

On the Kingsmere portage.

Lakes, and the ladies were thrilled to help us push the heavy load through it.

When we finally arrived on the shore of Adjawan, Grey Owl, dressed in buckskins, with an eagle feather in his hair, paddled his canoe across to meet us. When he laid down his paddle about fifty yards from shore, extended his arm toward us and said "How!" the English ladies literally squirmed with excitement. They had already accomplished everything they had dreamed of on their trip.

And now I hate to spoil this story by telling those of you who don't already know, that after Grey Owl's death it was discovered that this buckskin clad Indian with the long braids and the eagle feather was not really an Indian at all. He was born in England, of noble birth, and had turned his back on all that his inheritance would have provided, to live a fulfilling and rewarding life as a lone Indian in a land and environment that he loved.

Those of us who were close to him found the revelation of his ancestry hard to believe, but after the initial shock, we respected this great man all the more for his success in changing the life that was given him to one that we all loved and respected. There was, after all, really no deceit in him, because he never deceived anyone for material gain, and his many animal friends loved him for what he was.

Grey Owl and Jellyroll.

127

THE ICE TRAIN

During the winter of 1941-42 I worked for Big River Fisheries, hauling fish by cat train from northern lakes into Big River.

Winter fishing on those far northern lakes was a big industry, usually carried out by native Indians. They produced hundreds of tons of whitefish, trout, and other top grade fish for the Canadian and American markets. It was not a viable summer industry because of lack of transportation and refrigeration.

The fish were netted under the ice. Long nets were fed through a hole cut in the ice, and propelled to the next hole by a unique system of a line-actuated ratchets dogged along the under surface of the ice. Cutting thick ice and handling wet nets and wet fish in 40 below zero weather on the open wind swept expanse of a big lake was frigid work, but those tons of fish were always there, boxed and ready to go, when the cat trains arrived.

Freight had been hauled north and fish south for many years by horse teams. Long strings of sharply shod four-horse teams had braved those winter temperatures for weeks at a time, stopping each night at stables and bunk houses built and provisioned along the rivers and lakes that were their highways. The biggest hazard was not only frostbite for men, but frozen lungs and consequent pneumonia and death among the horses.

When Cat trains began to compete, and ultimately replace the horses, they ignored the fifteen mile stop-over bunkhouses and stables along the route. They hauled their own bunkhouse at the tail of the train, worked in shifts around the clock, and never stopped except to refuel from their own stores.

Our route that winter was a five hundred mile round trip, Big River to Buffalo Narrows and back. Ninety percent of the travel was on the ice of the river and lake chain heading northwest, with occasional rough cross country portages between river systems. (It would help your understanding of this story if you could locate our route on a map.)

We could travel only during the ice months, but ran day and night around the clock at 4 1/2 miles per hour all winter. Our train consisted of an open caterpillar tractor, three twenty ton freight sleighs, and a heated caboose with fuel barrels ahead of the cabin and wood piled on the back deck.

On ice, to reduce the risk of going to the bottom, each part of the train except the caboose was separated by, and towed by a sixteen foot cable fastened to the leading end of the tongue of the following sleigh, so the train spanned over one hundred feet. The lighter caboose was hooked short to the sleigh ahead by its eight foot hardwood tongue, and we tongue hooked all the sleighs on portages.

On the trip north we hauled and delivered freight to Hudson's Bay Co. trading posts and Indian settlements. We frequently experienced forty below zero weather, sometimes colder, on that open Cat. We were a four man crew, working in two teams. On a working shift of eight hours, one man drove the Cat while his partner spent his time in the caboose preparing meals, cleaning up, tending fire, as the other team slept.

The driver was relieved about every forty five minutes, depending on the weather. When it was time to change, the driver slowed to a crawl as his partner donned outdoor parka, mitts, and whatever extra clothing the weather dictated, dropped off the caboose and ran up the length of the train to the drawbar of the Cat.

At each eight hour change of shift the Cat was unhooked and driven back to the caboose, shut off, fuelled and lubricated. On the way, the Cat hooked by a snatch cable to each sleigh in turn and bunched them up, leaving the haul cable slack between each of them.

It usually took less than ten minutes to gas up and have the new crew take over, but during that time every one of those sixteen 8 foot steel shod sleigh runners would freeze to the ice. When the Cat driver got back and hooked to the lead sleigh he took a full speed run the length of the first slack cable, hoping the jerk would break the first sleigh loose. If successful, the second sleigh was hit with a jerk, and so on down the line until the train was on the move again. Sometimes it took a series of jerks, unhooking and bunching sleighs again before they all broke free. Once freed, the train moved easily.

A V snowplow on the front of the Cat took care of snowdrifts and ice heaves, although we upset the caboose three times that winter. I was in it, asleep, each time,

129

and landed twice on my head and once on my feet. Everything including the stove was bolted down, so we didn't burn.

I was driving one soft, warm moonlit night , with the Cat chuckling along easily at 4 1/2 MPH. My partner was preparing to take over from me, and before leaving the caboose he stood on the back platform of the caboose to relieve himself, dressed in heavy clothes with mitts under his arm.

When he went to put on his mitts, he had only one. By the time he searched the platform, his bunk and the caboose, and decided he must have dropped it overboard, several minutes and hundreds of yards had passed. With no communication to the driver, he dropped off the moving train and trotted back along the track. By the time he found his mitt the tractor was half a mile ahead, and in heavy clothes he had no option but to run as hard as he could to try to catch up.

Fortunately I had slowed down during his race, thinking he was on the caboose and ready to come up. After a time, when he failed to show, I assumed he had fallen asleep, and had just stopped the rig to check on him when he collapsed, exhausted, on the platform of the caboose.

Winter daylight was short, and the dark nights were long, with eight hour days and sixteen hour nights for much of the winter. One stormy night, in a heavy wind with snow piling up, the wire to a headlight loaded so heavily with ice it pulled out of its socket, shorted out all the lights, and left us in a black dark blizzard.

Orville was driving, and he and his partner worked with flashlight and screwdriver to insert the wire back into the socket. With bare, freezing fingers, Orville dropped a tiny screw and lost it beyond recovery in the snow. There was no substitute, so they decided to go to bed until daylight and either melt a few cubic feet of snow in the caboose to find their screw in the water at the bottom of a pot, or find some other way to recover their headlights.

Morning dawned bright and clear, and as Orville walked back up to the tractor he spied from fifty feet away the tiny screw standing up on a snow tee, sparkling in the sun. Its warmth when it was dropped the night before had melted, then froze, a sliver of ice on which it stood as the blizzard wind blew the snow from around it.

Our turn-around in Big River was as fast as we could unload, restock our supplies, load for the Indians and trading posts, and head north again, noon or midnight. We arrived in Big River at four o'clock one frosty morning with our sleigh runners screeching in the snow and our tractor snorting at full throttle in a 60 below zero temperature. When we reached the icy streets, our deep snow lugs precisely turned each twelve inch section of ice between lugs upside down as they came off the back of the tracks, so we converted an ice track to a gravel track.

Now our runners really screamed, and pulled so heavily we had to unhook and pull one sled at a time through the sleeping town. Our exhaust stack turned red hot as the laboring tractor snorted each load through, and the whole town must have been kept awake for the rest of the night.

One of our loads for the Hudson's Bay post at Buffalo Narrows included a large case of brightly colored, fleece lined women's bloomers. The factor opened the case and set it on the counter as he busied himself with the rest of the load.

Our arrival always filled the store with Indians, and the fifteen or twenty squaws in the store tore into that box of bloomers at once. There was a storeful of laughs as the women held them up for display, modelled them, traded for size, then took their choices to the sales counter. The whole box sold out in minutes.

Another time we had a hustling little eight year old Indian boy among the volunteer crew helping us unload, and he hurried every trip from sleigh to store, always on the look-out for a load he could handle. An eight inch, sixty pound canvas bag of lead buckshot was part of the load, and his eyes lit up when he saw it. He hurried to the little bag, grabbed it, and was going to start away, but his bum came up in the air and nothing else moved. We had a hard time hiding our laughter as he walked around it, checked to see if it was nailed down, tried it again, and gave up with a puzzled look.

As spring approached, our loads changed from frozen to fresh fish, which brought premium prices in the Eastern American market. They were packed in chipped ice, in sixty pound boxes as they were taken from the nets, kept from freezing, and shipped as far as Big River in covered, heated, insulated sleighs. We had to ensure that they didn't freeze in spring ice storms or lose their ice covering in warm spells as we carefully monitored temperatures and kept heaters going as necessary in each sleigh. Our heavy load of ice and wood fuel cut our train from three to two sleighs and a caboose.

As we crossed Dore Lake one afternoon in early April the tractor and first sleigh cracked the ice, and the second sleigh and caboose broke through. Their broad racks settled on the surrounding ice, with runners and running gear down at least two feet in the deep water. Those of us in the caboose baled out on Orville's shout, "GET UP, WE'RE IN THE LAKE!!" and walked through water spreading rapidly over the surrounding ice.

Fortunately we were within a couple of miles of one of those old horse-days stopover depots, with bunkhouse and stable. We hauled the front load to the old depot, unloaded the several tons of boxed fish into the bunkhouse, and lit a big fire in the barrel heater.

Back at the train we approached as close as we dared with the tractor and empty sleigh, and transferred the load from the sunken sleigh to the empty one. The caboose was hooked to the sleigh ahead by its eight foot hardwood tongue, now under water and almost hidden by the overhanging rack of the fish sleigh. Since we had no hope of moving them both, and would have to go under water to unhook it, we sawed off the connecting tongue under two feet of water. The open water had frozen by this time, so we had to chop clear whatever we worked on.

Using fifty feet of cable, we hauled the sleighs out one at a time, but had to reach two feet under that icy water to hook cable to the stub tongue of the caboose. By the time we got everything to the depot it was after midnight. We spent the rest of the night bunked in there amid many tons of fish.

Our main problem in the morning was replacing the hardwood tongue. Finding a suitable birch tree and cutting a pole to size was relatively simple, but drilling six bolt holes for drawbar and braces was something else. We heated all six bolts red hot in the stove, then drove them one at a time as they burned their way into the green wood, withdrew them as they cooled and replaced them with fresh red ones. By the time we finished we couldn't see in the bunkhouse for smoke, but that makeshift tongue hauled us safely to Big River.

We were a day and a half beyond our scheduled arrival at the Big River depot, but their worry changed to praise when they found those two big loads of fish in prime, iced, unfrozen condition.

The ice train on a portage in spring, with two sleigh loads of fresh fish. This is the train that went through the ice.

I'll tell just one more little story before turning the story telling over to Bill:

THE STRIP TEASE

When my wife (Bert) and I were married in 1942, I thought it would be nice to show her the old ranch on our way to a Waskesiu honeymoon. Travelling a forest trail, we had run into rain and slippery roads. When our car slid off the road I had to drive through a lightly wooded area to find a spot where we could get back on the road again.

When a half decayed old log blocked our trail, Bert hopped out of the car and rolled it out of the way. A few minutes later she began to squirm on the seat, then suddenly shouted "STOP," leaped out, and in the privacy of those woods she did the fastest, fanciest strip tease any new bridegroom could hope for. As I sat, mouth agape, watching my bride throwing off all her clothes in time to a fast and fancy thigh slapping, high stepping dance, I could hardly believe what I was seeing.

It wasn't until she leaped back into the car and asked for my help that I realized the dance wasn't for my benefit after all. She had stirred up a nest of fire ants in the log, and needed my help to slap the last of them.

BILL KITZUL'S TALES

My earliest memory is that I was an unwanted child. I lived my early life on the defensive, picked on and cruelly treated by a bitter, vindictive grandmother who, reluctantly, raised me.

I was born six months after my father died in the 1919 'flu epidemic on a homestead farm thirty five miles west of Yorkton Saskatchewan. My mother married again before I was three, and since my stepfather would not accept any of her four children, we were all put up for adoption. My three sisters were adopted into distant families, but I, as the baby boy, was fought over by my grandmothers, (not for who would have me, but for who would not).

There was long standing enmity between my paternal and maternal families. My paternal grandmother, after raising me for about a year, decided to dump me on my maternal grandparents. Arriving in their yard by horse and buggy, she shouted, "Here he is. You can have him!" then dumped me out, turned her horse, and whipped him out of the yard to the shouts and imprecations of my other grandmother.

This woman was a cruel, hard, bitter mother of eighteen children, aged from departed adults to a baby. She certainly didn't want another one, and made that fact known at once. She shouted, "You don't belong here. Get out! Go with your grandmother!"

At age three I didn't understand what was going on, but certainly understood that I wasn't wanted in that yard. I fled out the gate and down the road vainly chasing the distant buggy, and ended up in the woods by the roadside, crying my eyes out and surrounded by a milling herd of curious cattle.

As my grandfather returned at dusk from his day's work in the field, his curiosity was aroused by the milling cattle. He walked among them, expecting to see a coyote or a newborn calf. When he found me there crying, he picked me up, put me in his wagon, took home and laid down the law to his wife. He told her that I was there to stay and that he didn't want to hear any argument about it.

I grew up hating my grandmother for her cruelty, and she must have hated me, for she never ceased to treat me

134

sadistically. I received an untold number of vicious beatings, most of them for no reason. If anything blame-worthy happened on the farm, it didn't matter who was responsible, I was the one whipped for it. Most of these I didn't deserve, a few of them I did, but the frequency and unfairness of her beatings created in me a deep feeling of insecurity and resentment that I didn't lose until I grew up and was out on my own.

To understand the people who raised me, we have to go back to their origins in the Ukraine. My grandparents were born in a village there in 1870, under the feudal system of Tsar Nicholas and the domination of the Russian aristocracy. Their village of five thousand serfs was governed by a family who had complete control over all these people. A season's work on the land yielded one sheaf to the serf and seven to the lord.

My grandparents had been married under these con-ditions, and my mother and one boy were born in the Ukraine. My grandfather, who had learned as a youth to work unceasingly, had not only carried that 4:00 A.M. to dark work ethic with him to his grave, he expected everyone under his control to do the same.

This small family came to the New World under Canada's settlement policy of free homestead lands. When my grandfather arrived in Winnipeg in 1898 he trekked on foot over three hundred miles to his new homestead in the present day Yorkton district. With his hard work and rapidly growing family and eagerness to acquire new land his homestead grew over the next fifteen years to five quarter sections, two of which were free homestead grants. During their first twenty-three years in Canada this family grew to eighteen children, and I became the reluctant nineteenth child.

This area was predominately Ukrainian, mixed with a few German and Polish homesteaders. Most people of their generation maintained their simple European culture and customs and their need to be self sufficient. As a boy, all my socks, sweaters, mitts, were knit at home from homespun wool taken from our own sheep, and most of our clothing was woven from our own wool. My straw hats were made using a Ukrainian technique of weaving seven wheat straws into a continuous reel, then sewn into a flat, circular weave that, when formed into a hat, was water-proof. Our ample garden produced not only our own bins

135

of vegetables, but our barrels of sauerkraut and our kegs of homebrewed white lightning.

By the time I reached my teens there were only four boys at home, myself and three uncles, two of whom were a year or two older and one younger. Our five quarter sections were a very big farm in the days when all field work was done with horses, and all of us worked hard. We had a couple of acres of garden, all of it planted, cultivated, and harvested by hand labor. We had eighteen work horses and fifteen milk cows. Every morning before I left for school I milked several cows, fed horses, cleaned stable, and carried several buckets of water up a steep hill from a creek a couple of hundred yards away to fill the household water barrels.

My grandfather had a phobia about keeping us busy, to the point that we were regularly forced to do dozens of hard jobs by hand that could easily be done by horses. Work was his whole life and his only interest, and we boys looked on him as very stubborn and maybe even a little stupid in his demands on us.

For instance, he planted timothy hay and alfalfa in his three acre farm yard, then forced us boys to cut it by hand, (scythe), as stock feed, when he had a perfectly good horse-drawn hay mower sitting idle in the yard.

We were teenagers and becoming rebellious before he allowed us to properly utilize horse drawn and power machinery. From age six or seven we carried hundreds and hundreds of buckets of water from the creek, until as fifteen year olds we convinced him to allow us to use a horse-drawn stoneboat to haul the water, a barrel at a time, to provide the eighty to one hundred gallons a day for household and yard use. He had a good tractor, but he used it only for belt power, while we boys almost broke our backs breaking land with horses who were stopped in their tracks every time the plow hit a heavy stump. It took us years to convince him that tractor power with a breaking plow made more sense.

We boys had to beg hard, generally without success, for time off on a Saturday or Sunday afternoon to go to a community picnic or ball game. I was generally the one delegated to approach Grandfather with our common demands. The others for instance would shove me forward on a Saturday night to ask for fifty cents apiece for the local dance, with the promise that if I got the money,

136

they'd take me with them. I was the one to demand horse power for hauling water and cutting hay, and tractor power for land breaking.

When I was fourteen and preparing to go to school one morning he said to me, "You've had enough schooling. You can read and write. Hitch up a six horse team and start plowing the west quarter."

At about this time, probably looking forward a few years, Grandfather adopted or took in another grandson, a son of one of his oldest boys. I now had a sibling cousin as well as three uncles, all near my own age.

Due to our lifestyle we were more or less spared the trauma of the great depression. Except for the black clouds of dust drifting across our horizon from distant lands, obscuring the sun for weeks at a time, we experienced little of the blowing winds and drifting soil of the dustbowl years. Most of our land was fairly heavy, and sheltered by belts of trees left from original forests. Much of our soil though was very rocky, and one of Grandfather's edicts was that we pick rocks as part of every move we made in his fields. We children picked and carried and piled tons of rocks, until all our fences were lined with walls of rocks, heaped to the third wire. Sloughs and potholes in the fields were filled with rocks, covered with soil, and incorporated eventually as crop land.

Anyone who has farmed in the horse days is familiar with harrow carts, towed behind the sixteen foot harrows for the operator to ride during his daily miles of harrow travel. My grandfather had harrow carts too, but we boys didn't ride them. He replaced the seats with wooden rock boxes which would hold five hundred pounds of rocks to be loaded and unloaded into rock dumps. Instead of riding all day behind the harrows as our neighbors did, we walked all day and hustled back and forth across that moving sixteen foot swath to pick rocks while keeping up with horses walking at normal speed. That was one more point of rebellion among us.

A four horse team on the drill (seeder) and six on the harrows.

RIDING THE RODS

In 1935, when my cousin and I were fifteen and sixteen, we decided we'd had enough of farming, and made plans to run away right after harvest. We packed a bit of food, an extra jacket and our harvest earnings of $30 apiece.

In Yorkton we found the "hobo jungle" near the railroad tracks to be packed with about one hundred and fifty hobos and drifters. Many of them had been riding the rods for years, picking up the odd job here and there, working for a meal, visiting city soup kitchens, moving from city to city and coast to coast. Most of them were honest, bitter men.

Luckily, we were befriended by one young man who taught us the ropes re catching moving freights, dropping off before the train reached switching yards to avoid railroad bulls, carrying a strap to tie ourselves to a ladder or the top walkway so we could doze without rolling off, and so on.

When our freight stopped to take on water in Minnedosa, we decided we had time for a quick meal in the Chinese cafe across the street. The three of us had gulped down our main course but still had our large pie servings untouched when the freight started to move. We each snatched our pie and ran for the train, ignoring the shouts of the proprietor as we dashed past his cash register. Stuffing our mouths full of pie and hotly pursued by the Chinaman, we ran beside the fast moving train, each caught a ladder and swung aboard, almost pulling our arms from their sockets.

Riding the roofs of freight cars was fairly pleasant in the autumn sunshine, but became bitterly cold in the wind when the sun went down. We walked back about six cars to a flatcar load of lumber and found sheltered cubbyholes big enough to crawl into between the piles of lumber. We could feel the lumber shifting as the freight sped around sharp curves, or when the couplers rattled and banged as the accordion of the train shortened on heavy application of the brakes. Knowing we risked injury in the lumber, we returned to riding the roofs as soon as the sun warmed the day.

We weren't as well prepared for the cold as the old hands, many of whom carried coats and even sheepskins to ward off the bitter wind. We listened to stories of men found frozen to death, strapped to ladders between cars, or to the roof walkway. While that wasn't a risk for another month or two, we knew we'd have to have more protection soon.

On our third day, travelling the lake country of Northern Ontario, we were really suffering from the cold when a brakeman, walking the cars to the engine, stopped by the three of us and said,

"I'm not supposed to do this, but I hate to see you boys freezing up here. There's a passenger car ahead of the caboose carrying a few cattlemen who look after the carloads of livestock on the train. There's room for you there, but don't be caught. If I give you the word, get out in a hurry, and don't stay in there on stops, or you'll get me into trouble."

Except for occasional brief returns to the outside, the rest of our trip to Toronto was relatively comfortable, and I've always had a warm spot in my heart for that brakey.

When we reached the Toronto freight yards our friend left us two boys on our own. We walked the streets for days in a vain effort to find work, scrounged a few meals from soup kitchens, and began to realize there was no hope of finding work. If we weren't to spend the winter as homeless tramps, wandering the streets and alleys of an unfriendly city, we'd better grab a freight for home before it got too cold to ride the rods.

We were more experienced on our long ride west, but we didn't enjoy any favours. There were only a handful of us on the westbound freight however, so there was little competition for good locations. We didn't have a dollar between us when we sneaked sheepishly back to the farm and into the house. Our first confrontation with our grandfather was at the supper table, where we listened to a long lecture about being bums.

* * * * * * * *

I worked on the home farm for another couple of years. After another harvest I left for Regina to visit my sister, and look for work.

An Ontario pulp company had a representative in Regina recruiting men and farm horses for winter work in the pulp camps in the Hawkes Junction area north of Sault Ste Marie. I signed on as an experienced logger, but when I reached that one hundred and eighty man camp I quickly discovered there was a lot of difference between pulpwood logging and cutting trees for stovewood on the farm.

The men were housed in one long bunkhouse, with ninety men to a side in four tiers of bunks along each wall. The only heat was one big central stove, and in that bitter cold weather the men at each end were yelling for more heat as hoar frost froze their blankets to the walls, while the men roasting in the center bunks were yelling to shut down the fire.

The snow was knee deep or more, and the weather was bitter cold. When it reached 45 below zero they kept the horses in their stables, but still sent the men out to work. Our timber was Ontario spruce, with trees about forty feet tall and eight inch diameter at the butts. We were required to cut, limb, buck the logs into eight foot lengths, and assemble and pile our cutting into our own piles. We were in a poor cutting area with scattered trees, and in that bitter cold, even the old time pulp cutters were cursing a bad season.

When the log boss looked over my very modest pile of logs after a few days he said,

"Son, I don't think you're going to make grub money, and I'd advise you to pack it in. Why don't you try for a warehouse job in the junction?"

Our camp was one of eight big pulp cutting camps totalling about fifteen hundred men in a twenty five mile radius around their central supply and distribution camp. Freight came into the warehouse by rail, and was distributed from the hub out the eight spokes to the various camps by caterpillar sled train.

I was lucky to arrive at the central warehouse just when they needed a warehouseman, and was hired. For the rest of the winter I slugged hundred pound sacks of sugar and flour, hard frozen quarters of beef weighing up to one hundred and fifty pounds, and cases and sacks and kegs and barrels of other supplies from freight cars to warehouse and out again to cat sleighs. We were well housed and well fed and at $5 a day plus grub, well paid. I didn't spend a dollar all winter, so I had a pretty good grubstake by spring breakup.

The camps closed when the huge piles of pulp logs stacked on the ice of the local rivers started down to the mills as the ice broke up in spring freshets.

My old pulp camp boss came in to the warehouse at layoff time and recognized me as the prairie boy he had sent in months before. He said,

"You're from the Prairies. How would you like a free ride back to Saskatchewan? I have six carloads of farm horses to ship back to Melfort, and I need a man to go with them to see they're fed and watered every day. If they don't get back to their owners in good shape, the farmers won't hire them out to us again next winter."

So - I ended a very good winter with a job that took me home again, riding legally in the train's caboose.

* * * * * * * *

PLACER MINING

I had another cousin who worked three summer seasons with Yukon Consolidated Gold Corp., driving steam pipes into the permafrost to thaw the gold bearing gravel for their big dredge and sluice system. I went north with him that spring of 1939, but instead of going with Yukon Gold I was hired out of Dawson City to work for a small American company dredging and sluicing the gravel of Clear Creek Valley. My job, among other things, was to drive a small cat, hauling machinery and supplies from camp to the work area.

This was hydraulic placer mining. They had gone back up Clear Creek about five miles, built a dam, and diverted the water into a ditch that followed the contours of the creekside hills with just enough fall to flow the water to a huge storage tank about two hundred and fifty feet above the diggings. From the storage tank a twenty four inch steel pipe dropped two hundred and fifty feet to the valley below, where several eight inch reducing pipes fed the water to high pressure six inch nozzles (monitors) about twelve feet long. The water left the monitors under a pressure of sixty pounds per square inch, with enough power to reach one hundred and fifty feet and roll a three foot boulder out of its bank. The monitor operators swept their hissing stream of high pressure water back and forth against the river bottom gravel, digging and rolling and sweeping it into the sluice boxes.

These boxes were four feet wide and sixty feet long with riffles three inches high and an inch apart. Every day, as the wash of gravel and water tumbled down the sluice boxes, the heavy gold dropping between the riffles produced an ingot of gold weighing at least twenty pounds.

There was inevitable horseplay with the monitors. Their six inch stream of high pressure water would blow a man off a machine or roll him head over heels, so no one dared aim that hundred and fifty foot blast directly at anyone. However, anyone foolish enough to stray into their range while the boss wasn't around was apt to have an icy blast of mud blown over his head.

The moss in our mining camp area was twelve inches deep, with every cubic inch of moss sheltering a cubic inch of mosquitos. If you stamped your foot you got a swarm of them in your face, and during the day there was always a howling cloud around us. The only way one could work among them was with tightly closed clothing, elastic wrist bands, pantlegs tucked into boot tops, and all exposed skin doused and soaked in repellant. There were quarts of it always available, and we stayed wet with it.

Many tall mosquito stories went the rounds of the camps. The best I heard was in Dawson, where a miner working his claim overheard two mosquitos talking about him from behind a small knoll. He heard one say, "Shall we eat him here, or carry him back to camp?" to which the other replied, "Let's eat him here. Maybe we can pick up another one on the way back."

Old Harry had a lifetime of experience as a crane operator. He worked here operating a big crane with a two yard bucket on a ninety foot boom, moving the continuous supply of waste gravel away from the bottom end of the sluice boxes.

Harry was a little long in the tooth to be climbing his ninety foot boom every day to grease the blocks, so that became one of my jobs. I was up there one day still pumping grease when suddenly the boom trembled as the cable started to sing. I just had time to grab a brace cable on each side when the boom bounced several feet as the bucket was slung out to swallow its load, then it sagged and lurched and swung around at terrifying speed in its ninety foot arc, jumped and dropped and shook as it dumped its load, and swung back again so fast I could scarcely hang on, all the time with lethal cable singing back and forth at my shins.

I shouted and screamed at Harry, and threw my grease gun down at his cab, but couldn't get his attention. On my next whirling, stomach churning trip I saw a distant man running toward us, but it seemed forever before the cables suddenly went slack and Harry came out of his cab to look up at me. The poor man was horrified when he realized that for the first time in thirty years he had operated that long boom with a man bouncing out on the end of it. It was several days before I got my voice back.

We were eating lunch one day when we heard an explosion, and the foreman leaped to his feet saying that the big pipe was gone. The pressure was so heavy on that huge downpipe it was alive, and had to be cabled down to keep its movements under control. This day, while the monitors were shut down for lunch and no one was watching it, the bottom end had blown off and drained the huge storage tank in an awesome flood of water and scattered equipment.

Strangely, most of the two hundred and fifty foot length of that heavy pipe was crushed flat when the last of the great weight of water rushing out the bottom closed the top valve and created a vacuum in the pipe. That was the explosion (implosion) we heard. We lost a couple of weeks production, building and installing a new pipe system.

When placer mining was closed by snow and freeze-up in early September, I headed for the outside world with a good grubstake. The company flew us to Whitehorse, where we took the narrow gauge railway to Skagway, and the Princess Marguerite down the coast to Vancouver.

I had never seen the ocean, or a ship, or those beautiful mountains and fjords and islands of the Alaska and British Columbia coasts, and was hugely impressed by it all. Little did I know that my future was right here, that all these islands and inlets and harbours and coastal towns and deep, rolling water would become as familiar to me as the rocks and fields and gullies of my grandfather's farm.

I was impressed again as our ship approached Vancouver on a September evening, passed Point Atkinson lighthouse, moved slowly under Lions' Gate Bridge, rounded Brockton Point in Stanley Park, to reveal the lights and downtown skyline of that busy, beautiful city and harbour.

This was 1940. I was 21 years old.

* * * * * * * *

LOGGING

I didn't know a soul in Vancouver, and had no set plans for my future. After a night in what turned out to be a run-down skid road hotel I moved to the Castle Hotel on Granville Street, and used that location for all my many Vancouver stays in future years.

The beer parlors were full of loggers. I made two or three friends among them in the next few days, and when one of them suggested I try logging, I dropped in to the Queen's Reach Timber Company hiring office and signed on as a chokerman.

Queen's Reach Timber Co. was a small (gyppo) company logging the high mountain forests of Queen's Reach Inlet off Jervis Inlet, a hundred miles north of Vancouver. We travelled by ferry to Pender Harbour and from there by large water taxi delivering loggers to camps up and down the various inlets.

Queen's Reach had beautiful timber, but was very difficult to log as it was real mountain goat country. From our camp on the beach we travelled eleven miles by crummy (camp bus) up very steep mountain grades to reach our work area. We carried lunch and came back down the mountain every night.

This was high lead logging, with cable systems operated by stationary donkey engines moving the logs from the falling area to log decks on the landings, for transport down to salt water booms by logging truck and from there by big tugboats hauling log booms hundreds of feet long to the mills in Vancouver.

To help you to understand my logging experiences I'd better take a few minutes to describe the equipment, the jobs, and how the system worked:

The crew consisted of several skilled groups of men who had to work closely together, with confidence in one another in this very high risk work.

The company's timber claim was marked out by blaze marks on boundary line trees. Their timber cruiser then walked the ground, laying out the access roads, the falling areas and their sequence, the spar trees, the log landings.

The falling crews, consisting of fallers and buckers, were next on the ground after the access road was built. The fallers undercut and backcut the huge

145

trees to fall them in precise patterns, generally all parallel on the ground and pointing down hill. They avoided dropping them across other fallen trees, and were careful to avoid breakage by missing stumps and rocks.

As soon as the fallers moved on, the buckers moved in on the fallen trees, limbing and bucking them into log lengths. Chainsaws were not yet in use here, and all the heavy cutting was done with axes and crosscut saws.

Both these jobs were extremely dangerous. Many fallers were killed or injured every year by falling limbs, unpredictable snags, (dead trees), kickbacks or barber chairs (trees splitting at the stump as they started to fall, and kicking back to catch a faller with thousands of pounds of force). Buckers were at risk from rolling logs, especially in such steep country. Falling trees often slid down the hill to pile up in draws and gullies or hang up on stumps or rocks, and were a problem to buck and to know what each heavy log was going to do when it was bucked off. Bucked logs, suddenly freed, could swing or roll and crush anyone below.

When an area was felled and bucked, the rigging crew moved in to string their cables for moving the logs to the landings. Heavy anchor stumps were chosen around the top perimeter of the logged area, and blocks (heavy steel pulleys) were chained to these stumps in turn as the work progressed. Light cable, carried up through the steep tangle of logs, limbs, broken trees, and other debris was used to haul up and string the heavy haulback cable.

While the rigging slingers were working, the high rigger chose the tallest, strongest tree in the central landing area. Donning spurs and a steel cored rope belt to which were fastened his axe, saw, and light line, he climbed to a height of eighty to one hundred and twenty feet, limbing as he went. Standing on his spurred boots and leaning back on his belt, with axe and saw he cut off the top forty or fifty feet of the tree above him.

When the top came off, his biggest risk, as he swayed back and forth in a fifteen foot arc, was that the tree wouldn't come off clean, because if it hung and split at the cut, his steel lined belt would crush him to a quick and painful death.

A heavy block was chained to the top of the spar

tree, and 1" cable strung through it. Several other spar
trees were selected and prepared around the logged area,
Each in turn became the outside spar for the high lead or
skyline strung between it and the base tree as they
cleaned up the set.

Several chokers were attached to the high lead line.
A choker is a sixteen foot, one inch cable with an
elongated ball fastened to its end and a sliding socket
that can be quickly connected and disconnected from the
ball. Chokermen moving among the tangle of downed logs
took a choker when it came to them on the cable, formed
a noose a few feet above the log's end, snapped the ball
into the socket, and got clear before the cable tightened
up.

The donkey engineer might be several hundred yards
away from the chokermen, but as he ran his cable out,
dropped it slack among the logs, tightened it up, lifted
the several logs and whizzed them down by drag line and
skyline to the landing, every movement he made was
precisely controlled by the whistle punk.

This man had the important job of co-ordinating the
movement of rigging slingers, chokermen, and engineer so
that the cables moved out and in as quickly and safely as
possible. He stood where he could see the log area and
the chokermen clearly, (usually on a high stump), and
communicated to the engineer by a whistle system that is
common to all high lead logging. The engineer spun his
cable drums in, out, slow, stop, tighten, fast, by
different, clearly audible signals.

Loggers begin as chokermen, and move up through the
hierarchy and pay scale to rigging slinger, and if
interested in falling, to bucker, bull bucker, faller.
Other jobs include engineer, high rigger (the highest
paid job), timber cruiser, whistle punk, log truck
driver, crummy driver, boom man, cook and helper.

I received quite an initiation to high lead logging.
I had never been in high mountains, so the crummy ride up
the steep, narrow, winding road with drop offs into the
dark of bottomless canyons had me hanging on with white
knuckles. When we got out on the ground at the landing I
thought to myself as I smelled the fresh morning scent of
torn up earth and the strong perfume of crushed branches
of fir and cedar that I was here as a chokerman but
didn't know the difference between a choker and a piece

of rope. As I looked away above me at the tangle of downed trees, logs, debris, I thought a logger would have to be a mountaineer to walk about in this country, let alone carry heavy equipment with him. I soon found out!

The rigging slinger called me over, pointed out a pile of logs several hundred feet above me in the tangle of debris, and said, "Take this block up to that log pile. I'll meet you there."

When I picked up that huge twelve inch steel block I figured it weighed about eighty pounds. After almost half an hour of hard climbing, when I finally reached the logs I was so winded I could hardly talk. The boss was sitting there on a log smoking a cigarette, and I knew that he knew that I was certainly not in shape for logging.

He didn't say anything except, "Move the block around to the far side of the pile." I started around the end, but got into such a tangle I took a shortcut up over the ends of the logs. At the top I laid the block down to get my balance, and heard a tinkle and a bump as the retaining pin holding the eye of the block closed fell out and disappeared ten feet below, among the logs. It was impossible to reach.

The boss didn't seem concerned when I told him where the pin was. He just told me casually to go back down to the landing and ask the engineer for another one.

The trip down was bad enough, but by the time I got half way back up again that one by eight inch pin seemed to weigh forty pounds. I was beginning to wonder what I was doing in that mountain goat country, but after ten days I scarcely noticed the steepness of the terrain.

With so many experienced loggers away to war, and logging companies, patient with inexperience, willing to hire any able bodied men they could find, logging was especially dangerous during the early war years. We lost two chokermen to cable accidents, one by a cable that dragged and crushed him against a stump, the other caught and flung in the air by a tightening cable. We lost two logging trucks to brake failures on the very steep road down to the saltchuck. Maximum grade was fourteen percent, and much of the road was that steep. The trucks carried hundred gallon water tanks behind their cabs, with hoses running to the brake drums to try to keep them cool. Those trucks came down smoking and steaming, in conditions that wouldn't be tolerated today.

When we were shut down by heavy snow in mid December, we came in to Vancouver with instructions to report to the company office next day for our paychecks. That evening a few of us heard a rumour in the beer parlour that Queen's Reach Timber Co. had gone belly up.

I couldn't sleep that night. Five of us who were at the office door when it opened the next morning got our full pay. The men who reported later in the day never got a dime.

* * * * * * * *

I decided gyppo logging was too risky, financially and physically, and my next job would be with one of the big companies. So, after Christmas I went with Elk River Timber, a big logging show on Vancouver Island. This was railway logging in a big valley, cutting big, first growth, virgin timber.

My job now was helper to a four man falling crew, bringing up tools, gas, doing odd jobs, and training to operate a chainsaw. These saws had only recently come into use, and in the monstrous trees we were working in, the saws too were very large, and very heavy by today's standards.

They were two man saws, with cutting bars from four to eight feet long. The saw had a heavy end with the powerful engine and two handlebars with the saw controls, and a light end with a single handle extending beyond the end of the bar. It weighed one thirty five to one hundred and fifty pounds. The head faller, holding the single bar, guided the cut while his helper, with a handlebar extending past each hip, ran the motor and provided most of the beef.

Within two or three weeks I graduated to faller, operating a saw. Our timber ran from eighteen inches to eight feet diameter at the stump, and there were lots of six footers. We didn't bother cutting anything smaller than twelve inches at the stump, but most of these trees were smashed down in the falling or skidding anyway. The tops were bucked off at twelve inches, and the rest was waste.

One tree in particular was a giant among trees, and

the other crews gathered to watch when we felled it. The biggest blade in camp was eight feet long, and we had to trim the four inch bark off the tree at the cut to span it. Two hundred feet tall, it shook the ground like an earthquake when it came down. As a favour to the buckers we bucked the first two forty foot logs off it with our eight foot saw. It scaled out at over fifty thousand board feet.

We were paid by piecework, each crew falling about fifty thousand and as high as eighty thousand board feet per day. Our pay rate varied with the quality of the timber, but our daily average of $12 per day after paying for grub and idle days was fairly constant. That was excellent money in those days. We didn't stop for rain or snow, but if the tops of those tall trees were moving in the wind, we didn't work.

During the five months I was there before my accident I helped pack out two other loggers the mile or more over logging slash to our crummy train for the eleven mile ride to camp and on to hospital. When my inevitable turn came, we'd had a normal start that morning in very thick timber. We felt like ants in a field of wheat, as one by one we felled those very tall, eighteen inch diameter trees, laying them in neat windrows. There was no wind, and except for the fact that the stumps were unusually close together, nothing to worry about.

My head faller and I had completed the undercut and were well through the back cut on our twentieth tree when it happened. He always watched the top of the tree, and made last moment adjustments to the cut to swing the tree's fall exactly where he wanted it. Normally we just stepped well back with our saw when the tree started to go, and watched it fall, but he had trained me to throw the saw and run if he yelled "RUN!"

For some inexplicable reason, as this tree started to move it twisted on its stump and brushed other branches a hundred feet above. When he yelled "RUN!" I found the saw jammed tight in the cut, my handlebars on each side jammed against the stump behind me, and no place to go.

As I scrambled out from between the handlebars by going backward over the stump behind, the tree kicked back, caught my leg and threw me twenty feet. I landed with a compound fracture of my right leg, and ended my logging career in that moment. I was fortunate I didn't also end my life.

A stretcher trip over logs and stumps and windfalls took me to the crummy train which took me down to camp, where the first aid man set and splinted my leg, and sent me on to the Campbell River hospital. Due to complications I had to have the leg rebroken after a month, and I spent four and a half months in hospital.

When I came out in July 1941 I was sent to a bone specialist in Vancouver, who eventually allowed me to return home on rehabilitation pension. So, with a gimpy leg, a good sized monthly compensation check, and nothing to do but get well, I once again met my grandfather,

When I left home originally my grandfather labelled me as a bum. When I returned two years later with my pockets full of cash and a three hundred dollars a month compensation check coming in, his attitude to me changed dramatically. He couldn't believe anyone could make the kind of money I was talking about, and probably as a test he said, "My harvest expenses are running pretty high this year. Can you loan me some money?"

"How much do you need?"

"Can you spare two hundred dollars?"

"Sure!" I hauled a roll out of my pocket, peeled off two hundred dollars, and put the rest back. From that moment Grandpa showed a lot of respect for me.

I received an army call up, reported to Regina, and was classified L4 category due to my broken leg. I never received another call.

I was still limping as harvest season approached.

Grandpa asked, "How would you like to run my threshing outfit?"

"How much?"

"Five dollars a day."

"Hell, I'm making more than that on compensation, doing nothing!"

"Okay then. Eight dollars a day."

For the rest of the time I knew him, Grandpa treated me as an equal, sharing his bottle of white lightning, repaying his loan without quibbling, conversing with me and talking over his plans, showing affection and regret when I left again for Vancouver.

* * * * * * * *

DEEP SEA FISHING

Loggers and fishermen always had good rapport. We had a high regard and respect for one another's jobs, as we met and socialized in huge numbers in city beer parlors and camp towns.

In the 1940's for instance, Comox, Courtenay, Campbell River, and Nanaimo were all fishing and logging towns. Nanaimo, at about a quarter of today's population, had twenty-six downtown and harbor-front beer parlors. Fishermen couldn't meet loggers in the woods, and loggers couldn't meet fishermen on the ocean, but we all made many friends on the weekends along the whole east coast of Vancouver Island.

When I left the farm again I returned to Campbell River, with the thought that I'd like to switch from logging to fishing. A taxi driver told me that Jimmy Pope had just fired his cook on the forty eight foot dragger "Welcome Pass", and though I didn't know how to boil water, that afternoon I joined his three man crew of cook, engineer, and skipper.

Jimmy had been on a big bender the night before, and he was hung over and very dry when I approached him for a job. His only question was, "Have you got a liquor permit?" (Wartime liquor was tightly rationed to one 40 ounce bottle per month, and you needed a government permit to buy that). Jimmy had obviously drunk his quota.

When I admitted that I didn't have a permit, he said, "Come with me to the Liquor Board and we'll get that fixed up right now." Within fifteen minutes I had my permit, a bottle of booze, and a job.

Jimmy fished a cod reef off Cape Mudge Lighthouse that winter that produced a twenty five thousand pound load of fish every two days. Since he transferred his fish to a packer, we had a day off every three days, and the boat made good money. Jimmy and I became very good friends, and I fished with him until the summer of 1945.

After the war Jimmy bought a war surplus seine boat, the "Willow Point", and put me in charge of the Welcome Pass on a twelve percent share of its earnings.

Fishing was good. I had learned a lot about the technique of dragger fishing, the productive fishing areas, and the ocean bottom. Knowing the bottom is critical in dragging, as your gear is sweeping only a few inches above it, and if there is a reef down there or even a good sized rock you're going to hang thousands of dollars worth of gear on it.

Ling cod, a prime market fish, favor reefs and rocks, moving with the tides. A successful fisherman has to know the contours of the bottom to avoid tearing his nets apart, and learn the movements of the schools of fish that ebb and flow with the tides in and out of the reefs, in order to fish near enough to the reefs to capitalize on the big schools in the area.

This was long before the days of satellite navigation and electronic sounding equipment which in later years allowed us to pinpoint our location anywhere at sea within a few yards, and to read the bottom of the sea with precision. Good fishermen in those days though learned to locate themselves very accurately in their fishing grounds by taking bearings and cross bearings on landmarks - mountain peaks, islands, unusual trees, anything visible and identifiable on shore. We used a sounding lead line to read the bottom for depths and obstructions like rocks and reefs. The lead weight on the end of the line had a concave bottom filled with tallow that not only told us our depths, but brought up a sample of the bottom, be it sand or mud or bare rock. All this was carefully charted, so we could return to a start point by cross bearings on two or more landmarks, and set our nets for an accurate bottom tow that we knew was hazard free.

While good fishermen knew their favorite areas like the back of their hand, it was not uncommon for others to hang on the horizon and watch, copy their navigation and follow a few miles behind to encroach on their grounds. One of the worst offenders was an old Scotsman we called Crazy Louie, who was known and admired throughout the fleet for his toughness and eccentricities but disliked for his habit of taking advantage of other fishermen's knowledge by sneaking into their grounds and following their sweeps to avoid the risks and trouble of charting his own.

Normal fisherman used a strong wooden fid for splicing rope. Louie used his finger as a fid. and could separate the strands of a tightly twisted, heavy line with a bare finger. A story that went the rounds of the

153

fleet told of Louie working on the stern of his boat with a big pipe wrench when he was knocked overboard and came up to the surface swimming with the pipe wrench clenched in his teeth.

In view of our reputation for success on our reef, Louie became a pest to us. We tried to guard our secrets carefully, especially our special tows, and resented Louie hanging on the horizon trying to get a bearing on our movements. We finally put an end to it and moved him out of our area by short cabling him, a rather dirty trick.

Seeing him in the distance one day lining up on our bearings we shortened our normal 125 fathoms of haul cables to fifty fathoms and headed across a series of eighty fathom rock piles. When Louie came through a couple of hours later with his gear on the bottom he tore everything to ribbons.

* * * * * * * *

What is a dragger? or a seiner? or a gillnetter? or a troller? or a long liner? These are the basic types of boats in the fishing fleet, fishing for salmon, herring, cod, sole, hake, skate, snapper, flounder, shrimp, halibut, even dogfish, in several varieties of each. I should take a minute to help you understand the fishing trade by explaining them:

Some species of fish live on the bottom, some wander mid ocean depths, some swim surface water, and most move through a variety of depths and a wide variety of location according to season, tide, temperature, and so on. Good fishermen study and chart all these factors as they experience them, anticipate their movements and use the right gear at the right place at the right time. Good fishermen come in with full holds regularly; poor fishermen, working the same water, struggle to make a living.

Most of the larger boats are equipped to handle more than one type of gear, and can change back and forth between seining and dragging and gillnetting, according to the season and the market. Some of the smaller boats might work as trollers or gillnetters in different seasons.

A dragger or trawl boat hauls a large trawl net on long cables a few hundred feet behind, and usually right down on the bottom, fishing for cod, sole, hake, and other bottom fish. The net is held open vertically by floats along its top and weighted line on tiny 8" wheels along its bottom, to make an opening twenty feet high. It is held open horizontally by paravanes or "trawl doors" on each side of the net. These hold the opening one hundred and fifty feet wide, with the trawl doors three hundred and fifty feet apart.

The trawl net then is a net bag about one hundred feet long, with an opening twenty feet high by one hundred and fifty feet wide, sweeping along inches above the ocean floor. It is hauled from a large drum on the stern, with cables out at an angle to the trawl doors and back down to the net.

When the skipper estimates he has a load back there, the drum winds in the cables, the doors are uncoupled, the net load of fish is picked up by a deck boom and winch, the bottom of the net is released, and several thousand pounds of fish spill onto the deck for sorting and stowing below in crushed ice. It might take a week to load the boat with from 25,000 pounds to 300,000 pounds, depending on its size.

Seiners fish closer to the surface, seeking schools of herring, cod, salmon, shrimp, in different seasons. When fish are located, the boat drops its 20 foot power skiff into the water to circle the school of fish with a close-meshed net. This circle might be several hundred feet in circumference. When the circle is closed around the fish, a cable strung through the bottom of the net closes it into a purse, from which there is no escape. The net is then closed more, to concentrate the catch beside the mother ship, which then brails or pumps the fish into the hold.

Gillnetters lay a long vertical net into the water, held on the surface by floats and held down in a wall formation by lead weights. It is usually used where fish are migrating and trying to reach or pass up a river. The mesh is sized to the type of fish, allowing them to get only their heads through the net. When they try to back out, the mesh holds them behind their gills. The net, with a few or with hundreds of fish, is brought in over a stern roller, and the fish are individually detached and tossed into the hold.

In salmon season, hundreds of gillnetters fill the open waters of Juan de Fuca Strait and salmon rivers such as the Fraser, boats and nets drifting with the current, moving occasionally, jockeying fiercely for position.

Long liners fish the deep waters of the northern ocean, the Gulf of Alaska and Queen Charlotte area. A heavy line, hundreds of feet long, is baited with short leaders every few feet, and laid on the ocean bottom. Each boat will put out several miles of lines, each marked by buoys. When they are picked up the next day, there may be several dozen 50 to 100 pound halibut on each line - or a good catch of cod.

Long liners' biggest risk, other than the fierce weather they encounter in northern waters, is sea lions. These mammals love to come upon a long line of captive fish. They eat only the liver, so one sea lion can destroy a whole catch by taking one bite out of the belly of each fish.

Trollers are usually small boats with a one or two man crew. They troll several baited hooks over each side of the boat, held outboard on long spars with steel line and pulley. The steel line on each side has a leader line every few feet, all held down to proper depth by a heavy lead ball on the main line. Trollers catch one or two fish at a time. Each time the bell rings, signalling a fish on the line, it is reeled in by a small winch, catch removed, rebaited, and returned. Catches are counted in dozens, rarely in hundreds.

These then are the main types of fishing off the West Coast. My fishing was successful from the beginning. I regularly brought in a full load of fish every week, (25,000 pounds for the Welcome Pass), and often had a few thousand extra pounds of deck load.

* * * * * * * *

156

I married during that time, and Winona and I spent all of our savings in building our home in Burnaby. I was still working on Jimmy's shallow draft, 48 foot Welcome Pass, but in 1947 I began to plan on owning my own boat.

I found a good one. The Western Maid was a fifty foot, wide beamed, deep hulled boat, at forty-eight thousand pounds almost double the capacity of the Welcome Pass. Its $17,000 price though was about $15,000 beyond my cash assets. My fishing record and credit rating were both good, so my bank agreed to match as a loan whatever cash I raised, and between us we turned up $15,000. I got the rest of it from a fisherman friend, on a handshake. I felt as though I were the skipper of the Queen Mary as I took my fully equipped dragger out through Vancouver harbor, under the Lions' Gate Bridge, and headed for the fishing banks to fish for myself.

My experience as skipper of the Welcome Pass stood me in good stead, as I continued to load my boat every week. I had learned that fish behave in a predictable pattern, according to tide, moon, and season, and kept a careful log of all conditions wherever I found fish. After a few years of this I paid little attention to other boats, but could often turn up with a quick, full load of fish that were right where I expected them to be.

Fishermen watched each other closely, and moved in quickly when they saw brisk action in the distance. There was little sharing of big haul information, although a few of us did communicate on our radio phones by code.

I recall talking to a friend a hundred miles away one evening for instance. We had just put the gear out when he told me by code that he was in heavy fishing and would be loaded by morning. The boys were puzzled when I ordered the gear hauled in a hurry, and we took off at full speed to travel for several hours.

When we arrived, there were eight or ten boats dragging the area. I left my gear aboard as I made two or three passes among them, studying my sounder. When we let our gear out we picked up forty thousand pounds on the first tow, and filled our boat in the midst of ten boats who had been fishing there for several days. It was all a case of fishing the right depth. Ten boats could be trawling in a line abreast, and one boat might pick up as many fish as all the others put together, because his nets were at the depth where the fish were.

There were many American boats among us. In fact the American boats frequently outnumbered the Canadians. They didn't fish inside the three mile limit, but we seldom fished that close to shore either. Many of them were high line (skilled) fishermen, and I had several friends among them. One of them made me mad one day though, but he inadvertently did me a good turn.

We were fishing a bank a few miles off Ucluelet, with about a dozen trawlers crowded into eight square miles. The American boat was running parallel on my port side, and wanted to get over to starboard. When he couldn't pull ahead to pass, he dropped back to pass behind. I had big gear out, with a three hundred foot spread, much wider than he anticipated, and he crossed too soon and caught my net with his trawl door.

As soon as I felt the catch I stopped my engine, called him to pull in his gear, and brought mine in. I had both his fifteen hundred pound doors in my net, with lines broken and my net torn to shreds. We cut him loose, brought in our gear and headed for Ucluelet.

He called on the radio and offered to come in to the harbor and put his crew on my boat to repair the net, but I told him we were rigging our spare net, and weren't going to repair the torn one.

I decided to try a shelf a few miles further north, even though my log indicated we were probably a few days early. There was nobody on it, and as we passed over it my sounder showed a "beehive" of fish. We quickly dropped the gear, and scooped up forty thousand pounds on the first pass. We loaded our boat, and passed the others, still fishing, on our way to town.

It took about two days to unload a full load of fish, load fuel, ice and provisions, and head back out, and two days was our usual stay when fishing was good.

I remember fishing in a group off Ucluelet one time and topping off my load in stormy weather. I set out for Vancouver while the others headed for shelter. On a hunch I could get another quick load off Barkley Sound, I headed back out in continuing rough seas. When we reached our bank, every time we let out the gear we brought it in loaded. It took only one day to load the boat and another to travel back to the fish plant. They couldn't believe we could load up so fast, and asked if we had a spot off the mouth of the Fraser.

When we got back off Ucluelet two days later, the rest of the fleet thought we were returning from the first trip. The word eventually got out that we'd unloaded two loads while they were in harbor, and the general remark was "That lucky Kitzul! He's still got a big horseshoe hanging around his neck!"

I had my third boat by this time. I turned the Western Maid over to a member of my crew, a good fisherman, on a share basis with the option to buy it from his share income, and put in an order to the Vancouver Shipyard to build my sixty foot, wood construction, ninety thousand pound capacity Charlene K, named after my little daughter. This was in 1954.

Fishing continued to go well for me, so well that in just two years the ninety thousand pound capacity of the new Charlene K was limiting our catch. We brought her in to drydock in 1956, had her cut in half, and added twelve feet to her length.

This was a major contract, and cost almost as much as to build her in the first place. Every pipe, cable and wire had to be spliced. Almost every beam was rebuilt, every plank along the new lines was removed and replaced, and a lot of new tanks, storage capacity, and bigger gear had to be added. She was now seventy two feet long, with a capacity of one hundred and twenty thousand pounds.

The larger Charlene K served us well for ten years. In 1966 I put in a shipyard order for a new steel ship, eighty feet long, of two hundred thousand pounds capacity. When the new ship was delivered I retained the name, and leased the old one to a Scottish crew member. He renamed it the Bon Accord, ran it for me on shares for two years, then bought it.

* * * * * * * *

THE EGG WAR

One of the boats we worked closely with was the Renown, and we many times radioed one another to share information on fish concentrations.

Fishing crews, spending long days of isolation in a mix of idle boredom and frantic activity, welcomed the occasional brief passing visit with crews of other boats that passed by within shouting distance.

In the days before I exchanged the Western Maid for the Charlene K, the crews of the Western Maid and the Renown knew each other well. Their conversations, jokes and challenges yelled across the water, over the noise of engines and surf, gave shipboard comedians and practical jokers an opportunity to do their stuff, with a big laugh from one crew at the expense of the other.

This took a different turn one day. As the two boats, with both crews lining the rails, were cruising slowly past one another, we were suddenly ducking and dodging about a dozen raw eggs hurled across the water from the Renown and splattering us, our decks and gear and wheelhouse windows as the boats drew apart to gales of laughter from the Renown.

They sneaked up and caught us again a few days later when we were busy hauling gear and too busy to fight back. While we remained friends and worked together and were able to laugh about it when we were ashore, the Western Maid and the Renown fought the Egg War for a good part of that season. Egg maneuvering became as important as net management when the two boats were near one another. Our provisioning always allowed for a few dozen extra eggs, and tactics became important to all of us.

Sitting around on deck one afternoon while waiting to haul gear, our crew were talking egg tactics when one of them said,

"If only we could figure some way to keep out of their range and still blast them with eggs. How about rigging a big catapult?"

"No good. An egg wouldn't stand the strain of being hauled back against the tension of the launch apparatus, and you'd end up with egg on your face."

At this point the engineer said,

"How about an air gun?"

"What do you mean? Can you rig one?"

"I think so. We'll take a piece of two inch plastic pipe, close one end, rig an air line to it from the compressed air tank, hook a quick release valve into it, and blast eggs at them with compressed air."

"Awe, you'd have eggs dripping out the end of the barrel!"

"I don't think so. You know how impossible it is to break an egg with pressure on an end. You remember that old trick of locking your fingers together, putting an egg between your palms, end on, and squeezing as hard as you could - you couldn't break it? Well, I think we can blast eggs out of a pipe with air without breaking them."

"Well, it's sure worth a try. Go for it!"

The engineer built an air valve into a three foot length of two inch pipe, attached an air line from our 150 pound pressure air tank in the engine room, slid an egg down the pipe to the valve, and snapped the valve open.

Well, that egg sailed out of the pipe in a long arc and splashed into the sea 300 feet away! There was a cheer from the crew and a round of high fives as other crewmen tried the gun and practiced for accuracy. They could hardly wait for the next meeting with the Renown!

We saw her approaching from a distance, and the boys hurried to hook up the air line and lay it out from the engine room to the gun lying by the rail. They had a couple of dozen eggs lying at their feet as they innocently lined the rail watching the distance close.

The crew of the Renown were armed with eggs, but long before we got into their range there was a "phttt" from our deck and an egg splattered their wheelhouse. Another and another and another sailed past and into the startled crew who ducked and fled through their wheelhouse door and watched in amazement through the yolks and whites of several more eggs splashing against their windows as their skipper turned and fled.

The Renown gave us a wide berth for the next few weeks, never did figure out how we blasted them, and eventually sued for peace.

So ended the Egg War, with a lot of laughter between the crews whenever they met ashore.

* * * * * * * *

TERROR AT SEA

Early in my fishing career I learned that the sea demands respect from those who would sail upon her and fill their boats with her bounty, and that her punishment is severe on those who disregard her warnings.

When I was skipper on Jimmy Pope's Welcome Pass, I first experienced the fury of a raging sea, and I needed patience, skill, and luck to win our long battle. The Welcome Pass was a shallow draft boat, not built to venture into the open ocean.

Fishing off Comox in the Strait of Georgia, as I turned for Vancouver with my boatload of fish, the weather report forecast 30 MPH winds. We were well on our way home, when off Ballenas Island a huge black cloud filled the horizon, and the boat began to rise on big swells running under a choppy sea. If I'd known then what I know now, I'd have turned back.

We were suddenly hit with a full gale with seas rising fifteen to twenty feet. As the gale increased in the dark of that terrifying night we could see nothing but black water and white spume, with raging seas sweeping the length of the deck and crashing over the wheelhouse in howling wind. As I fought the wheel I was frequently up to my knees in sloshing water.

The loaded boat was so low in the water it would have been suicide to turn around. We were in the middle of the gulf, with no shelter, and just hanging on, throttle eased half speed forward, back easy, half forward, back easy, as the boat continued to meet high cresting seas sweeping over us in the roaring blackness.

The decks, not built to be a roof, leaked like a sieve. Both my crewmen were seasick, but they worked feverishly all night manning the hand pumps to maintain all the flotation we could manage. Realistically, we could have gone under any minute, but the gallant little boat staggered out from under every punishing wave.

It took twenty-one hours to make the four hour trip, and as we limped in to dock in the cold, dirty grey of a stormy day, our radio announced that the gale had crested at 85 miles an hour, and that several boats were still unaccounted for.

Even though that taught me a never forgotten lesson, the sea caught and punished me other times. I was better equipped for the battle though, with better boats.

I was north of Cape Scott with the wooden Charlene K one calm winter day, heading for Hecate Strait. While I normally would have taken the inside passage for that long trip, the sea was dead calm with a good weather forecast so I decided to take the short route across the open sea.

We were out of sight of land when we were hit by a strong, unannounced, bitter wind, outflowing from the land. When it increased to sixty miles an hour, mountainous seas built up, and as we turned to run for the shelter of Hakai Pass and Fitz Hugh Sound they were right in our face.

Our progress was ten feet forward, six feet back in choppy fifteen footers whose crests and spume heavily iced our decks and our gear. During the twenty two frigid hours it took to go thirty miles we chopped tons of ice to lighten our deck load. As we finally approached our narrow, dangerous sheltering passages in the dark, our radar sweep was iced up and immobilized, so we had to chop it free to restore our night vision.

* * * * * * * *

We sheltered from a storm one night in the harbor at Ucluelet. It wasn't a serious storm. The wind was blowing off shore, so we set only one anchor fairly near the lee shore, and went to bed.

I awakened in the middle of the night to a heavy thumping at the stern, and as I leaped out of bed and hurried on deck I was startled to have to push the leafy branches of a tree out of my way!

The wind had shifted 180 degrees and swung us stern first toward the rocky shore, then blew hard enough that we had dragged our anchor, and were on the rocks. As crewmen struggled sleepily on deck, I shouted orders to get the life raft inflated and overboard. (This is a large ten man seaworthy raft, instantly self inflating, with emergency supplies and a covered top).

When I hurried forward I was amazed to see that we were between two huge slick rocks towering above each side of the bow, with only a few feet of leeway. We had apparently backed into that narrow passage like you would back a car into a parking stall.

I put out a MAYDAY call on the wireless, but got no answer from the Canadian Coast Guard. However, after a few minutes the American Coast Guard came on the air from Port Angeles. They asked my condition and position, and said they would stand by and send a boat if needed. (But they were several hours away.)

With our boat still thumping heavily on the rocks, I knew that unless we could get free quickly, we would be holed. I decided to try to power ourselves off, as even if I tore off the propeller we would be no worse off than sitting there doing nothing. When I started the engine and eased it into forward gear there seemed to be no propeller contact with the rocks, but no response either. I gave it more power, but we still didn't move.

The boat was rising a couple of feet with each wave, and thumping down again, so I timed the next wave, and as the stern rose I jammed on full power. We broke free, brushed past the towering rocks on each side, and wiped our raft, which the boys had tied overboard, right off the boat!

The boat was steering strangely, so I opened the well above the rudder to check it, and found the huge bolt that secures the shoe protecting the rudder was driven about four inches up through its supporting beam. Since the propeller clears the rudder by only six inches, I wondered how close it was coming to the rudder as we moved. I figured we had better get tied up, so headed for the dock a mile away, reporting my move to the American Coast Guard as I did so.

We had to buy our life raft from a couple of Indians the next day. The price was two cases of beer.

* * * * * * * *

The storm that probably came closest to sending us to the bottom hit us in the Strait of Juan de Fuca. We were fishing off the west coast of the Island, and as we neared a full load, I made one more set to top it off. However the last tow came in bulging, and we not only filled the holds, we piled a 20,000 pound load of fish on the deck.

A strong westerly blew up as we headed into the strait, and as the wind increased, huge rollers swept us along. I knew we'd be in trouble if those rollers encountered a strong outflowing tide, and when I checked my tide book, the news couldn't have been worse. When tides meet rollers head on, the pattern of the waves breaks down, they crest in all directions in a wild jumble of water, and you never know where the next one is coming from.

We were between Port Renfrew and Jordan River, with only one possible harbor on that long stretch of coast. However, the shoreline there lay very low in the water, with a reef in the harbor entrance that would be impossible to see in these conditions, so I decided the lesser risk would be to pass it by and try to get into safer shelter further on.

As the seas got higher and wilder I posted a man at the door at the back of my wheelhouse to warn me of any combers coming from behind that might break over the deck, telling him to be sure to slam and bar the door in time. Well, it wasn't long before he yelled and slammed the door, as a huge wave broke over the stern and swept the deck clean of fish and everything else that was moveable.

It was only a few minutes before he screamed. "Here comes a monster!" and we were literally submerged! The stern went down as the water roared over the wheelhouse and drove the whole boat under the sea at a 20 degree angle. I jammed the throttle wide open and swung the wheel for a 180 degree turn, and as the boat responded sluggishly to the rudder and the powerful thrust of the propeller, she slowly, slowly fought her way back up out of the sea. It was only the propeller that brought us back to the surface, and we were seconds from sliding stern first to oblivion.

Now headed back into the gale, I decided to risk the reef to get into shelter. We made safe harbor, and counted our future days as a gift from the sea.

* * * * * * * *

Herring fishing was the most dangerous type of fishing, and took many boats and many lives. There were numerous reasons for this:

Herring are small, slippery fish that when confined in the hold of a boat, ebb and flow like a heavy oil. In the early days of unpartitioned holds, a half load of herring, reacting to the roll of the boat, often turned a boat over, as just when it needed to recover from a roll, the tons of herring sloshed to the low side of the hold and increased it. The only safe load of herring was

165

one so full that the fish could not flow. That problem was partially solved by dividing holds into many partitioned sectors, and spreading the load among them.

Herring boats going out to the grounds with empty holds and heavy deck gear of seine nets and winches and cables and spars and power skiff and life raft were top heavy, and very vulnerable to storms. Even when the nets were stowed in the hold, they were tipsy. Several of them rolled over in moderate seas, and were lost. When holds were partitioned and pumping systems improved, most boats went out with water ballast, which stabilized them.

The biggest risk in herring fishing was the catch itself. A seine net could surround and bag two hundred tons of fish, suspended in the water by a spar holding the net. As long as the fish could swim, the boat was fairly safe, even with a big load overboard, but two things could change that dramatically:

If the fish panicked and all those tons of them sounded at the same time, they put a two hundred ton force against the bottom of the net, and that quickly turned the boat that was holding them on an extended boom upside down in the water, and took it to the bottom. On the other hand, if the seine were tightened up and the fish concentrated for brailing, they quickly died and sank, and two hundred tons of dead fish in the net could also roll the boat over.

The huge quantities of herring in a net were a boon to some boats, and a tragedy to others. Fish had to be taken from the net and loaded quickly, yet suspending the seine on your spar when you already had your holds half full of oily fish could be hazardous. Brailing them meant closing the net pretty tight and raising it to "dry" the fish as you worked, since the brail could reach only a few feet into a net that might be forty feet deep in fish.

Modern boats developed a pumping system. An eight inch pipe inserted into the mass of herring pumped them aboard at a high rate, and reached deep into the water to avoid lifting the net.

Herring fishermen were prepared to come quickly to the aid of others who had a full seine, and their help was usually welcomed. They helped support the net, and took on the surplus load, if any, at a percentage of its value. Occasionally a lucky fisherman preferred to wait for a particular friend, and his luck sometimes turned bad if he waited too long.

This happened on the grounds one day when a boat seined in a huge load. Nearby boats offered to help, but he turned them down, saying he had a friend on the way. Well, his friend didn't arrive before the whole bag of over a hundred ton of herring worth over a hundred thousand dollars went through the bottom of his net, and he didn't land a fish.

I, too, had a very close call. A friend gave me an urgent call for help one day, saying he had a big bag alongside, estimated at four hundred tons. We tied to his net, and both boats started pumping fish. We had about seventy-five tons on the Charlene K when she started to list as the huge mass of herring milling in the net suddenly sounded.

I had warned my deckhands to have their knives sharp, and to cut the lines without hesitation if I ordered it. Well, when those fish sounded, our rail started to go under before any of us could move, and as I yelled "CUT!" and we all rushed to cut lines, we were waist deep before the bag let go and headed for the bottom. Our top rigging was just touching the other boat's top rigging when they slowly parted as the boats righted. Had they tangled or either of us been slow in cutting free, we'd have gone to the bottom.

The power skiff, twenty feet long with a nine foot beam, was still tied to the net. As it was drawn on its beam end by the plunging net, the deckhand in it jumped overboard and was eventually picked up. However the skiff went down with the net, and we figured it was gone, when with a swoosh it almost leaped out of the water! Its flotation tank buoyancy was strong enough a hundred feet down to break its line and free it for a fast trip to the surface.

We both got fair sets, but lost about three hundred tons of herring at $600 a ton. However we were thankful to save both crews and both boats, and a partial load.

* * * * * * * *

THE RUSSIAN EXPERIENCE

In the mid '60's a huge fleet of foreign vessels began encroaching on our fishing grounds. They were predominately Russian, with a few Polish and Japanese ships. At that time the twelve mile limit was in effect, but our rich fishing banks extended far beyond that.

As fishermen, we knew from the first time we saw them on the horizon that we were in for trouble. We had heard of their operations on the Grand Banks off Newfoundland, but this was to be our first experience with them on our coast.

Our biggest draggers were less than one hundred feet long, with a crew of six to eight. Theirs were one hundred and fifty to three hundred feet long, with crews of one hundred or more men and women aboard. They were supported by huge factory ships processing their catches right on the grounds, and thirty thousand ton packers hauling full loads of frozen fish to Russia.

They claimed at first that they were concentrating on rock fish and hake, but, fishing among them, we could see they were taking our salmon, our halibut, our cod, our herring, everything we fished for was being swept up in vast quantities.

They were using the same type of dragger gear as ours, but theirs were immensely larger. The eighty foot Charlene K had a hundred and fifty foot net, theirs would be three to five times as large. They swarmed over the whole West Coast, from the Gulf of Alaska all the way down past Washington and Oregon to California.

They became so aggressive they even fished inside our twelve mile limit, paid little attention to boundaries and no attention to our fisheries regulations, laws and limits. They moved in on our restricted herring fishery, sweeping vast tonnages that were off limits to our own boats in our own waters. They pushed us around on our own grounds, plowed right through our fleet and stripped gear off our boats, and we had to get out of their way to avoid it.

One boat had its gear picked up by a Russian dragger, and the Russian didn't stop hauling his gear until he almost had the Canadian boat on his deck. Formerly we anchored on the grounds and went to sleep at night, but the Russians fished all night, so we had to keep a man on watch and be prepared to move in a hurry any time. I sometimes counted as many as forty of their boats within my horizon, and we felt as though our whole industry was being gobbled up.

The international cold war was very cold at that time, but it became icy on the West Coast, then suddenly heated up. We had appealed to our Fisheries Department and directly to Ottawa to do something about it, but our appeals were bogged in bureaucracy until we took the matter into our own hands. Some of our boats started carrying high powered rifles, and when a few shots were fired across the bows of encroaching Russians, that made the international news. Within days we got action from both Ottawa and Moscow.

A fisheries conference was arranged, to be held in Ottawa. Our Fisheries Department asked for a representation from the fishermen to attend the conference as advisors to their delegates and I was chosen to represent the draggers.

We were flown to Ottawa, and spent five weeks in intense bargaining before a tentative agreement was hammered out. The Russians knew our coast as well as we did, and better than most of our government representatives, so we fishermen had to keep our delegates aware of the areas of prime fishing grounds, and be alert to subtle changes between talks and charts. We took no part in the bargaining, but sat in on all meetings, and took an active part in backroom strategy and discussions.

An agreement was finally hammered out and lines drawn, restricting their areas dramatically. We were quite satisfied with the charts we studied in our rooms that night, but when they were exchanged and passed around the next morning I noticed there was a major change in the red line that didn't correspond with the line agreed to the night before.

I passed a note to Dr.Needler, our chief negotiator, who called a recess and met us in a private room. We proved that the line had been moved four miles toward our coast, to take in a major fishing bank, but when the meeting resumed and Dr. Needler pointed it out, the Russians denied there had been any change.

Our Minister stated that unless the line were restored to its original position he would not sign the agreement, and would call off the conference. An icy staring match between their chief and me followed, but he finally called a recess and came back to sign our version of the chart.

The October meeting in Ottawa ended with arrangements for a follow-up meeting in Moscow in January to sign the Fisheries Treaty between Russia and Canada. I was again appointed as an advisor to our delegates, and flew with them to Moscow for three weeks of meetings.

The Russians were generous hosts. All formal meetings were interspersed with dinner meetings, cocktail parties, sight-seeing trips, embassy parties, banquets, where service and food and drink were lavish. A waiter stood at my elbow constantly, with his vodka bottle at the ready to refill my glass after each of the innumerable Russian toasts. When we tried to slow our drinking with only a sip in acknowledging a toast, our host countered that with a mandate that we must turn our glass upside down and rub it on our head after every toast. We left each dinner very tipsy.

After days of meetings and dinners and sightseeing in Moscow we boarded a luxury car on a high speed overnight train trip to Riga in Latvia, where we were to inspect the Russian Atlantic fishing fleet in harbor. The fleet in Riga consisted of a towering forty-five thousand ton factory ship supported by a dozen huge trawlers. I can imagine the tonnage they swept up off the Grand Banks every week.

Our access to the factory ship was via a rather rickety stairway against the side of the ship, something like climbing a seven storey stepladder against the side of a swaying apartment building. The ship though was huge and impressive, with accommodation for three hundred crewmen, a twenty bed hospital, and a few locked doors that were off limits. A banquet room for sixty accommodated our party.

Our cocktail party had at least the usual number of toasts. I had worried about my climb up that tall stairway over the water when I was sober, but have no remembrance of my trip back down. Perhaps I floated.

The Russia Canada Fisheries Agreement signed in Moscow in 1967 is still in force today. One of the terms was that after the first year they had to stay two hundred miles off our coast, and that took them right off our fishing grounds.

Sorting a bag of fish on the Charlene K.

Running out the trawl net. Note the trawl door (lower
right), one of two that will spread the net wide.

SHIPS, CHARTERS AND FILMS

During my fishing years my equipment, boats, expertise and catches all grew steadily, and with that, my income and recognition among my peers.

I have already told of the move from skipper on Jimmy Pope's Welcome Pass to my own Western Maid, to the sixty foot Charlene K, rebuilt to seventy two feet, then to the steel eighty foot Charlene K., rated at two hundred thousand pounds capacity. That, too, became too small, so in just four years we again went to the shipyards for more tonnage, adding sixteen feet and one hundred thousand pounds capacity to the Charlene K for a new capacity of three hundred thousand pounds. My boats grew then in twenty nine years from twenty five thousand pound capacity to three hundred thousand, for more than a tenfold growth in size and fish landings. I now had one of the biggest, best equipped boats in the fleet.

During those years my son Billy grew up. He started making summer holiday trips with me when he was twelve, when his main interest was trolling a salmon lure over the side. As the years passed he began to take an active interest in the commercial aspects of our trips. By the time he graduated from university he also graduated from part time crew member to full time employment on the boat. He eventually qualified as skipper, and took over the boat during my absences on business and hunting trips and holidays.

In the meantime my daughter Charlene married, and my son-in-law went through the same apprenticeship, as crewman, part time skipper, and qualified skipper. Bill and Randy bought the Charlene K on shares when I retired, and operate it in partnership, taking turns working at sea and holidaying ashore.

(But that is still in the future in my story.)

* * * * * * * *

In 1968, when my eighty foot boat was new, the Department of Fisheries called for bids to charter a ship to test herring stock on the whole B.C. coast. They were looking for a large vessel as they would be fishing the outside waters. I put in a bid, but made it a high one to cover the loss of a whole fishing season. Our bid of $260,000, though one of the highest submitted, was awarded the charter.

Our crew was cut to three deckhands and skipper plus government people, including biologists from the Nanaimo Biological Station. We had an easy summer, just cruising around, making about three sets a day and keeping only a few dozen fish from each set for biological examination. Every trip was seventeen days, and we rotated our crew so none of them were out of work. Though as skipper I was in charge of the boat, Fisheries directed our movements through their grid of the whole coast. We moved from one grid to the next, from the west coast of the Island up the inland waters and Queen Charlotte Sound to Hecate Strait and on past Prince Rupert, and back down the next set of grids.

We were using experimental mid-water gear, similar to our bottom trawls except we could control and monitor the depth we were trawling. There were electronic sensors on it reading the depth and registering on our monitors the catch going into the net. We fished as far as fifteen hundred fathoms depth off shore, though we never trawled below 350 fathoms, and saw few fish at that depth. The only place we found commercial quantities of fish was on the continental shelf, down to eighty fathoms. However the biologists were happy to examine and record every tow, whether it was a few rockfish or a full bag of cod.

As a result of our charter we not only had an easy, profitable season, we were the first to use the mid water trawl, which eventually became a mainstay in the trawling fleet. Following my Fisheries charter I adapted my gear to mid water as well as bottom trawling, and since I had the electronic gear to find fish at any depth and the trawl gear to fish any depth, I found great success with it.

* * * * * * * *

We were approached one day by a producer from the National Film Board, with a request to put a filming crew aboard the Charlene K to film the fishing sector of a National TV production to be titled "THIS LAND OF OURS". Logging and mining sectors of the film had been completed. There would be a five man film crew.

When I asked "What's in it for us?" he replied "Nothing". I felt they would crowd our accommodations and be a handicap to a whole fishing trip, so I told him we weren't interested.

He came back a week later and pleaded with me to take them on, saying our boat was ideal for the job. I was still opposed, but my crew, hearing they would be on national television, were all for it, so I reluctantly gave my consent.

The week was perfect for them. As we moved under Lions Gate Bridge we headed into the most beautiful sunset I've ever seen, making a spectacular introduction to their film.

When we reached the grounds off the west coast of the Island we tried a few sets, but fishing was poor, so we moved up past Cape Scott into Queen Charlotte Sound. We made several good sets in the next couple of days, while the film crew filmed all our activities from the time we got out of bed until we went back to bed. They were a nice bunch, very friendly and easy to get along with, and I was glad to have them aboard.

The weather had been dead calm and the sea like a mill pond until one night the wind came up, a south east gale at about forty knots. The sea got rough, and though we were taking some seas over the rails, it was not too rough to fish.

We made our first set at daylight. An hour or two later, as we hauled in and dumped a good load I looked around for the film crew, and couldn't see a soul. When we got the gear overboard again and the load sorted and stowed I went down to see what was the matter with my film crew, and found all of them in bed, seasick!

I said, "Hey, I don't want a film that shows fishing to be just a ride in the harbor on flat calm water. There's finally some weather action out there and I want you out on deck to get it on film!"

So the camera man got up, and a couple of his crewmen got up, green faced and ill. They came out and filmed

174

us bringing in the next tow, a real good haul of fish with lots of action as the boat rose and fell in big rollers breaking over the deck, then they hurried right back to bed.

They were all back in action next day, and during our successful, ten day trip they shot ten thousand feet of film. This was edited down to two thousand feet of excellent footage. It became part of their TV production "THIS LAND OF OURS", shown several times on CBC. It is now in the National Archives in Ottawa.

* * * * * * * *

THE CABLE

One memory I'll never lose had international implications:

Until the space age and satellites made inter-national communication easy, the world was laced with direct wire lines that spanned continents and dipped under the oceans in huge, heavy cables. One of these ran for thousands of miles under the Pacific from Bamfield, B.C. to Melbourne, Australia, linking our continents. It skirted our trawl fishing grounds, but it was marked on our charts. Since we could pinpoint our position within 100 yards, we stayed clear of it. There was, however, an uncharted old miles-long length of derelict cable in the area that was cursed by every fisherman who hung up and abandoned gear or anchors on it. We could never be sure where it was, as it seemed to move about.

One evening as we were hauling in our last set of the day, we hung up. I was puzzled, as I knew there were no rocks in the area, and we were over half a mile from the Australian cable. When I ordered the boys to power the winches again, the boat was hauled back toward the trawl, so I knew we were really hung solid.

I thought I might have a wrong reading on my Loran set, so I phoned a friend who was half a mile away. I told him I might need help, and would like confirmation on my reading. He finished hauling his set, came along-side, and confirmed my location to within a few yards.

We hauled back until the straining cables were almost straight down. Nothing moved. There was a heavy swell running, and with the winches at full strain we could hold the load as the boat rose on a swell, then gain a few feet as it fell in the trough. Well, that went on for half an hour, with the cables tight as a fiddle string and the winches turning and stopping with each swell.

Finally one of the paravane doors came to the surface with a heavy, black, four inch cable draped securely over it and heading off forward and aft in a shallow angle. I could see half a dozen anchors with trailing cables caught on the fifty feet of cable fading away into the depths.

My friend leaned over his rail and verified again that we were more than half a mile from the Australian cable. He confirmed my suspicion that we were hooked into a long length of the old, abandoned cable that the fishermen had been cursing for years. Mine was the first boat with power enough to bring it to the surface.

By the time we got the door alongside, the load was so heavy our stern was only inches from the water, and something had to give, soon. I told a crewman to get the fire axe and chop the cable off where it hung over the door. His swings of the axe were ineffective as he thudded here and there into the heavy lead sheath, so I took the axe from him and started swinging.

My third swing into an earlier cut produced a sudden hissing column of fire and smoke! As sparks flew and my crew fled, I had the awful realization I'd cut the live cable!

Well, we were still almost awash with the strain, and the damage was done, so I continued to chop. New sparks flew with every blow, until it dropped in half and sank into the sea as our boat slowly righted itself.

When I called home on the radiophone the next morning, Winona said, "Did you hear about the Australian cable?"

"No, what about it?" (I wasn't going to admit over the air that I knew a great deal about it.)

"Well, I was listening to the nine o'clock news last night when they interrupted it with a news flash that the cable shut down at ten minutes past nine, cutting all communication between Australia and Canada."

"Gee, that's serious. I wonder what happened?"

A day later the Vancouver Sun reported that a cable

ship was coming from Midway, three thousand miles away, on the other side of the Pacific. When this big ship eventually arrived in Vancouver harbor it had a huge thirty foot cable drum on its stern and hundreds of feet of heavy cable on deck.

When they reached the fishing grounds their instruments quickly located both ends of the cable, which they brought up and spliced after a couple of weeks work.

I was very concerned for a few days, but no attempt was made to discover who had cut the cable, and this is the first time my part in it has been revealed outside a few close friends. However, the cable company, aware of the mass of fishing gear on the cable, put out a notice to all fishermen asking our opinion as to where they could safely lay it. (Obviously it had already been dragged over half a mile across the sea-bed, and the abandoned cable that fishermen had been cursing for years really didn't exist, but was in reality this cable they had been dragging around.)

A gully, 80 or 90 fathoms deep crossed our grounds about eight miles from the cable location. We never fished that area, so on our recommendation they somehow moved the cable into it, and we've never seen it since. It has been dead for years of course, replaced by satellites.

Another good consequence of the cable episode was that the cable company, B.C. Telephone, and others with cables and pipes under the sea all asked that if we hung up on their under-sea equipment that we cut our gear free, put in a claim, and they would reimburse us for the loss. Many claims have been made and collected, with both sides happy.

* * * * * * * *

RIPPLE ROCK

The awesome power of the Pacific's tides funnels constantly back and forth through the inside passage linking Queen Charlotte Strait and the Gulf of Georgia, between Vancouver Island and the Mainland. Tides that have freedom to rise and fall and go their way present little problem to shipping, but when that immense flow of water is restricted to narrow channels it builds up and forces its way through anyway, creating powerful currents and huge tide rips that must be reckoned with.

Johnstone Strait is a long, very narrow passage, with tides running at twelve to fifteen knots, (about eighteen miles an hour), eddying around islands with cross currents and surges and boils that change by the minute. Most boats time their passage to slack tide through the worst tide rip areas, as the alternative requires a powerful motor to make headway against the tide, or being swept through at breakneck speed with the tide. Any motor trouble can quickly result in disaster.

Up until the early 1960's, this very dangerous waterway was made more deadly by a submerged rock, right in the middle of the narrow passage. No ordinary rock, it was the size of a ten storey building. No one ever saw it though, as its summit was barely submerged at low tide, and was only a few feet below the surface at high tide. Tide rips surging and swirling past carried untold numbers to their deaths, as its very hard surface became furrowed and scarred by the hulls of ships and boats that ripped their bottoms out and sank around it.

As Ripple Rock became a gravestone to more and more ships and men it gained international notoriety, and many attempts were made to remove it. Plans to drill and blast twenty or thirty feet off the top were foiled year after year, as the massive flow swept drilling barges back and forth in spite of every effort to anchor a steady drilling platform. While the deadly toll continued, the government was forced to heroic measures. The final engineering plan called for drilling and blasting the rock from under the sea!

Hard rock miners would drill a large shaft down one hundred and fifty feet in a nearby island, then drill and muck out a tunnel under the sea into the base of the rock, come up inside it to hollow out a huge cavern

178

thirty feet under the surface, fill it with high explosives, and blast it out of the water.

The progress of the work was followed avidly by the news media and the whole western population, as Ripple Rock's notoriety was widespread. The drilling and blasting and mining and mucking were extremely dangerous, as ton after thousands of tons of rock were mucked out of the passage under the sea.

When the final excavation was made, many tons of high explosives placed and fused and wired and the tunnel sealed, almost all of Canada were glued to their television sets while the widely publicized 10:00 A.M. zero hour counted down. All of us who witnessed it still remember the suspense, the relief, the pride in success and the celebration as the monstrous explosion filled our screens with immense volumes of rock and water surging massively out of the sea, rising and spreading and falling back in a cauldron of gigantic proportions. Ripple Rock had finally been overcome, no longer to reach up and snatch its toll of ships and men passing through that racing sluiceway of the sea.

* * * * * * * *

WINNING THE FISHING LOTTERY

The herring fishery was very big until 1979, but it was also the biggest gamble in the business. It paid huge returns to those who had the good equipment, know-how, and lots of luck, but it cost many fishermen their gear, their boats, and their lives.

With two or three hundred boats fishing herring, the annual quotas were reached quickly, so the season was very short. Sometimes an hour or two made the difference between a boat's very good season and a poor one.

The Federal Department of Fisheries controls the size of the fishing fleet through its licensing system for each type of fishing, and controls the volume of the catch by opening and closing the season on particular species.

In the mid 1970's it stopped the burgeoning growth of the fleet by cutting off the issue of new licenses. This meant that the number of boats fishing any species would remain steady, and the only source of a license for those wanting to get into the business was to buy it from a fisherman who was retiring, or who, for a price, was willing to give up fishing that species of fish. Anyone buying or building a boat to get into the fishing industry must first find a license or licenses for sale within the existing fleet.

Talk about capital gains! Most of us paid little or nothing for our licenses, but now due to a limited supply and a voracious demand, our licenses would sell for almost any asking price. For instance, the current market value of my herring license is about a million dollars, and my four licenses would go for over two million. I didn't transfer my licenses to my boys with the boat on retirement, as we'd have paid hundreds of thousands of dollars in capital gains, but if I were to sell any of them, they could no longer fish for that species.

Well, to get back to fishing: We were well equipped for the herring fishery, with one of the biggest, fastest boats in the fleet, excellent gear, and a good crew. We had done very well in the short time herring were open each season, and looked forward to the scramble for our share each year.

The price of herring had gone up over several years from six hundred dollars a ton to about two thousand at the beginning of 1979, as the demand for herring roe in Japan grew by leaps and bounds. As we headed out from Vancouver to start the 1979 season, fierce competition for the catch developed among fish buyers. This glued us to our radios, as one buyer after another announced new offers and rapidly escalating prices.

The first offer started at twenty four hundred dollars a ton. Within an hour another buyer offered twenty-six hundred, then came an offer of twenty-eight hundred plus girls to entertain the crew, and by the time we reached the grounds, the price had climbed to three thousand dollars a ton!

Everyone was champing at the bit, but no one could set a net until Fisheries declared the season open. It would open off either Tofino or Barkley Sound, with rumours flying over the air that it would open at 8:00 AM at one or the other, but not both. There were dozens of boats at both places, and more running back and forth on the strength of new rumours.

I was caught up in the rumour chase myself, and was about half an hour off the Tofino grounds when my radio announced that the season had opened there! As I approached the frenzied fleet, some were seining up, some were pumping, and a few were still milling around looking for fish. I figured we would be lucky to get in on the rush.

As I cruised slowly among them my sonar picked up a huge school of herring tight against, but outside another boat's net. I ran my net along his and circled a beautiful set, and pumped two hundred and sixty ton into our holds. Right in the middle of the fleet, we took out the largest load of the day. I radioed a packer, who picked up my load, worth over seven hundred and fifty thousand dollars for one day's work, and the highest priced load in the history of West Coast fishing!

We went on during that very short herring season to bring in a total catch of one million two hundred thousand dollars. That was ten days work in that year, and of course we already had a good season on dragging and salmon seining.

I sold the Charlene K to Bill and Randy on a share basis, and retired.

* * * * * * * *

Nowadays, as I sit at my desk and my telephone, dealing with investments, making reservations for world travel, I often think back to my grandmother, and to my grandfather as he scrabbled for a living, and to those tons of stones, and wish they could see how much my life has changed since the day Grandfather took me out of school to hitch up a six horse team on that far away farm.

* * * * * * * *

And now, here's Ed!

ED WHITLAM'S STORIES

I was born in 1917 in the city of Edmonton, Alberta, and grew up there in a complete farm environment on our farm in the city. Contradictory? True!

When my father left the family homestead near Morden Manitoba as a young man in 1895, he headed West to make his fortune. After a brief look at Chilliwack, B.C., which he considered too wet, (many years before the Dutch immigrants' canal and diking systems transformed that area into a Garden of Eden), he turned back to the Prairies, where he built up a freight business hauling north from Edmonton to supply the pioneer settlements in the Peace River district.

His freight train was a string of eight Red River carts loaded with groceries, dry goods, hardware, building supplies and farm machinery, hauled by eight yokes of oxen. His plodding, patient oxen were content to follow the cart ahead of them, so he had no trouble on his lone, two week trips to Grande Prairie.

Dad stayed in the Peace River country after his last trip every fall, proved up on a homestead, broke land with his oxen, bought, broke and sold farm land and homesteads, and made enough money to send for his two younger brothers. In partnership with them he opened a real estate office in Edmonton on 1909.

This business prospered and expanded rapidly over the next three or four years. However the real estate market slumped in 1913 and collapsed completely on the outbreak of war in 1914. It caught them with a huge sub-division development in Edmonton, extensive farm holdings at Mundare Alberta, and several houses in Vancouver B.C. With absolutely nothing moving, the brothers divided up the business assets. One took the Alberta farm land, one took the houses at 12th and Granville in Vancouver, and my father took the Edmonton property, known as Edmonton Heights.

His holdings in Edmonton Heights consisted of one hundred and forty city lots plus ten acres of undeveloped bush land. Though most of the lots and all the bush land were still treed, some streets had been laid out, cleared, and rough graded. Mill Creek ran through the property.

When the real estate market remained dead, Dad

eventually fenced the whole development and converted it to a farm. He had married in the meantime, and built a house at the corner of present day 85th Street and 65th Avenue in modern suburban Edmonton. He went into partnership with Harry Bell, raising Clydesdale horses, training them as Whitlam-Bell fire horses, sold all over Alberta to haul fire engines racing through city streets. He also pastured Standard Bred sulky pacers and race horses for a Mr. Johnson, who owned the horse barns at South Side race track.

The half mile length of the streets on our property, fenced off at each end, held no traffic except for the thunder of fire horses in training, and pacers and race horses being exercised. Old race horses and show horses were also retired to pasture here, and my boyhood memories are filled with beautiful horses.

When motorized fire engines put fire horses out to pasture in the early 1920's, things started going down hill for us, as the subdivision property was still not selling. With taxes eating away at it, the City of Edmonton began seizing a few lots for back taxes every year, so our farm fences began creeping inwards. By the late 1920's we were raising a few dairy cattle, hogs, chickens and turkeys. We delivered milk, and sold eggs, butter and garden produce in the city market.

My brother and I worked very hard from our earliest years, milking cows, tending livestock, hoeing, picking and selling garden produce, hauling water from Mill Creek by the barrelful for the livestock in 40 below zero weather on an ice covered stoneboat. We had no time after school and on weekends for the games and sports that other children played, though we did play ball, and ski and toboggan on the local hills in our "farm" area, today solidly built up as part of the city.

By the time the great depression settled in earnest in the early 1930's I had earned the nickname "Patches" for the patches I wore on my clothes. We had a few fights over that, and a few laughs, but there were lots of kids worse off than I, and we got by.

I had an early interest in things mechanical. My teenage ambition was to become a mechanical engineer, but it was obvious that there was no money for a university education, so I settled for technical school. Here I learned motor mechanics, woodworking, machine shop, sheet metal, and mechanical drafting. These skills were to serve me well for a large part of my working life.

As the depression deepened, the winter of 1933-34 was a disaster, so my father decided to move. We settled on a 40 acre farm near Chilliwack, in the lush Fraser Valley of British Columbia, but our fortunes didn't improve much. I had to get out and find some sort of work, and ended up with the only thing available - working for farmers at a dollar a day. I had determined I was never going to get back to milking cows, but I had to take it. I worked for one farmer that winter who expected me in the barn at five o'clock in the morning, and I was usually still working there at eight at night, earning $25 a month and board.

I decided after a couple of months that this was just no good. I was lucky to find a job with an Italian chap who was dairy farmer and part time Italian consul. He made cheese in large quantities for weekly delivery to the Italian colony in East End Vancouver, and spent a few hours once a month in the consul office in the Vancouver Hotel.

Mr.Ferrari took a liking to me, and I spent a happy eight months there. He took me with him on cheese delivery trips, and soon had me doing all his driving for him. He even loaned me his car on Saturday nights, saying, "Take the car and have a good time!" I was eighteen, and I did.

My cousin came down from his coal mining job at Blakeburn that Christmas, and suggested I go back with him and try for a job in the mines. When I arrived in that high mountain valley in late March, the snow was still up to the eaves of the buildings, and there was very little doing.

My uncle, who was the millwright at a sawmill producing lagging for the mine, suggested I see a Mr. Barnes, who was doing the hauling for them. (Lagging is short boards, about 3"x6"x4', used to jam in and fill the uneven spaces between the ore body and the timbers supporting it in underground coal mining.)

Barnes took me on as a truck driver, driving a 1934 five ton International on his eight mile bulldozed track between the mill and the mine two thousand feet above. This was mountain driving on dirt road, mud and ice. Brakes were of no use in many parts of it, and it was a case of gear down and steer! I often had my windshield still plastered with mud as I negotiated hairpin turns more or less by guess. I dinged up a fender or two, but that was normal for the job. Anyone surviving a few months of driving on that road was pushing his luck.

The mine personnel office sent word after a couple of months, and I left Barnes to start work as a coal miner.

* * * * * * * *

UNDERGROUND COAL MINING

Before I take you underground on my first shift, let me share with you some of the things I learned about the job and the world of darkness that miners live and work in.

When I came up Blakeburn Mountain to the mine site I came into a huge open area filled with empty mine cars on line after line of rail, with a line of loaded cars moving down an incline to the tipple. An aerial tramway led from the tipple up a slope, over the crest and down two miles or more to the big dump tipple and rail loading docks at Coalmont. The tramway resembled an oversize ski lift, with loaded cars on the way down passing empties coming up in a steady stream.

A shift of miners, their battery powered lamps on their hard hats throwing narrow beams of dusty light, were hopping on the skip or tram train, to ride into the tunnel and down one long incline after another. Their skip was controlled by cable and drum as the hoist man and the rope rider maneuvered their progress from one level and drift to the next, dropping men and cars off at their various work stations.

The miner, often lying on his side in dark, dusty, confined space that would give claustrophobia to a mole, worked his air powered twist drill to drive his holes, loaded them with a small amount of powder and very small caps, and set them off with a low voltage battery. (He constantly had to guard against spark or flame, as the resulting coal dust or gas explosion would spell one more mine disaster.) With pick and shovel he mucked out his ore and loaded his coal cars, pushing them by hand along the rails to the station where they'd be picked up.

He kept his tunnel shored up to guard against bumps or collapses. Stout timbers on each side of his drift supported the timbers he placed as close as possible to his roof. He then filled any space above his roof timbers with lagging, driving the short boards in and tightening it all with driven wedges. When everything was secure he crawled in to drill his next face and start over.

To avoid explosions, all underground power to operate drills, hoists, cable drums, pumps, fans, was air powered, serviced by high pressure lines from huge compressors at the surface. No lights except the miners' sealed, battery operated lamps illuminated the dusty stygian darkness of thousands of feet of underground slopes and stopes and drifts branching like a huge inverted tree driven down into the heart of the mountain. It was all serviced by miles of cables and drums lowering and raising cars on their tram-railed slopes.

On my first trip into the mine the skip passed #4 drift and reached a huge underground flat with dozens of cars and the hoist system servicing the cars for #5. It was from here that they dropped us down into #5 mine on a long steel cable. I was to go down to the 5000 foot level. (Levels are counted as height above sea level, so on our 7000 foot mountain I was actually 2000 feet below the surface).

When they dropped me off they told me my rope rider would be along to tell me what he wanted me to do. He showed up on the next skip and said, "You'll be operating the hoist. I'll be riding the last car down on the skip, and I have to jump off and kick the cable around guide pulleys as the skip goes around curves."

He focussed his lamp down the slope and said, "You see the four pulleys bolted to that tie on the corner there? Well, the cable has to be kicked onto those pulleys. If I don't get it on, then you're going to pull a car or two off the track, and it's a hell of a job getting them back on."

He showed me how to operate the huge cable drum hoist, then said, "When I get to each corner I'll give you one ding on the bell, and you stop the drum. When I give you two bells, you proceed slowly, and when I've passed the last pulleys I'll give you three dings and you proceed at normal speed. If you're not fast enough I'll let you know when I come back."

When I stopped the train on his bell at the first corner I watched him kick the cable onto the pulleys, then eased his skip around the corner and listened to it rumbling down into the inky darkness. I marked the cable with chalk each time I stopped it, but found later that chalk didn't last or show too well, so I tore up a rag and wrapped a strip of it on the cable for all my stops. That made all my later station stops easy, and as time went by I was able to ignore the markers altogether.

Well, this was still my nervous first shift. When my rope rider came back up on his first trip he said, "Well, that's not too bad. The next time I go down, when I come to these stops you just slow down. I won't ding you, but if I do ding you one bell, stop in a hurry, because I'll have missed a pulley and you'll have a car off the rails."

Everything worked out pretty well, and he and I got along fine except the odd time when I slipped along a little too fast and he missed a pulley and derailed a car. It happened only when he was going down empty, because I never allowed any slack in the cable. Once it was on, it stayed on all the pulleys, and when I was hauling a loaded train back up, there was lots of tension to keep it there.

As the skip got down to different levels the rope rider dropped off empties and picked up loaded cars, kicked "frogs" to switch his skip into different drifts, and managed his train so that each station was constantly supplied with empties and had loads picked up. He was helpless without power, stops, starts, slow and reverse, all supplied in the dark by the cable drum hundreds of feet away. As I learned to read my cable I always knew where he was, and we learned to work together with a touch of the bell.

Now down in these different levels below, the miners were working in dusty, dirty, dangerous darkness, as I described earlier, some lying on their sides, with a "thump" or an explosion a constant possibility. Their timber supports and lagging had to be tight, because coal and its surrounding material are not stable. Thumps sometimes just filled air spaces, sometimes signalled the collapse of old, rotted timbers in an abandoned part of the mine, but they got your attention, and could be felt for hundreds of feet.

After I had been working some time and was promoted to rope rider, I was riding my skip one day when a thump occurred right over my head. It was a pretty big one, as a broken timber came down. I was still moving, and caught my head between the broken timber and the car. It gave me a scrape along one side of my head, and a mess of slivers on the other side, and if that broken timber had been half an inch longer, I just wouldn't be here to tell any story today.

Talking about explosions, I want to go back a bit to when we passed #4 mine. #4 mine blew up in 1932, killing forty men and five horses. It so happened that my cousin was the last man to come out of that mine alive. He was the rope rider on the train, and as the blast came he was just pulling out of the mine. The blast blew his hat off and speeded up his exit. One of the timbers that was blown out of the mine ended up on top of his load. It was a long time before they got #4 back in operation.

The explosion was caused by a runaway rail car that raced down the track until it crashed, causing a flash of sparks that set off a huge underground blast.

I went down in #4 one time because I was interested in seeing how they used horses. Six horses at that time spent their lives down there, hauling coal cars on rails from the face several hundred feet to the cable station.

We miners worked in the beam of light from our lamps, but the horses had no light, and worked a lifetime in stygian blackness. They were gentle, smart animals, who learned to perform their jobs on their own, as though they could see perfectly. (It was said that after a year or two without light they went blind, and if so they were doubly blind). They walked steadily, hauled their cars to the station, waited to be unhitched, turned and walked back in the dark, stopped and turned in precisely the right place and waited to be hitched to their next load, totally blind, whether from lack of eyesight or the stygian underground darkness. They were washed, well fed, well cared for in their underground stable, where they lived and died.

When the big hoist brought the coal up to the surface, the cars ran out and were parked on sets of rails, waiting their turn to move to the main haulage track heading down a slope to the tipple. The rail yard was sloped, the cars (with no brakes) moved by gravity, controlled by the spragg man.

Spraggs were sharpened wood about a foot long and 4" diameter, placed in piles every few feet along the track. Old Sparky, the spragg man, would stand by a pile with an armful of spraggs, tossing them underhand between the spokes of the moving train wheels, locking them into a skid. He was so precise he almost never missed a wheel, and could spot each skip of loaded cars pretty well where he wanted it. A cable was then attached to the cars as they were let down on the main haulage track leading to the tipple.

The cars had a quick hitch system that allowed them to be picked up and hung on pulleys on a huge two inch stationary cable. This ran on pylons over the ridge and down two miles to Coalmont and back. The movement of the cars was controlled by a second, running cable. The weight of the two miles of loaded cars running down the slope drew the short run of loaded ones up the slope from the tipple, and the two miles of empties coming back up. This was top grade steam coal, used exclusively by the Canadian Pacific Railroad to fuel their steam engines across Canada.

Eventually we were working only three days a week, and at $4.50 a day, by the time we paid our room and board, we had little to spend. However, it gave us days of spare time, and I played a lot of baseball. We were in the Similkameen ball league, playing in Hedley, Oliver, Coalmont, Princeton, and Osoyoos. There was no Hope-Princeton highway in those days, so we travelled narrow, dirt, mountain roads. I had a Model A Ford, and those roads were my training ground for the thousands of miles of back roads I would drive on hunting trips in the mountains in future years.

Things eventually slowed down at the mine until we were working only two days a week, so I figured I'd better look for another job. I went over to Copper Mountain, on the other side of Princeton, applied for work, and was hardrock mining the next day.

The Copper Mountain area has produced copper and silver ore in huge amounts for over fifty years, in my day as an underground hardrock mine, nowadays as an open pit operation.

I'll describe hardrock mining later in more detail, but since I was at Copper Mountain for a very short time I'll limit this part of the story to my experience there:

As miners drill and blast and muck out their rock they frequently encounter rich ore, which they are directed to follow. This results in "glory holes" which may grow and extend upwards from the stope until it is the size of a two or three story house. All loose rock clinging to the sides or roof of the glory hole has to be scaled off with bars, and all cracked rock checked and anything moveable pried off after each blast.

This was my first experience at hard rock mining. I was mucking rock for the miners, and everything went fine for about three weeks.

One day they put me in a huge glory hole that extended up about fifty feet. When I looked up, I spotted a huge rock up there that looked loose, and had to come down. With my longest ladder and longest bar I couldn't reach it. While I was looking around for a longer bar, the shift boss came along.

"What are you looking for?" he asked.

"I'm looking for a bar long enough to bring that big rock down."

"We don't have a bar that long! It'll come down."

"What? Supposing I'm underneath it?"

"Oh there's always someone else to take your place."

"Is that right? You're not going to do anything about it?"

"No."

"What the hell, I'm through right now!"

I picked up my lunch bucket, and out of there I went. So ended my three weeks experience at Copper Mountain.

I went back up to Blakeburn, but after working short shifts for a couple of weeks I figured I could do just as well back home in Chilliwack. That was the spring of '38.

* * * * * * * *

191

I spent the following year at several jobs, including cat operator, carpenter, and auto mechanic at the old gold rush town of Wells, where I had tried unsuccessfully to get work in a placer mine. We built a big theater there, and at the same time that I was driving spikes on the theater job I was working nights in a garage on motor repair.

I had applied some time before for work at Island Mountain gold mine, and in the spring of 1939 I got word to report for work as a mucker.

They put me with a miner who specialized in following up small seams of high grade ore. This resulted in tiny, narrow stopes with just enough room to crawl through. Working in the dust and sharp rock in those areas on my belly or my knees, mucking back the rock by hand and short handled shovel after each of his blasts got to be a bit much, so I spoke to the foreman. He put me on a new drift with another mucker named Rayner, who in spite of a bad leg, could sure move a lot of rock. We were about the same size, and worked well together. However, we had drawn one of the most miserable, contrary miners to work with you would ever meet.

Hardrock mining involves the licensed miner drilling a set of deep holes in the face of his stope, packing his fused charges in the back of the drill holes, and setting them off in a pattern that will remove the next six feet or so of rock. The muckers then load the several tons of fractured rock into ore cars, which are moved on rails to the crusher. Here they are ground to a powder consistency and the mineral (gold in this case) is chemically extracted.

The drifts were usually about six feet high by seven or eight feet wide, with a fairly level floor. A set of four or five 4x8 foot steel plates were laid on the floor to receive the bulk of the rock blown out of the face, which made the muckers' work easier.

The miner's drill had two hoses attached. It was air powered, using a combination pounding and turning action on the drill steel, which might be anywhere from two to twenty feet long. Each drill steel had a three eighths inch hollow core, through which a pressurized stream of water kept the drill cool and washed the drill dust back out of the hole in a continuous shower of mud. The miners wore slickers and boots to stay more or less dry.

In spite of the water, drilling did create some dust, and blasting and mucking always filled the stope with choking clouds until the fans cleared some of it.

The miner usually took one shift to drill, pack and blast his next set, and the muckers took the next shift to load it out, so they never worked together.

The miner drilled his holes, usually about six feet deep, in a precise pattern to keep his line and move the rock. He drilled a row of four holes across the top, about five or six down each side of a six foot stope, and four close together in the center. He then drilled one hole in the center of those four, and finished with a row of four holes drilled a few inches above the floor down in a slope to the back of his set.

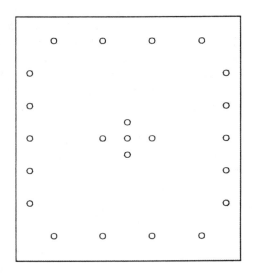

The center holes were the burn holes and the bottom holes were the lifters. He left the centre hole empty, then packed and fused the four around it, and all the perimeter holes, cutting the length of his fuses so the different sets blew out in a particular sequence. The burn holes blew first, making space for the perimeter rock to blast toward the centre. The lifters at the bottom were the last to blow, moving the whole face of shattered rock out onto the plates for the muckers to pick up.

Well, Dusty, whether through contrariness or plain cussedness, would often drill his lifter holes so low that his blast caught the steel plates and lifted them in a tangle within the tons of broken rock we had to muck and load. We not only didn't have a decent floor to work from, we had an awful time contending with heavy, contrary steel mixed in the rock. Many's the day his ears should have been burned to a crisp with our cursing.

Sometimes on the weekends we'd come across him in the beer parlor, and we'd give him hell about the plates. He just laughed, because he was making lots of money, being paid for every foot he advanced the face of that drift.

Ray and I loaded twenty two to twenty five cars of rock per shift. We trammed our loaded cars out to the shaft, where they were left until they went up in the skip. I'd take out a loaded car (by hand, on track) and bring back an empty. By that time Rayner would have one loaded, and he'd take that out while I loaded mine, and so our day went. At the end of each shift we had to have everything cleared up, lay track up to the new face, and move our heavy steel plates up, so that when Dusty came in he could set up his liner (drilling machine) at the new face. It was a lot of hard work,

These liners are bolted onto a bracket that goes up a bar on a twist screw to the driller's required height for the holes he's drilling. The bar is jacked tight between an air pressurized foot and ceiling, so when it is set and the air turned on, the miner can turn a screw and keep pressure on his drill bit while it is chewing into the rock face in a shower of mud and water.

The whole thing weighs well over a hundred pounds. When it's operated in a glory hole that might have grown to a cavern fifty to seventy five feet across and thirty to forty feet high above the main drift, where the miner has to climb a long ladder with that load, drag fifty feet of water and air hose behind him, set it up and secure it and start drilling, all this in the beam of his light while surrounded by total darkness, spattered with high pressure mud and water, he, too, earns his pay.

When I looked at our mucker's wage of $5.50 a day against the miners' $10.00 a day I spoke to the mine superintendent about getting a blasting certificate. He gave me books and notes to study, and when the mine inspector came from Victoria six weeks later I wrote the exam for a blasting certificate. In passing that, I qualified as a hard rock miner. This was '39.

The pit boss put me mining a vein of high grade ore, similar to the one I started on here as a mucker. It was precision work, but tough conditions, drilling and blasting and mucking out with the help of a mucker in cramped, confined conditions, working on my knees or my belly.

After two months I had a chance to go drifting, where I would be drilling a large face, driving a drift seven feet wide and eight feet high. I worked all alone, played baseball, skied, hunted, fished Bowron Lake where I could limit out in the half hour before I was driven out by mosquitos.

When I was on night shift (night and day were the same underground), I often spent my days taking prospectors out to their diggings. I loaded my Model A with their gear, chained up that tough old car and got out to some awful areas that had no roads for miles. We followed paths and game trails, cut trees where necessary, followed creek beds, and got in and out of some seemingly impossible driving situations. The car and I both survived and grew smarter, and that experience refined my skills for the driving I was to do many years later on trips from creek bottoms to mountain tops with my hunting friends.

Eventually the mine slacked down to a three day week, so I started looking for another job. A Wells friend told me about a job in Prince George as spare driver-swamper for Wood and Fraser, hauling freight from Vanderhoof to Vancouver. I quit the mine and got the job.

We were driving a 1936 five ton Fargo. The Caribou road and the Fraser Canyon road in those days were very different from the modern highway. They were dusty, narrow, climbed and dropped down precipitous slopes. The canyon road for many miles was one-way, frequently overhanging the cliffs on propped wooden trestles. One car might have to back up for hundreds of feet to let another by.

I'm going to digress here to tell a story about my brother. Dunc and I were coming down to Chilliwack in my Model A for Christmas, when we came upon a Saskatchewan car stopped in the middle of the road on Jackass Mountain, (named in the gold rush days, when a pack mule fell for hundreds of feet off the trail and was killed.)

When we checked, we found the driver so terrified of the road he declared he wasn't going to drive another foot. (He had only taken over the driving at Lytton, a few miles back, when the man who came out with them dropped off there.)

Dunc and I went back to my car to talk it over.

"You're going to have to drive his car down through the canyon," I said.

"Hell, I've never driven a car in my life!" (And he hadn't.)

"Well, we can't get past him, and we can't leave him here, and I can't drive two cars. You've driven lots of tractors. It's about the same, and you know how to shift. Just take it easy, and I'll follow you."

So Dunc got in, got the car going, and away we went. I'm not sure what that man would have done if he'd known that Dunc's first car driving experience was to take him and his wife through the Fraser Canyon, but he thanked us profusely when Dunc delivered them safely into Hope.

* * * * * * * *

Well, back to my new job:

I had been working about three weeks, when I took over the driving at 100 Mile House one day, and the other driver went to sleep. Coming over the very winding 70 Mile House road, I guess I also dozed off, as I woke up with the truck rattling through the bush.

They were small poplars, on fairly level ground. I could see the road ahead, so I geared down and kept going until I got back on it, as my companion, now wide awake, hung on. There was no damage to the truck or the load, and I thought no more of it than of many of my bush trips with the Model A. However, the driver reported the incident in full to the boss when we got to Vancouver.

Well, he told me I could go as swamper back to Prince George, where I could pick up my check and my car. That was a quick end to a brief job.

* * * * * * * *

Jobless in Vancouver after picking up my car in Prince George, I dropped in to the Britannia Copper personnel office and was hired as a hardrock miner. The trip to Britannia in '39 was by Union Steamships, as there was no highway along the cliffs of Howe Sound beyond Horseshoe Bay, and no B.C. Rail this side of Squamish.

This was a huge mine, with thousands of feet of workings entering from both sides of the mountain. I rode into the mountain on a mine train, dropped off at my stope, and checked my gear.

I would be following up a vein in a glory hole, drilling and blasting. As I hauled my heavy "widow maker" up a ladder, set the foot of it on rock or planking by the light of my lamp, jacked it tight to the ceiling and powered up my drill and high pressure water, and worked hour after hour in the mud storm blowing out of my drill holes, you might wonder why anyone would work in those conditions.

Sometimes when drilling in very hard rock the drill bit would come across veins of soft rock angling through it, and would tend to follow that until it bound. That meant hard work with heavy wrenches and hammers, trying to free the drill. Occasionally it had to be abandoned, hopefully to be recovered in the rubble after the blast.

After I completed my drilling pattern and loaded and lit my charges I'd clear out my gear and retire around a corner of the drift, to count my blasts and account for all of them, then turn on the fans to clear the clouds of dust and fumes out of the dark drift. I was responsible too for any dud charges, which had to be found, fused again and blown before the rock could be mucked out.

If I were doing only a small blast the shift boss might ask me to go back and drill and blast two or three sets before mucking - or he might ask me to drill and blast twenty five or thirty holes in one set, bringing down so much rock it would take two mucking shifts to clear it.

If they wanted to bring down a really big volume of rock and had a glory hole to accommodate it, they used the old fellow called "the coyote hole digger". He had spent so much of his life in a three foot tunnel that he walked with a permanent 50 degree stoop, but was apparently comfortable spending weeks at a time by himself in his coyote holes.

He drilled, blasted and mucked out a long 60 to 80 foot tunnel, about 3 feet square, in a series of 15 foot zigs and zags. He mucked out all his rock on a little rubber tired trolley (no tracks) and might take weeks to do it. When a coyote hole was loaded and blasted we felt it all through the mine, as hundreds of tons of rock came out in a pile 20 feet high and 30 feet across, with hundreds more tons of loose rock behind it.

There was talk of building a main haulage tunnel right through the mountain to link Incline Camp overlooking Howe Sound with Victoria Camp on the back side of the mountain. At this time, ore from Victoria Camp was coming out on a long haulage track around the back of the mountain. The new tunnel would be twelve feet wide, ten feet high, and four miles long, to accommodate large ore trains. Three quarters of a mile of it was already in use from our end.

This job paid by the foot, and if you could make good time you could earn almost three times miners' pay. I applied and got on, on a shift of two miners and one mucker, drilling twelve foot holes. We made good time, using a large mucking machine to load our cars, but in spite of constantly watering down with spray hoses, dust was a serious problem.

The mining engineer, who checked after every blast for alignment, did a good job, as the four mile tunnel was only a foot out of line when the two sides met.

I worked on the tunnel job for four months. Frenchy, my partner, stayed on the job, didn't worry about dust, (gave me hell for constant watering), and died of silicosis a year or two later.

I went down to Vancouver for Christmas 1940, and so ended my hardrock mining career. It had been hard, heavy, dangerous work in what you might consider awful working conditions, but I think it made a pretty good man of me.

Ed (left) and Rayner, waiting to go underground.

WARTIME

When I came down to Vancouver for Christmas 1940 I found my brother working as a machinist for Boeings on Sea Island, manufacturing PBY flying boats for war service. I took a course on aircraft construction and repair at the Aeronautical Technical Institute, and started work for Boeings in April 1941.

We were repairing planes damaged in service or in training - Hamptons, Beauforts, Lochheed Hudsons, Bollingbrokes, Grumman Goose. I started as a draftsman in the engineering department, drawing up sheet metal repairs, moved to working on the floor as a lead hand in hydraulic lines and later on the assembly and replacement of nose sections and controls, rebuilding planes wrecked in crash landings.

My aircraft trade ended in the assembly and engine overhaul section of Canadian Pacific Air on Sea Island in December 1943. Working with friend Leo Bibby (Bib), we got fed up with the continual service deferments secured for us by our employer, and tried to enlist in the RCAF, in our skilled trades.

Strangely, in spite of the urgent air force demand for skilled aircraft mechanics and repairmen at that time, and their giving my cousin, for instance, a quick course in air-frame mechanics when he enlisted at about the same time as a green hand, they turned us down, offering us air gunner postings. We were as well or better qualified in our trades as RCAF servicemen with two or three years experience, but apparently they didn't want our skills, and they never gave us a chance!

So - we joined the navy as confirmed petty officers. I was given a five week diesel course, and posted as a qualified motor mechanic (diesel and gas).

After four months in the machine shop at Cornwallis N.S. I was drafted to the Sans Puer. This was formerly the Duke of Sutherland's yacht, now armed with a four inch gun, loaded with depth charges, and used not only on anti submarine patrol, but to train officers on depth sounders, asdic, and radar in actual combat conditions. We were based in Digby, N.S., and usually had 10 or 12 trainees aboard.

One happy memory is the time we were two days off the East Coast with two corvettes when a big storm blew up. Forty foot waves and a wall of mast high spume obscured the other ships for half an hour at a time, though we were only a thousand yards apart.

Of eighty-seven men in the crew, there were only seven of us on our feet, and it wasn't hard to bargain the two tot issue of rum for standing a man's watch . I stood so many of them that when we got into Rimouski I had fifty-three ounces of rum which I sold for a dollar an ounce, good money in those days.

Bib and I were drafted off the Sans Puer to go on full time U Boat patrol in the North Atlantic. We were on one of a flotilla of four Fairmiles, very fast ships that specialized in sub chasing. Eventually I was thrown down a gangway in heavy seas, with a bad break in my shoulder. I ended up in a body cast for five weeks, was given a four week pass to Vancouver, and was there for the wild VE Day celebration.

But of course the war wasn't over. I returned to Halifax and was posted back to the Sans Puer, now working as a mother ship to a flotilla of Mediterranean class subs, waiting posting to the Pacific and the war with Japan.

While on this posting a German U Boat came in with its colors struck and surrendered to us. We escorted it into the base, were allowed to go aboard, and were most interested in exploring the many refinements in their equipment and armament that had made them so deadly during the long sea war.

I was posted back to Vancouver in December 1945, for discharge from the armed services in January, 1946. Jobs in that post war winter were hard to find in the flood of returning servicemen, and wartime industry layoffs.

* * * * * * *

On board the U Boat that surrendered to the Sans Puer. Note the snorkel.

WORK AND PLAY

My first post war job was with Star Shipyards, using my navy diesel engine experience for the installation and repair of engines on fishing boats. The shipyard superintendent knew me from CPA, where he had worked for me. It took that kind of break to find a job in the post war market crammed with returning servicemen and workers laid off from wartime industries. I was bumped off the job after only five months by a former employee with union seniority.

"Lucky", another fellow-worker from CPA, ran into me one day. He had a contract with the big Malkin trucking fleet to install exchange motors in their trucks, and needed a hand. That six weeks job lasted a year.

In 1947 Hilda and I married and established our home.

I was anxious to get out of the garage business, but it wasn't to be. My next job was with Docksteader Motors, where I was promoted to shop foreman with a crew of twenty-two men in the garage and body shop.

After five years with Docksteader I took my head mechanic with me in partnership, to open our own garage and service station in Vancouver in 1953. Jim was a good man, and business boomed, but trouble started for us after he hired his son, newly discharged from military service.

This guy was an alcoholic, and it wasn't long until they were both into it. Jim and his son would take in a lot of work, promise the customers they'd do it at night, then not turn up to do it. I would find myself with two or three of their repair jobs promised for morning, and no one there to do the work. I often had to work all night, and phone Hilda to come down to open the service station at seven in the morning while I went home to sleep after a twenty hour shift.

I was very unhappy with the situation and told Jim I was thinking of moving out. Things improved some, but not an awful lot, until one day my uncle came along and kicked my foot that was sticking out from under a car and said, "Come out of there Ed. You've been under these cars too long. I've got a proposition for you."

Following a long discussion I went into the Whitlam Agencies insurance business with him as a partner. A lot of the fellows in the insurance offices said to me one way or another, "Ed, you're not going to make it. A mechanic just can't deal with the problems you'll be working with."

Well, I succeeded in the insurance business beyond my expectations. When my uncle passed away in 1956 I bought out his partnership from the estate, and I never looked back. I often thought, "These fellows never know what a person can do if he's got some initiative."

I sold the business in 1976 to Pat Anderson Agencies and retired, subject to one year with Anderson on a good salary. That was a soft touch, as I was just a good will ambassador to look after the customers that he had bought from me. Those customers included Bill and Gord and Cas.

* * * * * * * *

I have enough hunting stories to fill a book, but Cas isn't going to let me tell them all here, so I'll just add a few highlights that he didn't cover:

There was the hunting trip on McKay's ranch at Soda Creek that ended with Hilda and I fighting our way through a night time blizzard. We had been house bound for a couple of days of heavy snow and very cold temperatures, but when a howling wind came up after dark we knew we had to get out in a hurry to avoid being trapped in there for the winter.

Heavy, drifting snow had already wiped out any sign of our trail across several wide meadows studded with big rocks. We held a glove between us at arm's length to find and break trail for the wheels as we walked in the swirling, icy darkness of the blizzard across each meadow, avoiding the mounds that were rocks under the snow while seeking the bush opening on the opposite side. Returning to the car we would drive across the meadow and through the bush trail to the next meadow, and we did it again - and again and again.

We were bursting through three foot drifts that put snow over our hood, and had no one within twenty miles to help if we stalled or hit a rock or a tree, (or a deer, bouncing everywhere in our lights as they headed down to the shelter of the Fraser River flats).

* * * * * * * *

There was the first hunting trip Bill and I took together in 1964, when we borrowed Cas's new truck and headed for the Kootenays. Bill bagged an eight point royal, - a trophy elk that had the Fernie natives out taking pictures of it.

That was the quickest shot I've seen, and the easiest loading. We were two or three hundred yards above the road when we heard the rattle of antlers coming down through the alders at terrific speed - but we couldn't see a thing.

Knowing it was a bull elk, Bill lined up on a two foot opening in the alders, and fired as the flash of color broke past a hundred yards away. In the silence that followed, Bill figured he'd missed it, but we found it stone dead a hundred yards below, and nicely above the road. We had only to back the truck to the bank and slide the whole, dressed elk into it. That also impressed the natives!

* * * * * * * *

Cas left me to tell a couple of the yellow bug stories:

There was the time we three were up in the Quintette Mountain area, when Bill and I, sixteen miles from camp, had two flat tires at the same time, one front, one back. The spare was the size of the smaller front tire, but we replaced the small front flat with the huge, flat rear tire and put the small spare on the rear. That left us with a big tire and a small tire on the back, and a good small one on the left front and a big flat on the right front. Bill rode standing on the back left bumper to keep as much weight as possible off the flat, and when we got moving we found that the light load and centrifugal force kept the flat looking almost normal. After sixteen miles, it wasn't even warm!

That was the trip too, when Bill and I caught up to a coyote on the trail. We sped to catch up, and were surprised to pull along side the speeding coyote, who seemed reluctant to leave the trail. When Bill reached out and put his hand on the coyote's back, the coyote ducked under the bug to escape, only to be inadvertently run over and killed. We hadn't planned that.

When we got back to camp that evening we put the coyote on the seat of Cas's trail bike, under the tarp he had put there to keep frost off. We all had a big laugh the next morning when he peeled off the tarp, to find a passenger on his seat!

* * * * * * * *

We often forded streams with the bug, as it could negotiate steep banks, roll over rocks, and didn't mind water up to the floor. We bit off more than we expected though the day Bill and I tried to cross the Prophet River on a trip in from Trutch, on the Alaska Highway.

The river was about a hundred feet across, running fairly fast over a rocky bottom, with four foot banks. We checked out our planned crossing carefully. We found a way down and a way up on the other side, through water about eighteen to twenty four inches deep, as far as we could tell. No problem.

No problem until we were half way across and plowing water, when the front end suddenly dipped and water washed over the hood and the windshield. Knowing there was no turning back I instinctively gave it full throttle, the back wheels spun off the rocks, and in a sink or swim situation, the bug was swimming, in five or six feet of fast water!

The big lugged rear tires bit enough water to keep us moving, and threw so much water away from behind the bug that the rear motor didn't drown out. We drifted far enough down-stream that we missed our landing, but when the front wheels touched, and the rear wheels found something more substantial than water to work on, the bug scrambled and clawed its way up the bank without quite tipping backwards. I'm sure it was as thankful as Bill and I that it was high and dry instead of a yellow shadow on the bottom of the river.

Our return trip later required a couple of hours of rock dumping before we filled the channel enough to chance the second crossing.

* * * * * * * *

I think of the day Bib showed me how to bag grouse without a gun. Hunting together out of Germanson Landing on a dry hunting day, Bib suggested that if we couldn't get a moose, we might s well take a few of the plentiful grouse back to camp.

When I pointed out we had only our big rifles, he said, "No problem". He took a lace out of his boot, tied a noose in it, and tied that to a fifteen foot pole. He then chased a grouse into a tree, and as the grouse sat there, mesmerized by the waving noose, Bib carefully placed the loop over its head, and Voila! A grouse for the pot. We took half a dozen, and I learned a trick that I've used many times.

* * * * * * * *

Gord was with Bill and me the time we folded a whole moose into the huge trunk of my Plymouth, then almost had to take the car apart to get it out after it cooled out and stiffened up.

* * * * * * * *

There was the day Stan and I came upon Cas and Bill, standing very frustrated beside Cas's truck. They had stopped on the road to glass, spotted elk on the ridge above them, then found they had locked their rifles and their keys in the truck. The elk were gone and they were still trying to get into the truck when we came along.

* * * * * * * * *

Well, there are lots more memories of hunting trips over the years. We were privileged to have shared so many experiences, challenges and adventures with such great companions, and to have formed friendships that have lasted a lifetime.

* * * * * * * *

I agree with Ed, and am sure Bill and Gord do too. Now you know three of the fellows I hunted with for many years, why those years were so great, and why I had to write this book!

Cas.